The Duchess Diaries

Oh, most definitely, Lara was the sort of woman who would make his life complete. Except that Griff did not have that life anymore.

"Lady Lara, do not worry," Griff said with a forced smile. "There are many women who think of themselves above my station, yet find some sort of excitement in the idea of loving me."

"I do not love you. Don't be ridiculous. I just . . ." Lara stopped and looked away from him. "You're such a gentleman, sir."

"I am not a gentleman," he said quietly.

Griff knew that he had to show Lady Lara Darling that she was absolutely wrong about him. He could not have this young girl thinking she loved him. He did not deserve it, and he did not want it from her.

He grabbed her around the waist, lifted her to him, and kissed her. It was not a light fluttery thing, either, but a deep, dark taking.

"There," he said wickedly. "Am I such the gentleman now?"

Other **AVON ROMANCES**

MIA RYAN

The DUCHESS DIARIES

AVON BOOKS
An Imprint of HarperCollinsPublishers

This is a work of fiction. Names, characters, places, and incidents are products of the author's imagination or are used fictitiously and are not to be construed as real. Any resemblance to actual events, locales, organizations, or persons, living or dead, is entirely coincidental.

AVON BOOKS
An Imprint of HarperCollins*Publishers*
10 East 53rd Street
New York, New York 10022-5299

Copyright © 2003 by Malia Nahas
ISBN: 0-06-051969-X
www.avonromance.com

First Avon Books paperback printing: December 2003

Avon Trademark Reg. U.S. Pat. Off. and in Other Countries, Marca Registrada, Hecho en U.S.A.
HarperCollins® is a registered trademark of HarperCollins Publishers Inc.

Printed in the U.S.A.

10 9 8 7 6 5 4 3 2 1

This one is for Kela Blair,
Makena Pearl and Mitchell Kai,
for making me a mom,
and eating a lot of frozen pizza
when "Mom is writing her book."

And for Steve,
for being a good dad
to our Corn Children,
and racing into the city to buy a printer,
even though he had a plane to catch.

Prologue

"No," Lara Darling cried, jumping out of her chair. "Absolutely not. I will not do it."

"Lara, sit down."

Lara blinked at the solicitor standing before her, and placed her hand over her heart. "Well," she said. "I never." Actually, she had never in her life uttered such a completely inane phrase, but it seemed the best thing to say in the face of some young upstart telling her, Lady Lara Darling, to sit down. "Of all the . . ."

"No, no, I'm only reading what your grandmother wrote in her will," the young man said quickly and thrust the papers at Lara. "I promise you, Lady Lara, I would never even think of ordering you about."

Emma snorted. Lara glared at her.

"Oh, do sit down, Lara. 'Twasn't Mr. Grant who asked it of you, after all," Amanda fluttered her lashes at Mr. Grant. The man went a deep shade of red, and Lara rolled her eyes. "It was Nanny L," her sister continued, "who knew you would jump up and stomp about."

"I am not stomping."

"Given time, I am sure you will start." Amanda shook her head and shot a superior look at the now purple Mr. Grant.

"Breathe, man," Lara advised the solicitor.

He glanced quickly away from the beautiful Amanda and returned his attention to Nanny L's will as Lara sank into the leather chair behind her. "Bloody hell," she muttered as she did so.

"Watch your tongue, Lara," Regina admonished her quietly. "Rachel and Lissie are in attendance."

Lara laced her fingers together and held them tightly against her lap. Reggie was right, of course. Reggie was always right.

Eight-year-old Lissie, the youngest of the six Darling sisters sat holding her favorite doll and staring at Lara with large, round eyes.

Of course, ten-year-old Rachel probably had not heard the interchange at all, as she sat quietly in the back corner with her nose in a book.

"Proceed," Lara said to the young solicitor.

Mr. Grant swallowed and then glanced at the girls' father. But Lord Charles David Darling, tenth Earl of Ashton, was oblivious to everything but the nuts and bolts that he tinkered with at his desk.

"Father," Lara called.

Lord Ashton glanced up from his work.

"Tell the man to go on."

"Go on," Lord Ashton said and returned to his gadget.

Mr. Grant cleared his throat. The papers in his hands shook, and Lara rolled her eyes. Idiot man, all flustered because her sister had paid him a bit of attention. Lara sent a piercing glare in Amanda's direction, but the girl just smiled sweetly.

"I knew, Lara, that you would have a problem with the idea of going off to London for your season, much less marrying—"

"Marrying!" Lara cried as if someone had just asked her to walk into a burning building.

"Oh, do let the man read, Lara," Reggie admonished her.

Lara clenched her hands into fists, her entire

3

body trembling. She was now extremely afraid of exactly what her grandmother was getting at with all this talk of seasons and, heaven forbid, marriage.

Mr. Grant swallowed audibly. "And so I gave my solicitors instructions . . ." Here Mr. Grant glanced up and said, "That would be my father, of course. I never actually met your grandmother. But my father died last year, leaving his business to me."

"Oh dear, I am so sorry," Amanda said prettily.

Lara held her tongue, which, really, she was awfully proud of herself for, since she desperately wanted to smack them both and yell at the man to continue. Something really horrible was about to happen; she could feel it. Better get it done quickly and know what she was dealing with.

"Well thank you, Lady Amanda." If Mr. Grant puffed his chest any bigger, the man would explode, surely.

Lara grit her teeth.

"Anyway, to continue . . ." he said.

"Yes," Lara said, her voice a bit high-pitched with stress. "Please do." *For the love of all things holy*.

"I gave my solicitors instructions to read this

4

to you only a few months before the season starting your nineteenth year." Mr. Grant looked especially pained as he continued with, "Goodness, child, you do like to give me extra worry, do you not?"

Lara pushed her handkerchief against her lips, because, even though she was rather angry with her Nanny L at the moment, she did miss her terribly, and having Nanny L speak to her from her will did make Lara wish to cry.

And, anyway, it had been a while since someone older than she had worried about her. Quickly, Lara shook her head and closed her eyes against imminent tears.

Mr. Grant cleared his throat. "I have written guides for each of you, my dearest granddaughters, diaries, really, which will help you navigate your way through Society. I am sure you all cannot wait to read my wise comments on life in general. Am I right?"

"Yes, Nanny L!" Lissie piped up. Lara smiled at her youngest sister.

"Now, dear Lara." Mr. Grant looked up quickly, obvious terror in his eyes. "I am reading, I swear. It is what is written."

Lara desperately wanted to tell the man to quit being such a complete ninny. Instead, with a glance at her youngest sisters, she only nod-

ded at the solicitor. "I understand, Mr. Grant."
You complete ninny.

"You will not want to take this money and go
to London, of this I am sure."

Smart woman, her grandmother.

"You will want to use the money to the advantage of your sisters."

Yes.

"I am older and wiser than you, though.
Truth be told, at this very moment, I am actually dead. But, I am wiser still. And I am telling
you that the money I am giving you will better
serve your sisters if you take it and have your
season.

I will assure you all now, though, that I had
just enough to put aside an amount of money
for each of my dearest granddaughters to have
one season each."

Amanda let out a squeal of delight and
clapped her hands together. Her blonde curls
bounced against her slender shoulders and her
pink cheeks went even pinker, if that were possible.

Mr. Grant watched as if he were witnessing
an act of God. Lara just glared at him until he
noticed and went back to reading.

"So you see, Lara, you do not have to worry.
If you do not want to do this season, or if you

are so completely opposed to being married, you can, of course, reject this offer I am making you. Each of your younger sisters will be given an opportunity to find a suitable husband. It is not your responsibility to make this happen for them."

Lara should have felt better, but for some reason she did not. Nanny L had a way of doing that to her, wording things so that Lara ended up doing things she had been adamantly opposed to when first discussed.

"Of course, it will be difficult to find a husband in only one season, with no dowry," Mr. Grant continued reading. Lara couldn't help but shake her head. Here it comes, she thought, she could feel it. This was where Nanny L was going to make her do something she really, really did not want to do.

"In fact, Lara, if you, as the eldest, were able to find a husband of some wealth during *your* season, you would be able to make your sisters' quests much easier."

No, Lara thought desperately. *No*. A season was bad enough, having to pretend she wanted to marry. Having to dance and sit around drinking tea and talking to people who bored her to tears. Actually finding a man and then marrying him? *No, please no.*

7

"And so, my dear eldest granddaughter, I am going to say here in my will something which I know will galvanize you like nothing else I could say." Mr. Grant pulled a handkerchief from his pocket and blotted his damp forehead without daring to glance up from the papers he held.

"I, Lara Regina Farnsworth, Dowager Duchess of Marleston, mother of your late mother, *dare* you, Lady Lara Darling, daughter of my daughter, to find a husband of wealth in one season and with no dowry. I just dare you."

"Damn!" Lara said, not caring in the least that all of her five younger sisters were in the room. Nanny L knew her well, of course. If there was one thing in the world that Lara Darling could never pass up, it was a dare.

Chapter 1

Make no mistake, Lara dearest, you can do absolutely anything you put your heart into. I know you can. The problem is, choosing the right things in which to place your heart.

The Duchess Diaries, Volume One

According to local lore, the coachman they waited upon at that very moment was the best driver in Christendom. Since he was now exactly twenty-three minutes late, Lady Lara Darling was quite ready to fight that point on pure principle. But, no matter, she still wanted to prove it wrong by outdriving him.

Unfortunately, that lovely thought had to be banished to the nether regions. All thoughts of fun would have to go if Lara was going to find a husband, a rich one at that, in only one season and with no dowry to speak of.

To accomplish this, Lara had to be perfectly,

wretchedly, ladylike. At this thought, Lara's heretofore straight shoulders drooped. Her spine curved. And she had to fight the need to bury her face in her hands.

Oh, yes, her grandmother's dare had galvanized Lara through dress fittings, her third sister Amanda's etiquette lessons, and dance lessons from their late mother's dearest friend, Mrs. Richards, for the last two months, but now, sitting here waiting for the coach into Town, Lara had to keep reminding herself not to slouch.

And she most definitely had to fight the idea that outdriving the coachman was anything other than scandalous.

A lady. She would have to be a lady. The mere thought made her feel as if she inhabited a dream. She even had a lady's maid, of all things.

A horn sounded, bringing Lara's attention away from her contemplation of the straight hem of her gown. The young man also awaiting the mail coach, a Mr. Whitehead, stumbled out of the inn. He had obviously spent their waiting time with a tankard at his lips. Lovely.

"I say!" he shouted to no one. "'Tis the Baron!" And Mr. Whitehead took off across the courtyard.

The Baron. It was rumored that his name

came from the fact that he was actually a peer who had lost his fortune. It all seemed highly doubtful. In fact, Lara wanted to laugh when she first heard it, but she controlled herself. Ladies did not guffaw. Nor did they let on that they knew men to be the dumbest beasts on the planet. Well, okay, perhaps they were not the dumbest. But they were horribly close to it.

Take the chap falling on his face in the dust when the sun hit his eyes after a half hour of imbibing in the inn.

Or the Baron, as it were, racing hell for leather down a country road as if he might make up the twenty-four minutes he was late in the last second before he reached the inn.

Idiots, all.

Through the archway leading out from the inn's courtyard, Lara could see a throng of villagers gathered at the side of the road. Surely the entire town had turned out to witness the Baron's return. They cheered as the mail coach rattled along, then a hush fell over the crowd.

The Baron had crossed the Two Penny Bridge and was now galloping up Tisney Cob. Lara had already been informed by her maid, who, it seemed, had the amazing ability of learning every bit of gossip in a place within minutes of inhabiting it, that the Baron could race over the bridge, up the cob and through the inn's archway, with only inches to spare on either side, without ever letting up on his speed.

And, of course, the whole town turned out to watch such an amazing feat each day.

Lara inched forward, for though she had carefully showed no interest whatsoever in her maid's information, if the Baron could truly do such a thing, Lara wanted to see it.

And she wished with all her heart that she could try it as well.

Mr. Whitehead jumped up and rushed through the archway toward the road, brushing at the dirt clinging to the seat of his pants as he went. *That's it, man. Run toward a racing coach as you trip over your own tongue*, Lara thought with a roll of her eyes and a shake of her head.

Another cheer brought Lara's gaze back to the road. The coach raced over the bridge, but then disappeared from her obstructed view.

Still, her heart kicked into a faster rhythm. Lara finally stood and took a small step forward. And then another. She squinted at the archway. A tight squeeze, that's what it was. And the man was going to do it without cutting the horses' pace in the least.

Amazing.

If he did it, of course.

Lara curled her fingers into her palms and waited. She could hear the coach bars rattling, the horses' hooves pounding the ground and the silence of the villagers as the coach raced up the cob.

She couldn't help biting at her bottom lip as she stood staring at the archway, waiting for the sound of a collision.

But none came.

With a woosh of breath she hadn't realized she'd been holding, Lara watched the coach race through the archway unscathed.

Well, goodness!

The villagers erupted in excitement, and small children raced behind the coach as the Baron charged into the inn's posting yard and came to a halt in a cloud of dust.

Lara swallowed hard and fought the urge to rush forward along with everyone else. She also fought the need to run forward and beg to try.

Just once. To see if she could.

Because, she was pretty damn sure she could do it as well.

The Baron jumped down from his perch atop the box, and the villagers went mad, rushing forward and brushing his coat with outstretched fingers.

Oh, really, Lara thought, with a touch of disdain.

The envy that battled with disdain in her heart won out, but she kept it tramped down as best she could.

The man pushed back his beaver hat and smiled.

Bloody hell.

Lara could only stare. The Baron was, absolutely, the most beautiful man she had ever seen. He stood tall and lean with broad shoulders that were obviously not a trick of padding.

This Lara had been able to tell right off, but what made her stop and stare openly were the man's eyes: a piercing ice blue the color of a sky she had only dreamed of. They were set in a face darkened by the sun and made in the form of Adonis, surely.

Usually completely immune to men, their looks, money or bragging, Lara stood staring for at least a minute. And, she was rather sure, she actually had her mouth open the entire time.

Right, that was most definitely not ladylike.

Turning on her heel, Lara snapped her mouth shut and went to gather up her lady's maid and the one trunk she hadn't sent ahead.

The Baron was lovely to look at and could

take his carriage at a run through a place the size of a knothole, but he was still twenty-four minutes late. How good could he be with that hanging over his head?

"Did you hear?" Molly screeched as she clambered over to Lara.

Lara glanced up at her maid. "Hear what?" she asked, but continued without waiting, because she just did not want to know. "Where's the trunk? Let's be off, then."

"The reason the Baron's late is that he was waylaid! By highwaymen! And he took them down by himself."

Lara just snorted, she would definitely have to control that impulse when she reached London. "Surely, he did not take them down himself. What of the guard?"

"No, no, my sister's friend's friend is on the coach. She was sitting outside and said the Baron took down the highwaymen all by himself. After the Baron tied them up, the guard escorted them to the next town." Molly smiled smugly as if the damned Baron were her long lost brother. "He is that good."

"Oh, bloody hell."

Molly stumbled to a halt, her eyes blinking. "Excuse me?" she asked, obviously stunned at her lady's sobriquet.

15

"Nothing." It was the bane of Lara's existence to be the most *un*ladylike of all the Darling sisters. In fact, Reggie always teased that Lara was meant to have been male, surely.

Still, Lara *did* watch them, men that is, with utter disdain as her woman's mind marked off all the idiotic things they did and said.

But all the while, her heart hurt with the need to do everything they did.

Lara held herself very still as a part of her thundered with the urgent need to go yank the reins from the Baron's fingers and prove she could drive just as well as he. Better, even.

And how completely stupid that was! As if it would matter that she could drive better than the Baron; a man she had never met, and really ought not to care a fig about.

But *she* wanted to drive a coach and fight off highwaymen, damn it.

Instead she was off to London to find a husband. One with gout, no doubt. And one who would probably never allow her to drive . . . ever. Or shoot, either.

Damn, damn, damn. She would probably be forced to stop her swearing, too.

"Well, anyway, did you see him drive under the archway, my lady? Did you?"

Was there some reason her sister had engaged the most talkative maid alive, Lara wondered?

" 'Twas amazing, that's what it was. I've never seen the like."

Would the girl ever be quiet?

"Took my breath away! I must tell you that much."

Must you?

"And he is quite a figure of a man, to boot, don't you think? I nearly swooned when he made it under that archway without so much as a twitch on the reins to slow the horses. I don't think anyone else in the world can do such a thing!"

"I could do it."

Now she had done it. Opened her mouth and said the words. *I could do it.* What a stupid statement. Only men said such idiotic things and tried to prove themselves by acting like boys swigging their first pint.

Which she could also do better than any man alive.

"Really?"

Lara nearly tripped over her own shoes at the sound of the deep voice behind her.

She already knew who it was. She could tell by the lazy quality of his words and the deep timber of his voice. No one but a gorgeous man who could drive like the wind would speak with such complete antipathy about something he obviously felt so much emotion for.

And to put it all in one small word, too.

Lara stood a little straighter and turned around. There he was, even more beautiful close up. "You there," she said crisply, "I've a trunk to be loaded."

He just stared at her, the arrogant fool. Or rather, she was the fool, but he was still arrogant.

"You can drive, then?" he asked. He had the male pose down to a science, this one. One large hand balanced against a lean hip, weight on his back leg, his amazing eyes glinting with humor that took the last vestige of hers completely away.

She could usually control herself, or at least act like she had control. But men like this, men who were just too damn good at everything they did, melted away most of her common sense. They made it nearly impossible for her to pretend she didn't want a thing to do with them, their dares or their bragging.

Inevitably, she ended up acting just like them. A dismal habit: She knew this most definitely, for her woman's brain realized it completely.

Oh, Lord, it was times like this she really and truly envied Amanda's natural femininity.

Well, maybe she did not go so far as that.

But it would be awfully nice if she did not even notice the bravado in the man's voice.

"You could drive that carriage over the bridge, up the cob and through the archway? Without slowing down?" The Baron smiled. He didn't laugh at her. He just smiled, one side of his wide mouth hitching up and making her feel a touch faint.

Of all things, faint! As if she *were* some ninny like Amanda.

Lara raised her brows and faced the coachman. "Excuse me, driver." She *was* a lady, after all. He should not be speaking to her in such a way. "I have a trunk, and you're late."

That last part was probably not the best thing to say. It was just to goad the man. At least it would have goaded her, if she had been the coachman.

Which she wasn't, of course. *She* was a *lady*.

Though, truth be told, the thought of driving a mail coach every day between London and Wales nearly made her swoon. Whereas the thought of the husband-hunting season ahead of her left her absolutely cold. Damn it, she *wished* she were a coachman!

19

The Baron's expression did not change in the least as his clear eyes lingered a bit too long on her face. But then he just nodded. "Of course," he said and shifted his weight so that he could walk away. And then he winked at Molly before he loped off toward her trunk.

It was the wink.

At least that is what she wrote to Reggie later. Though she knew that it would only cause Reggie to make that horrible sound with her tongue against her teeth. Still, it was the only reason she could give.

He *dared* to wink at her maid.

She could have kept her mouth shut, really she could have. In complete control, she was. But the wink just pushed her right over the edge. No one would have been able to stay mute in such circumstances.

Well, maybe Reggie. Definitely Reggie, actually. But asking that of Lara Darling was asking too much. Much too much.

"I could," she stated loudly to his straight, tall back.

He stopped and she could just feel the smile that crept over that smug mouth of his. Oh, he was good at this.

Lara knew she ought to sit down quietly and take out her sewing. Right here, right now, she should just take out the handkerchief she was trying to embroider with her father's initials, and sit right down and work on it. In fact, her mind screamed at her to do that very thing.

Instead, Lara lifted her chin in the air and glared down her nose as the Baron turned, his eyebrows arching high over those disgustingly gorgeous eyes.

"I could do it," she said prettily.

"Go ahead, then," he said, obvious laughter in his voice.

She really wished she could, but how dare he pretend it was possible. "I can't!"

"I thought you just said you could."

What an irritating man, this "Baron." "Well, of course I am *capable* of doing it, you ingrate." *That* was not entirely necessary, but it did slip out. "I cannot very well drive the mail coach, however." Lara shrugged, making the action as dainty as possible. "You would be dismissed!"

The man shrugged as well, though his action would never have been called dainty. Graceful, yes: dainty, no. "No one here will tell. They don't want me fired, after all. I give them their daily dose of excitement."

"You are quite full of yourself, are you not, driver?"

"And you aren't?"

"Oh!" Lara blinked, and could think of nothing even close to ladylike to say.

"Fine then," she said finally. And she stomped off toward the coach.

Reggie would have been glaring at her, and Amanda would have fainted about ten minutes ago. Lara could even picture her youngest sister, Lissie, grabbing onto her skirts as she was wont to do.

But Lara kept walking toward the coach. This was wrong, she knew that, of course. She could get into trouble, she was sure. Whenever she felt this kind of excitement, whatever she was doing was inevitably wrong or bad or against some stupid rule somewhere. But she was absolutely *not* going to let this man think she would back down.

Anyway, she would not be allowed to go far enough to cause any trouble. The Baron would stop her before that happened, she was sure.

She just hoped the man would wait until she had at least taken the coach over the bridge. She needed to show him that she knew a thing or two about driving.

So there!

Lara allowed herself a mental eye roll.

A boy had already hooked up a new team of horses. He nearly swallowed his tongue when

Lara grabbed the reins, hitched up her skirt and pulled herself onto the driver's box of the coach.

She did love to shock men. Although, she had to admit, it wasn't nearly challenging enough for her taste. Lara carefully arranged the reins, which were a bit too big for her hand, between each of the fingers of her left hand.

"Let her be, James," the Baron said.

"Yes, James, hand me the whip, please." She looked up and stared levelly at the Baron as she held out her gloved right hand toward James.

Actually, their old groom would have given her a good dressing down for mounting the box without a whip already in hand. But, truly, if she had taken the time to find the whip this time, it would have ruined the affect.

Lara grinned, and what an affect she had established! The entire yard was quiet though full to the brim with local villagers. James stood with his jaw hanging open and the Baron had a fire in those blue eyes that made Lara feel truly alive.

Oh God, she loved this. It was like an energy that sped through her veins, making her head feel light and everything around her seem in sharper focus.

This was what she loved. This was exciting.

And, of course, it was something she ought not to be doing.

But she was, so she might as well get as much out of it as she could.

That's right, dare me! She smiled widely at the man below her.

Just make sure you don't let it go too far. And make sure your *pride takes the fall, not mine.*

Bloody hell, she thought suddenly. How was she ever going to make it though a season without Reggie at her side? Obviously, she wasn't even going to make it to Town. She swallowed hard, her bravado slipping with that thought.

James handed her the whip, and Lara folded her fingers around it without breaking eye contact with the Baron.

If the Baron were any kind of a gentleman, he would back down.

She didn't believe he had been a peer, but his speech at least attested to the fact that he was a gentleman. So he would stop her before it was too late. Of course he would.

Lara gave the man another chance, waiting a moment longer than truly necessary before lightly drawing on the reins so that they gently tugged all four horses' mouths.

No one stopped her. And so, nodding smartly

to James and flashing a wicked smile at the Baron, Lara cried out, "Stand away!"

The horses trotted off together perfectly. They were lovely.

Still she waited for someone to grab the lead's head, but again, nothing happened.

Fine. Lara took a deep breath and decided to concentrate on her task until that arrogant fool, the Baron, finally came to his senses.

Please, Dear God, let someone come to their senses, soon.

Lara urged the team back under the archway, and couldn't help the smile that spread across her face.

Oh, she did love to drive!

She concentrated on getting a feel for the sway of the coach, checked the responsiveness of the horses, gauged how close the sides of the small stone arch came to the edge of the conveyance.

The group in the posting yard of the inn followed her out, but Lara resolutely pushed them from her mind as she trundled down the road and over the Two Penny Bridge. She went a bit beyond the bridge, just enough to give her the length to get up a good run.

With absolutely excellent form, Lara cracked her whip and executed a turn that would have made the Ashton Hall groom puff up with pride. In fact, it made her sit a bit straighter on the box. Surely the Baron would see that she would not back down now, not with that bit of expertise proven.

Lara glanced up, and could see the man clearly. He was tall enough that everyone around him looked small in comparison. He had followed everyone out of the yard, and stood just to the right of the inn's entrance.

She stopped her team and waited. One of the horses stomped a hoof against the packed earth. They wanted to run as much as she wanted to drive.

From under her lashes, Lara flicked another glance at the tall man by the inn. He stood just like he had stood before, his entire being daring her to do exactly what she should not do.

Stop this while you can, Lara! her voice of reason yelled at her.

But her heart gave her head the cut direct.

With a grin of excitement, Lara flicked the reins and bent to the task of proving that she could drive that mail coach just as well as some man she did not even know.

God, she thought as they were off, she was such an idiot.

Chapter 2

Do keep your wits about you, Lara, for when you allow them to get away from you, which happens much more often than it should, dear, you do tend to get into heaps of trouble.
The Duchess Diaries, Volume One

The woman was a complete idiot. Griff watched, waiting for her to back down, and when she didn't, it was too late for him to stop her.

The only reason he had even let her get so far as to actually set the horses to a trot was because he watched her expertly take the reins before mounting the box, and then set them perfectly in her left hand.

If she had dared to hold the reins in both hands, he wouldn't have even let James hand her the whip.

Which she really ought to have had in hand when she mounted the box, but she obviously decided that she needed to swing herself up first and show off. It was exactly what he would have done, given the circumstances.

Still, now that she was at a full trot, she was going to kill herself—or worse, the horses. And she was definitely going to ruin the coach. Basically, he was going to be in big trouble when this was over.

All because of some idiot woman.

Damn, you'd think he could learn his lesson somewhere along the line. But no, just one headstrong mistake after another. He held his breath as he watched her rush over the bridge and toward the inn's stone archway with his precious coach. And he said a very ugly curse at the exact moment she reached the point of no return.

Fortunately there weren't any children around him. Anyway, no one was giving him even a tiny bit of attention as the lady driving his mail coach went roaring through that damned archway.

Silence gripped the villagers standing outside the entrance to the posting yard. And then a girl yelled, and they all began yelling and cheering and running under the archway to converge on the coach.

Griff followed them at a more sedate pace. He gave his lead horse a pat and glanced up at the woman. She just sat atop the box, her breasts heaving and her eyes more alive than any he'd seen in a very long time.

And damn if he didn't want to yank her down and take her right upstairs with him.

Either that or kill her.

Both of which would bring him even more trouble than this bit of muslin was worth.

Griff twitched a smile and then sauntered over to her side and raised his hand to offer the woman help down from the box.

She laid the whip in his hand instead and jumped from her perch. "I say," she said with a lift of her dark brows, "but that was a bit of fun now, wasn't it?"

Griff nearly laughed out loud. Definitely, he wanted to take her upstairs.

"Now, driver, my trunk, if you please." And the woman picked her way across the yard toward her maid.

Good job. Still, he had seen her fingers tremble when she handed him the whip, so he knew she was not quite as unfazed as she wished to seem. That said she was quite a woman.

An idiot, of course, but an idiot he wouldn't mind rolling beneath him once or twice.

Damn, but that thought made him absolutely randy. Imagine such a woman in bed! It would be like pure heaven, surely.

He started after her and couldn't help but swagger as he did. Oh yes, tonight was going to be interesting.

"My lady!" her maid cried, looking as if her world had suddenly come to an abrupt end. "My lady, what have you done?"

Griff frowned. Lady? A peer, then? That could complicate things a bit. Hopefully the woman was at the very least married, for her sake. As well as his, really. Though now that he thought of it, she did seem a bit young.

Oh God above.

"Molly, just get my trunk. I need a drink," the lady said.

Truer words were never spoken.

"Excuse me," Griff said quietly, stopping the young lady in her tracks. "What is your name?" No use abusing niceties at this point now, was there?

The girl glanced at him, and then raised her chin. That chin, a sharp spade of a chin that just cried out to be grabbed and hauled up toward his face so that he could take the pouty lips above it in a good, thorough kiss.

30

"I have already registered with the booking office."

"I heard this girl, your maid, I assume, call you *Lady*?"

"Yes." She actually had the good sense to hesitate. "I am Lady Lara Darling."

"Darling?" Griff echoed her. Darling. It sounded familiar.

"My father is the Earl of Ashton," she said.

Well, hell. If he remembered correctly, Ashton was a widower with a slew of daughters. Griff could only hope that Ashton had married again. And if so, the old goat had managed to marry a young one. Even as he thought it, though, Griff knew that wasn't the case at all. This pup was one of the Darling girls.

Griff couldn't help the groan that rumbled through his lips.

He could be in a heap of trouble.

"Are you Ashton's eldest, then?" *Please, God*.

The girl blinked at him, her round brown eyes fringed with the longest, darkest lashes he'd ever seen.

"Yes," she said finally. "How do you . . ."

"And you are not married, are you?"

At this Lady Lara Darling narrowed her doe eyes and straightened her spine. And a good spine it was, long and tall with a pair of breasts on the front that made Griff want to grovel at the girl's feet.

"Excuse me?" she said with just the right amount of shock. "That is no business of yours!"

"I thought not." Griff sighed deeply. "Tell me, at least, that you are not on your way to be wed."

That got him a stinging slap. Damn, that would leave a mark.

"So, you are on your way to your first season, then?" he said without missing a step.

She pulled her hand back for another blow, but Griff caught it quickly. "Don't you think you've given enough of a show for the villagers?" he asked quietly. "Shall we adjourn to the inn?"

"I don't know who you think you are, but . . ."

"Listen, Lady L, I'm a voice of reason. You've just done something utterly stupid. Grant you, I helped. But I had no idea a young *Lady* off for her first season would do something so thoughtless as to get herself ruined before ever reaching Town in the first place."

"I did not."

Griff just shook his head. "Oh yes, Lara Darling, you did."

She blinked, and he could see every thought that ran through her mind in the depths of her dark eyes. Her bravado staggered a bit, and then righted itself.

"I am sure, sir, that I have done nothing *too* horrible."

He just stared at her quietly. And she sighed. It was a beautiful sight, actually, the lifting and dropping of that incredible bosom.

"I have, haven't I?" she finally said. "Oh dear. I really ought to have brought Reggie with me. Or at the very least tried to listen to my own head more."

He knew that thought intimately. Listen to his own head. *If only*. It was the refrain of his life now.

But who on earth was this Reggie fellow?

Not that it mattered. Not that any of it mattered. This girl before him was nothing to him, meant nothing to him. He did not need to do another thing. He could turn around right now, load the coach and let her deal with the consequences of her actions.

It was as easy as that.

Of course, she would linger around the edges of his conscience for the rest of his life: just another person who would have been fine if he had not been born.

Damn. He had way too many people like that in his life as it was.

"Never fear, Mrs. Hastings." He grinned down at the lovely Lady Lara. "As always, I have a plan," he said to her.

"Who?" Lady Lara glanced around them. "What? Have you gone mad?"

"Already there, Mrs. Hastings. I didn't need to go anywhere at all, thanks."

She furrowed her brow and shook her head. "I don't understand."

"Trust me," he said softly, and then turned to the maid. "Take Mrs. Hastings's trunk to the coach, Molly." The girl smiled brightly and ran off to do his bidding with no hesitation at all. Good woman, that one.

"Come along, Mrs. Hastings," he said loudly, wrapping his fingers around Lara's arm. She, of course, dug in her heels.

Griff lowered his head and whispered in the girl's ear, "I am going to save your reputation right now. Don't fight it. Listen to your own head, Lara Darling."

But that was the last time the man ever said her name. From that very moment until he finally shoved them off in London, he called her Mrs. Hastings, very loudly, actually.

And since Molly would have run through Hyde Park naked if the man had asked her, her maid referred to Lara as Mrs. Hastings for the next four hours as well.

It nearly drove Lara mad.

Of course, she had to admit that the Baron, or, rather Mr. Hallsbury, as the man had finally introduced himself, was completely right, though she would never admit such a thing to him. If she had let anyone in Lower Tunsburrow know her true identity, her daring deed would have been known throughout London before she even reached the Town herself.

As it was, the place was abuzz with the story of the mysterious Mrs. Hastings. Lady Tattenbaum, her grandmother's best bosom friend, and the woman to whom Nanny L had entrusted her granddaughters' debuts, would not let the story lie.

"Did you meet this infamous Mrs. Hastings, then, dearest? Tell me you did! Although, of course, you cannot let on to anyone else that you did. I am just nonplussed that you actually took the mail coach to London. Who on earth does such things? Well, first off, women like Mrs. Hastings, that's who. She actually sounds like someone whose company I would enjoy very much. Though I would, of course, never admit to such a yearning." Lady Tattenbaum shook her formidable white wig with such venom, Lara was sure the plastic birds nesting therein would fly from their perch and join their counterparts outside the window.

And there were very many windows through which the birds might fly. Lady Tattenbaum's house was bright, with huge windows in every room, and not a single shade drawn.

And each room had a color theme. A color theme unlike Lara had ever seen in her life. At the moment they sat in a drawing room, the main color of which was purple and the undertones, mustard.

The front room was pink.

Lara's room was a circus of greens and fuchsia.

Actually, she was still in a bit of shock after going upstairs with her maid and supervising the unpacking of her trunks. She had realized very quickly that when one spent more than a few minutes in a room where the most predominant color is fuchsia, one did feel the need to run away to the circus or perhaps tread the boards as a singer of melodies.

Neither of which was really the best thing for Lara to consider for too long. Because, really, she just might do it.

"Now then, dearest," Lady Tattenbaum said with a shake of her head. "You mustn't do anything so thoughtless as take off on a mail coach ever again. Do you hear me? I will, of course, send a carriage for you wherever you might be. In fact, I cannot believe that I did not think of this in the first place. Although *really*, dearest, I *did* think you would write to me when you were ready to come.

Lady Tattenbaum deigned to take a sip of tea. "I am scandalized, absolutely scandalized that you would come to London, with no escort, in the mail coach. Well, *I'm* not scandalized, truthfully, nothing at all scandalizes *me*. But others would be, and I'm just sick at what could have happened."

She bit into a biscuit. "Honestly, dearest, that Mrs. Hastings character did you quite a favor. Without *her* story, yours would be all about town. Really. Arriving for your come-out on the mail coach, of all things. And without an escort."

"I had my maid." Lara blinked for a moment, amazed that she had actually been allowed to get a word wedged in between Lady Tattenbaum's terribly longwinded sentences.

"A maid will not protect your reputation, dearest. Remember that! For you have little going for you as it is. You must keep your reputation pristine. And I say that with all the love I can offer the dear granddaughter of my very best friend in the entire world. Of course, you are beautiful. Not quite exactly the thing, as it were, but beautiful all the same. A beauty you received, by the way, from your namesake."

Lady Tattenbaum stopped suddenly, her dull gray eyes filling abruptly with tears. "Oh, I so loved your grandmother." A moment of silence followed.

Silence now being at a premium, Lara reveled in it.

"Anyway, your grandmother was lauded by the *ton* in her day. And the men, well, the men found her completely irresistible. And, if I do say so myself, you have the same quality that she did. That little something that makes the men watch as you walk by."

Lara frowned.

"You do look very much like your grandmother, of course. You have her same regal bearing, which I'm sure has much to do with your height. You are lucky to have gotten your grandmother's tall, lean figure! And her eyes as well. And her hair! I did envy your grandmother for her hair, all those streaks of color! Blonde, copper and brown. And so thick. Ah, such lovely thick hair.

"I was born with hair so blonde as to be

white. Not an ethereal white, but a dull, lifeless color, and the texture of dry grass to make it even worse. It was the bane of my existence, truth be told. And that was the first thing I noticed about your grandmother. I was sitting with my mother in the receiving rooms and in walked this lovely girl with beautiful hair. So I asked her where she had bought her wig, and lo and behold, your grandmother told me that she did not wear a wig. That all that gorgeous hair was her own which she then powdered. And we were best friends from that day. Though, of course, I was always horribly jealous of her hair.

"Anyway, you are the very picture of my own dear friend." Lady Tattenbaum laughed slyly. "Of course, I used to tease your grandmother that the reason all the men swooned at her feet was because of her . . ." Lady Tattenbaum's cheeks actually tinged pink and she pressed her fingers against her mouth. "Well, I always told her that they were staring at her bosoms."

Lara actually felt her cheeks burn. She was not used to blushing. Usually, *she* was the one making someone *else* blush.

Lady Tattenbaum let out a laugh that could

have made the very trees outside tremble. "Isn't that awful of me to say? And of course it was not true. Well, not entirely? Because, as you see," Lady Tattenbaum gestured to her rather ample bosom. "I have my own as well, and the men never stared at me. Anyway, dearest, tell me how my darling Griff is doing."

Lara opened her mouth out of sheer reflex. There was a pause in the conversation, after all. Wasn't she supposed to say something?

"Who?" Right, brilliant. She would thrill all of London with her conversation.

"Griff, darling. Lord Trenton. Oh, and isn't he just a fine figure of a man? Such a shame, what has become of him, though to hear the young bucks talk, you'd think the boy had been made the prince of Hungary, I do say."

Boy? She could not be speaking of Mr. Whitehead, then, could she? He was the only boy Lara had met. Though, to call that gawky fellow a fine figure of a man was definitely giving him more than he deserved.

"Lord Trenton?"

"Anyway, we are off to the modiste, dearest."

Lara blinked. Lady Tattenbaum's changes in topic were quick! "Modiste?" she said, a bit perplexed, and then registered what the lady meant. "Oh, no," Lara said quickly. "I have already made sure that I have enough gowns for the entire season, Lady Tattenbaum."

"Not to meet the king, dear! I have secured your introduction, and believe me, no one with any taste at all has the right gown in their possession to meet the king."

Lady Tattenbaum laughed, her entire body shaking with the effort. "When one goes to be introduced to the king, one must be ready to wear something that would scare small children."

Lara couldn't help but be intrigued. "You can't be serious."

"Just you wait. We're off to concoct a monstrosity, dearest, a monstrosity. I must tell you, it is quite fun. We shall stand in the middle of the room and anything that we see which we would never dream of putting on a dress, we shall sew right into every seam! Bells and porcelain cherries. And, oh, we mustn't forget all that goes on underneath! You have to have hoops under your dress to meet the king."

Lara bit her bottom lip. "Really?"

"Oh yes, just you wait until you see what the other girls are wearing. There was a young girl a few years ago who sat down in one of the chairs as she waited, and she could not get back up. They had to tip the entire chair over and roll her out.

"Of course," Lady Tattenbaum leaned forward and spoke to Lara out of the corner of her mouth, "the truly scary thing is that some of them actually think they are the height of fashion."

Lady Tattenbaum made such a face that Lara giggled. *Bloody hell*, she thought. This season in London was shaping up to be more of a challenge than driving a coach through the eye of a needle. Lara smiled widely, every nerve ending tingling. What fun!

Chapter 3

I have this dreadful premonition that the London season shall bore you to tears. And so you will do something horribly scandalous. Try, at least, to be anonymous when you do so.
　　　　The Duchess Diaries, Volume One

Two thoughts struck Lara at once. And when one is teetering about on heeled slippers, and wearing a wig that is at least three feet high on one's head, having anything strike, even metaphorically, can be quite catastrophic.

As it was, Lara sat down hard, and she did stop and say a tiny prayer of thanks that there was a lovely padded chair just behind her.

Her hoops did fluff up rather high, however. Still, no one was paying her the slightest bit of attention, so probably no one saw the ankle and bit of shin she was sure she'd flashed before she slammed her hands down, shoving the white silk of her skirt back toward the floor.

Holding her springy skirt down with one hand, Lara covered her eyes with the other. The ballroom before her faded to black. She had been battling a horrendous ache in her head since being introduced to the king, and now, suddenly, with the thoughts that had hit her, the ache threatened to turn into a pain she wouldn't be able to tolerate.

The first thought had been niggling at her since she had arrived in London the week before, and that was that the London season was really not exactly as exciting as it was rumored to be.

The other had also been hovering about in her mind, but for much longer than the last week. Actually, her entire life, Lara had very much doubted that she wanted to marry.

And now, with a clarity that brought pain, Lara knew. London was a complete bore. And she absolutely did not want to give herself, her very freedom, over to some stuffy, boring man.

Good God, it would mean she would have to be ladylike for the rest of her life! The last week had nearly killed her. If she had to keep this up any longer, she might topple into insanity.

And coming right for her that very second

was one of the reasons she finally realized she did not want to marry.

"Lady Lara!"

The rather rotund Mr. Roddy Piperneil huffed into a seat beside her. He pushed nonexistent hair off his forehead and pulled at his creatively tied cravat. Roddy wasn't a bad sort, really, just a bit boring, which was horribly upsetting since he was the only man who seemed the least bit interested in her.

"It is rather hot in here, is it not?" he asked, but didn't wait for her to answer. "I'm sure it is worse for you, what with all that stuff under your skirts." He stopped for a moment, his high forehead creasing. "Goodness, that did not sound right, did it?"

"No," Lara said shortly. She had been to a few teas and musicales before her debut. This ball she now attended was her very first ball, a special one, actually, for all the girls that had just been introduced. And she was already tired of making small talk.

"Anyway, you did very well, Lady Lara. Did you see Miss Mellings lose her hair?"

Lara bit at her lip. "She did not lose her hair, Mr. Piperneil."

"Well, the concoction in her hair, at least. All

that stuff made quite a mess on the royal floor, I think. Poor Miss Mellings."

"Yes, poor Miss Mellings." Poor all of them, that the most exciting thing to happen in the last few days was that the porcelain birds in Miss Mellings's hair had crashed to the marble floor at her debut.

"Still, it was a right good show," he said. "I only attended tonight because my mother told me she wouldn't feed me for a month of Sundays unless I did. Otherwise, I'd rather eat my hat than go to such things."

"Really, Roddy!" Lara said. It was just beyond her to keep calling someone like Roddy, *Mr. Piperneil*. He surely had never matured past thirteen. Though, truth be told, not many males ever *did* mature past thirteen.

"What?" Roddy asked. And, unfortunately, he really did not understand why Lara remonstrated him.

She sighed. The man next to her was the only eligible bachelor who had shown any prolonged interest in her. And, as Lady Tattenbaum had said to her after Roddy paid his first call on her after a musicale at the beginning of the week, Roddy Piperneil's income was laughable and he had the wit of a dead duck.

Anyway, the very idea of spending the rest of

her life living in the same house as Roddy Piperneil and listening to his inane conversation for that long as well made Lara seriously contemplate entering a nunnery.

As Lara was not even Catholic, that seemed rather drastic.

"Can you believe that it hasn't rained in so long?" Roddy asked then. He shook his head. "Amazing, really. It is the driest season I've ever experienced."

Maybe not that drastic.

"My mother's roses are wilting horribly."

Yes, she was crazed with boredom. "I never thought I'd ever marry," she said.

Roddy blinked at her. He had pale, bluish-greenish-brownish eyes that were rather small. Lara bit her lip in the face of Roddy's obvious shock. She had not meant to say that last bit out loud.

"Really?" Roddy asked. "I thought that was the main goal of every living female."

Lara grimaced. "No, actually."

"But, then, what *do* you want to do?"

Lara thought for a moment, but she didn't really know. And the last person she wanted to have this conversation with was Roddy Piperneil—but if she was going to help her sisters, she had to marry. To say nothing of the dare her grandmother had thrown out, obviously knowing that was the thing that would get Lara into London, at least.

"I think I need a plan," she said.

Roddy blinked his pale eyes once again.

Lara rolled her own eyes, and realized that she really needed to get away from Roddy Piperneil, especially since she was trying to use her intelligence to figure out a problem.

The use of intelligence was definitely stymied when in the presence of Roddy Piperneil.

"There you are, dearest!" Lady Tattenbaum swept toward them. She was a vision in purple, her turban topped with a huge, sweeping purple feather. "I wanted to introduce you to Lady Belnap."

Lara realized then that there was a small woman with Lady Tattenbaum. Lady Tattenbaum did tend to overtake one's senses. People around her blended into the bland background.

Lara quickly stood to make Lady Belnap's acquaintance, and within seconds they were surrounded by three other ladies eager for the gossip that Lady Tattenbaum offered. Poor Roddy looked as if he wished the floor might open up and swallow him.

"I do say," Lady Tattenbaum said, "Lady Belnap and I have been bemoaning the state of our gardens. My poor roses look as if they have been breathed on by a dragon."

"Yes, where is our rain?" Lady Belnap said.

Oh Lord, when even Lady Tattenbaum began speaking of the weather, there really was something wrong with the world. Lara leaned most of her weight on one foot. Deplorable manners, yes, not standing up straight, but absolutely called for when one might fall over from boredom.

Roddy bowed and excused himself, and Lara watched him enviously. Oh, to be a man. To be able to go riding in the park without worrying about taking an escort.

Although, truth be told, Lara did not usually take an escort with her when she exercised Lady Tattenbaum's mare, Goldie, on early runs in the park. She worried about the fact that she should, though. It would be nice not to have to worry.

The ladies around Lara continued their intriguing conversation while Lara concentrated on keeping her eyes focused. And then she realized that she could now think more on her plan, with Roddy gone and the women around her droning on about rain.

Hmmm. She needed a goal.

"Don't you think so, Lady Lara?"

Lara heard her name and glanced at the ring of women around her. "Er . . ."

"I know *I* think so," said Lady Belnap.

"Well, I don't," said Lady Tattenbaum. And then she launched into a lovely long speech that allowed Lara to go back to her planning.

Now, where was she?

"The goal of every gardener in England, really, should be to find the right soil." Lady Tattenbaum was still going on and on about whatever the women were debating.

Goal! That was it. She needed a goal. Lara smiled at Lady Tattenbaum, who frowned at her mid-sentence, but did not stop talking.

Okay, a goal. Lara tapped her finger against her full skirt as Lady Tattenbaum droned on in the background. Her goal, thanks to Nanny L, was to be married within one season. Of course, she could probably achieve it by showing Roddy Piperneil the smallest amount of encouragement.

Lara shuddered at that thought.

No, she really did need to make this goal more palatable to herself.

"Did you hear," Lady Tattenbaum said then,

bringing Lara's attention back to the conversation going on around her, "that Miss Rosalie Wyndham is engaged, finally?"

"Really?" asked Lady Belnap.

"You don't say?" said Lady Tinshew.

"Yes, she has accepted the suit of Lord Stilton."

"Lord Stilton?" Lady Belnap blinked. "I thought he had died."

"He is quite alive, although I do believe he is the oldest man on earth, and now he is going to marry a twenty-year-old girl," Lady Tattenbaum said.

And Lara had the answer to her dilemma. "That's it!" she said. All three women turned to stare at her. "Sorry," she said quickly. "Do excuse me, please. I need a glass of punch." And she danced away from her companions.

Lara felt much better than she had just a few moments before. She had a grand idea, after all.

First, she realized, the man she would marry had to be wealthy. Disgustingly wealthy, so that she could set up her sisters and have some left over so that she could travel when her husband died.

During the Selfton's musicale, Lara had decided that she might enjoy traveling outside of

England. Roddy had told her that he had met a woman in Greece who swam in the sea from one island to the next. Now *that* sounded exciting.

Especially against the backdrop of the Selfton's musicale.

Lara shook away the memory of the musicale. That didn't matter anyway, because she had a plan. She was going to marry someone old. Very near death. As near as one could be, really, and still be alive.

Lara grinned and poured herself a glass of punch. Ah yes, such a good plan! Still, obviously, she would have to be with this husband of hers for a few months at least, though hopefully less, so she also needed a man that was tolerably interesting and not too awfully degenerate as to make her do anything that might cause her to wish to jump off a cliff.

Lara took a long sip of watery punch. She felt as if a great weight had been lifted from her shoulders.

Perhaps she could truly, successfully accomplish this thing she had set off to do!

Two days later, Lara was no longer dancing. More to the point, she was sitting in a chair in a gold ballroom owned by Lord and Lady Hard-ing. She had been sitting in that chair for nearly two hours.

Mr. Bradshaw was sitting across from her on a divan. His body seemed to spill over both sides, though the piece of furniture was not small. Lara had been speaking with Mr. Bradshaw for the entirety of the two hours she had been sitting in her chair.

Around them people talked to each other, danced, walked around.

Oh, how she wanted to stand. Her bum had fallen asleep nearly an hour before. Surely she would never feel her legs again.

But Mr. Bradshaw was extremely wealthy and very old. And sick, to top it all off. She glanced at him. He was wheezing and could barely sit up straight.

He was perfect, really. Exactly what she wanted. And so she sat with him, trying to will herself to be charming and ladylike so that Mr. Bradshaw might perhaps want to marry her.

She really wanted to cry.

Especially since Mr. Bradshaw was one of the more palatable choices for a husband, being that he was one of the richest men in London. Truly, she was becoming rather desperate. Every man she had been introduced to that could possibly meet her requirements for matrimony was either older than Hadrian's Wall, surely, or was the size of that same wall.

Both descriptions aptly fit Mr. Bradshaw.

Gout was prominent in London as well. Of that Lara had become acutely aware.

Lord Merser hobbled past her line of vision. His problem was opposite to Bradshaw's. She had never in her life seen a person in such dire need of bulk. The only thing keeping Lord Merser stuck to the earth in a brisk wind was the density of his proboscis.

That, of course, was incredibly contemptible of Lara even to think. But she had quite noticed of late that she tended toward bouts of complete churlishness.

Since she was usually quite an agreeable person, or at least she pretended to be, Lara decided that her moments of meanness were the result of sleepless nights—of which she had spent several since arriving in London.

As would be expected when one had to deal with a ghost every night.

Unfortunately, Lara's ghost was actually not one to make her sojourn in London more exciting. Oh, no, nothing so entertaining as that. Lara was plagued by the ghost of a memory: a memory of a man.

To her ultimate dismay, Lara had dreamed of Mr. Hallsbury, or the "Bloody Baron," as she had begun to refer to the man in her mind, every single night since meeting him. To make matters worse, the dreams were absolutely shocking.

Strange dreams in which he came to her in the darkness of night, and touched her, kissed her, feathered his fingers against her skin. And her skin was very much at his mercy, for it tended to be unclothed, of all things.

All together unsettling, that's what it was. And Lara had not slept a full night in more than a week.

She was going mad.

That is why, when she actually smiled in true delight upon seeing Roddy Piperneil making his way toward her, and then actually accepted his offer of a dance, she blamed the Bloody Baron entirely.

When one was in one's right mind, Roddy Piperneil was terribly easy to reject. Poor boy.

"Are you ill, Lady Lara?" he asked as he led her onto the dance floor.

Lara frowned at her partner. "No," she said.

"It is just that you seem to be limping, and you have been sitting with Mr. Bradshaw all evening. Surely no one would sit with that terribly scary man unless forced to by severe dizziness or some other affliction."

Lara really did wish to cry. She could not possibly marry Mr. Bradshaw, for Roddy was entirely correct. She would surely die of boredom before the man stuck his spoon in the wall.

"I am fine," Lara told Roddy. "But I think my foot is asleep."

They faced each other and Roddy bowed, his tight breeches causing him to wheeze as he did. Hiding her laugh behind her fan, Lara curtsied most prettily. She was getting quite good at being ladylike, if she did say so herself.

"You should dance more often, my lady," Roddy informed her. "It helps the circulation."

Lara just nodded, as she had to move down the circle and take another partner. The man looking back at her could not have been older than Reggie, certainly, and his cravat looked like something alive, the way it sprouted so from his neck and furled up, nearly hiding his eyes from view.

He bowed and spoke to her, and Lara could not make out a word, his mouth being covered by his neckpiece as it was.

How on earth was Lara supposed to find any of these men even slightly interesting? It baffled the mind that women married at all.

She went on to her next partner and then the next, and finally Roddy came into view again. Goodness, who would believe she would be glad to see him twice in one night? Scary, that.

He grinned and promenaded around her with a sprightly step.

She frowned at him. "You seem rather excited about a dance, Mr. Piperneil," she said.

He laughed, and it sounded very giddy. Lara's frown deepened.

"Oh, I'm always excited at this time of the month," he said and then stepped closer to her and whispered in her ear, " 'Tis the full moon." His eyebrows lifted. "Men in London have a fine pastime on the night of the full moon."

"Really?" she asked. And he was gone. Mr. Tall Cravat stood before her. *Bugger it*. Finally something interesting had come from Roddy Piperneil, and she would have to go through five promenades before she saw him again.

But then a thought occurred to her. "You're a man," she said to the boy in front of her. He looked a bit baffled. Obviously, he was not at all sure if he fit the description. "What are your plans for this evening?" she asked.

The boy sputtered and stuttered, and said not one coherent word. So, Lara tried with her next partner. "What is it that men do on the full moon in London?" she asked the next one straight out.

"Ah, you'll be talking about the races?" he asked. This one had a waistcoat that rivaled Lady Tattenbaum's front room in color. It was pink, very pink with blue stitching. And that was really the best part of his outfit. His breeches were green.

And he had lace coming out of each sleeve and every buttonhole. Even his high-heeled shoes had lace on them.

"Races?" she asked.

But of course she was handed over to her next partner, who was a doddering old fool of a man, married, unfortunately, or he would be perfect for her. It was Lord Rawlings, and she had already made his acquaintance and knew that he could not hear anything at all, but would not use an ear horn. She just smiled at him as he, of course, talked about the fact that London had not seen rain in these three months.

Honestly, what did people speak of when it *did* rain, Lara wondered?

Finally Roddy came back to her. "What are these races?"

He blinked at her. "Who told you about the races?"

"It doesn't matter, just tell me about them, and tell me now, quickly."

And Roddy complied. She had to admit in that moment, Roddy did have his good qualities.

"Oh, it's nothing that would interest you, Lady Lara. Just some races up at Hampstead Heath. Coach and four, they be."

"Really?" Lara felt her skin go hot and cold, all at the same time. "How divine!" she cried. Which, of course, she should not have done.

Roddy looked at her as if she had just picked up her skirts and done a lone dance across the floor. But then he just shrugged and told her. "We lay wagers, but the Baron always wins, anyway. When he comes, there is not much competition."

The Baron? Lara was used to her senses reacting to things they should not. She was used to the surge of excitement she felt as she clambered up on the box of her father's old coach, or the thrill as she aimed her father's gun and felled a rabbit on the run with one shot.

But the flush that crept up her neck, all hot and prickly when she heard the Baron mentioned was something else all together. And her heartbeat surely tripled in speed.

"The Baron's a coachman, the best there ever

was. He was also . . ." but he had to go on to his next partner and Lara had to dance with the boy with no neck. She knew that her palms were wet, for she had suddenly had quite a flush of heat rush through her. For once, she was very glad to be wearing gloves. Now she completely understood why one should wear them at all times.

She finally made it around to the dandy, who fortunately loved to talk, and did not seem to understand that there were some things about which you should not speak to women. She was becoming rather endeared to his pink coat after all.

When she asked him about the races, he said. "Have you heard of Mrs. Hastings?"

Lara nodded calmly, though she was quite ready to faint.

"Well, some of the boys have put her name in the book at White's. They want her to come out of hiding and prove that she can drive. They want to know if she can beat the Baron."

Oh! That would be so lovely. Lara experienced all the same feelings she enjoyed when she was faced with something wonderful that, of course, she knew she shouldn't do. *Couldn't* do! *Wouldn't* do!

I swear, Reggie, I won't, she mentally told her

sister, who would be giving her quite a look right about now if she had been there.

"Of course, the Baron has said she's not real. At the very least, the story of what happened has been exaggerated, I'm sure."

"What?" she cried.

But she was twirled around in that instance, and no one heard her. She went on to her next partner, endured Lord Rawlings's dronings about the weather.

And finally, Roddy bounced around her, obviously in high spirits, and suddenly she really did want to slap him. If she were him, she could go out there tonight and show everyone that Mrs. Hastings was not a story that was exaggerated.

Of course, if she were Roddy, she'd have to kill herself, but be that as it may.

Lara really was in a foul mood after that. She went home as soon as she could. Blast Mr. Bradshaw, anyway, she could not possibly try to get in his good graces, which, it seemed, only lamb in gravy and tarts with sugar could do anyway, but really, the thought of spending effort to get such a horrible person to ask her to marry him was just more than she could bear.

Yes, she was definitely in an awful temper when she tried to go to bed that night. And knowing that she would dream of the Bloody Baron anyway did not help matters at all.

Thus, when she found herself sneaking out of Lady Tattenbaum's house in the middle of the night, Lara once again blamed it entirely on the Bloody Baron.

So, he had put it about that Mrs. Hastings was only a story, had he?

Well, she would see about that!

Mrs. Hastings, wearing a mask, of course, would make the Bloody Baron eat his words this very night.

Lara hired a hack to drop her outside of London at Hampstead Heath and saw her nemesis immediately upon alighting.

The man *did* tend to draw the eye.

A group of men stood mingling about a bit of road shadowed by tall trees. Moonlight speared through the branches. The Baron stood in a patch of moonbeam, his hair shining blue-black, his face in shadow, and his shoulders wide under the thin lawn of his shirt, as he did not wear a coat to protect him from the chill of the night.

Bloody arrogant fool.

Well, she was actually more the fool. But the Baron was most definitely arrogant.

Lara stopped when she saw him, though, her

body reacting physically to the sight of him. Her dreams had caused her unease. But they were nothing next to the way her stomach seemed to roll over and her heart quickened when she spied the man in the flesh.

Amanda had read aloud from her romantic novels on occasion, and that is where Lara had heard the phrase about a heart quicken-ing. At the time, she had made a terribly sarcastic sound at the back of her throat and told Amanda that such a thing was entirely impos-sible.

And now, here she was, Lara Darling, feeling her heart quicken as she stared at a man she hardly knew.

Really, what on earth was wrong with her?

With a deep breath, Lara stood a bit straighter and marched toward the men.

"I say!" She heard some boy remark. The en-tire group turned toward her as if part of a male ballet.

She recognized Roddy, and she swallowed hard, fear making her stumble a bit. Her mask would be put to the test now. Fortunately he didn't show any signs of realizing who she was.

She smiled and tilted her face up. "You think Mrs. Hastings an exaggeration, then?"

There was a moment of stunned silence.

Again she felt that little charge of excitement when she was able to shock a bunch of cocky young men.

"Is it you, then?" a boy said. And a bit of her bravado slipped as she recognized him as the boy with the cravat up to his nose. He couldn't have placed her, could he?

" 'Tis Mrs. Hastings!" Another yelled.

She sighed in relief, that was more like it.

"Finally, Baron, you have met your match. And it comes in the shape of a woman, no less!" Loud, raucous laughter followed this statement, and Lara felt a grin spread across her face.

"That's right, Baron, you have met your match!" she said, as she swaggered closer to the group.

"For the love of God, woman!" And the Baron charged right for her.

She blinked at him, coming at her like a bull. He would not hit her, would he?

No, but he would grab her, it seemed.

She made an inelegant sound as the Baron's shoulder connected with her midsection, and then all she could see were the backs of his booted heels kicking up the dust of the road.

"You are some kind of idiot," he said quietly

as he stalked quickly away from the shouting group of boys behind them.

"Put me down!" Lara cried. "How dare you!"

But he only laughed at her. Of course, the laugh held absolutely no mirth whatsoever. The sound actually put a shiver of fear right through her.

It was probably the same feeling a young child would feel in the face of a very angry father. Of course, she was not sure, because she had never seen her father angry. Not from lack of trying on her part, of course. But her father had pretty much ignored her no matter what she did.

Well, she had someone's attention now.

Not that she had asked for it!

Well, okay, so she had. Lara sighed just as the Baron plunked her atop a very large horse and then followed her up without even the need of a footstool.

Goodness, the man was tall.

Later she decided that this was the main reason she completely forgot to fight him. For in retrospect, Lara realized that this was the moment she could have surely slipped down and run for it. Forcing the Baron to race her.

It was all because with each graceful movement of his large frame, Lara was that much more awestruck by the Baron.

He really was amazingly light on his feet.

"Ah, c'mon, man!" one of the boys cried out.

The Baron turned. "I'll not be racing this night," he yelled at them. Some laughter followed this statement, but a few of the men yelled out things obviously meant to fire up the Baron's ire.

They would have fired hers, for sure. But the Baron ignored them completely. Wrapping one arm around her chest and shoulders, he anchored her tightly against him, and took up the reins with his other hand. And then he kicked his horse into a very bumpy trot.

God, were they going to ride like this all the way to London? She would have a bruise across her backside that might rival Lady Tattenbaum's favorite purple turban in color. She tried to turn a bit, but her captor held her fast.

"Oh really, *must* you choose this moment to prove your masculine ability to overpower?"

"I am not proving anything but my gallantry at this point, Mrs. Hastings."

"That is the most hilarious thing I've heard in a week."

He didn't comment, and they bounced along for a moment in silence.

Stupid, silent man. "You may turn around now and take me back to the race. I am going to prove that Mrs. Hastings is very much real and definitely able to drive better than any of those young upstarts!"

"No, you are not," he said.

The worst part was how calmly he said it. How dare he be so in control. But, of course, he was. She had no hope of getting away from him. She was not going to drive tonight. A pity, really, she wanted to so badly.

"You have no right . . ."

"What? To save you? To make sure you don't ruin your life?"

Lara frowned. "I do not need saving."

"I completely disagree. You are out to ruin yourself, and you don't even realize it. Obviously, Lara Darling, deep down you want to ruin your prospects. But you have no idea how that is going to adversely affect the rest of your life. And for some reason, I just can't let you do it. At least not if I am able to stop it."

Lara wanted to say something extremely brilliant to rebut his point, but nothing came to mind. Especially since he seemed to be right. She bit at her lower lip and kept her mouth closed.

She did not want to be here in London, and

she did not want to be married. The Baron was right, some part of her was trying to make it all go away.

"I am most uncomfortable," Lara said, finally, rather petulantly, actually. She did hate it when she became petulant. It was terribly unbecoming, but it was a personality trait that tended to come out when she was wrong and someone else was right. So, really, she was petulant a lot.

Still, at least she realized that it was not a good trait, and she did try to curb her tendency toward it. That was something, anyway.

The Baron did not seem to notice her petulance, and in answer to her question, he just pulled her closer so that her bottom slid off the edge of the saddle and onto the cushion of his upper thighs.

It was actually much more comfortable, but altogether unsettling. If one could be ruined socially by simply driving a coach, surely sitting upon a man's thighs was reason enough for being deported.

And why on earth did it suddenly seem completely reasonable to turn around and press her chest into his, her face against his neck? And, goodness, she could then reach up and thread her fingers into the hair that curled at his nape.

Lord, she must have the heart of a trollop!

Well, actually, she already knew; as Reggie liked to point out, Lara had the heart of a man. And all men were degenerates. So, with that reasoning, she was part degenerate.

Lara then realized that if she turned her head slightly and reached up with her lips, she could kiss the underside of the Baron's jaw.

Sitting upon a man's lap was not a good position for a degenerate.

Especially since, suddenly, it seemed that all she wanted in life was to press her lips to any part of the Baron's body she could find exposed. His skin would feel good against her lips, she was pretty sure. Warm, rugged, manly.

She sighed, closed her eyes and tried to think of something else.

"Lara, I cannot always be there to rescue you. You must be more careful."

Good. Anger. That was much better than the strange buzz of awareness that had charged her nerve endings in the last few minutes.

"You are not rescuing me, you Bloody Baron."

"Griff."

"What?"

"My name."

Griff? There was something familiar about

that name. "Fine then, Griff, you are not rescuing me."

"Right."

Lara waited, but the man said nothing more. Ooooooh, she did so hate men who didn't speak. Her father could sit at his desk for an entire day fiddling with one contraption or another without ever saying a word. Even when asked a question, he did not feel the need to acknowledge it.

Maddening, truly.

"You are quite arrogant, sir."

"I'm not, actually."

"Then what are you, actually?" There was that damned petulance again. She tried to breathe slowly and find her soft, gentle, mature femininity somewhere. She knew she had a bit of it, even though it did tend to get lost at times.

He did not say anything, and she thought that he would ignore her again. But then he said very quietly and with complete sincerity, "I do not want you to get hurt, Lara."

And she started to cry.

Well, there was her femininity, in full, tearful force.

Fortunately, she did not blubber, but a tear popped unbidden from the corner of her eye and streaked down her cheek. And then another and another. Drat.

Now she wanted to turn and press her face into his neck for comfort. First a degenerate trollop and then a weepy child. This man did not bring out the best parts of her personality—but, confound him, the only other person in the world who had ever worried about her was Reggie. And, of course, her mother and Nanny L, but they were both gone.

And they were all women. It was their duty to worry.

And now this man, a man she did not know at all, seemed truly to be worried about her.

Strange and somewhat terrifying feelings were punching at her insides. Unsettling. Everything about this man and the emotions he raised was unsettling.

They rode silently as Lara composed herself. She had even surreptitiously wiped the evidence of her tears from her face when she realized with a start that they were back in London proper.

"Now we have a bit of a problem," Griff said darkly. "I can't just drop you off in front of Lady Tattenbaum's home. And I can't send you off in a hack."

"I left in a hack."

"And you will never do so again."

Lara frowned.

"You've never left Ashton Hall, have you? You have absolutely no idea how dangerous it is here. Not only could you be hurt or taken for an urchin and sold into slavery, but you absolutely could be found out. And then your life would be completely ruined."

"How on earth do you know about Ashton Hall?"

"A pertinent question at this time of great danger," Griff said, with irony so thick it stood by itself.

"Ha! Danger. I sneaked out, and I can sneak back in."

"Good lord."

"I dare any man to try and overcome me. I'll take him with one hand tied behind my back." For the love of pete, she was sounding like the cocky young son of Ashton Hall's old butler, Yates. Reggie liked to point that out when Lara was at her worst.

"You, my dear, need a keeper."

Lara choked on her sharp intake of breath. Of course, from the perspective of her wise female brain, Lara realized he was completely correct. But how dare he!

"I know, I know. I'm arrogant," he said with a low chuckle.

"And completely without guile, sir."

"Right, so back to the problem of getting you into your room without the world knowing where you went tonight."

Lara shrugged. "I'll climb back up the same trellis I climbed down."

"Tell me your room is on the ground floor."

"Second, actually."

His arm tightened around her. A reflex, obviously. But she did have to fight her own reflex to snuggle back against him. "Don't worry," she said, as some strange part of her yearned for him to worry horribly.

"Well, we shall not see if you can climb back up the trellis. And if you climb down again, I shall take a switch to your backside."

All thoughts of snuggling grew instantly cold and hollow. And it wasn't anger that caused the reaction, but a sadness that startled her. All these strange feelings roiling about in her stomach, surely an unwanted case of attraction her woman's body was having to this man, and he only thought of her as a child who needed to learn a lesson.

With that wash of realization, Lara lost all of her fight. "Just drop me at the back door. The servants won't question me. I've been restless since I arrived, and I tend to wander the halls at night."

She could feel his hesitation, and then the slight pressure of his chin against the top of her head. "The ghost of Dryer House."

Lara frowned. "How do you know the name of Lady Tattenbaum's home?"

"I am all-knowing."

"Tsk."

"All right, then, I'll drop you at the back. But we'll have to be very careful that no one sees."

The horse's footfalls echoed in the street as they passed a lone man driving a cart. He didn't even glance at them. They rounded a corner and there was the gate to Lady Tattenbaum's back garden.

Lara scowled. "How did you even know that I am staying with Lady Tattenbaum? And how on earth do you know where her home is?"

Griff pulled his horse to a stop behind a tree, and then he put two fingers under her chin and gently tipped her head up so that she was scowling right into his magnificent eyes. And she just could not keep that scowl on her face.

Honestly, she felt like swooning. At the very least, she kept that inclination in check. Though she did feel herself lean slightly toward him. God, he was breathtaking.

"Now listen to me, Lara Darling." He sounded, once again, like a tyrannical father. Lara couldn't help the exasperated sigh that escaped her lips. "I do actually know a bit of your circumstances, and I know that you cannot squander the opportunity of this season."

"How . . ."

"It does not matter." He leaned closer to her face, so that his breath feathered against her cheek. It was nice, warm against the chill and actually smelling of mint. He must chew it. How nice.

"I know you, Lara Darling. I see in you the same spirit I had once. And it is a good thing, if you use it wisely. But you are being foolish. Do not be foolish."

"You sound like Reggie," she said.

He frowned. "He is looking after your own good, then."

"Reggie is my sister."

He laughed outright at that. "Good, I am glad. Now, go enter Dryer House without being seen, a feat that shall be child's play for you, I'm sure."

Lara sat a bit straighter and smiled.

"And do not be foolish any longer."

That deflated her, though he was completely right, of course. She really needed to be better.

Especially if she were going to win Nanny L's wager.

Griff leaned even closer and his soft warm lips caressed her forehead with a kiss.

Lara closed her eyes as a delicious heat shot through her like the time she had taken a surreptitious sip of her father's brandy. Oh, yummy! It was her first kiss from a man, and it made her shake.

She wished, suddenly, that she could feel the warmth and softness of his lips against her own lips. Somewhere deep inside, she even found herself wishing he would kiss her neck. She imagined leaning her head back as this man's wonderful mouth ravaged her entire body.

A shiver trembled over her.

"I know what you are thinking," he said softly.

Lara blinked, her eyes opening wide in the dark of the night. "You do?" she asked warily.

"I can see it in your eyes and feel it in my heart, which I think is very much like yours."

"Oh, no," Lara whispered. Her face heated with the thought that the Bloody Baron could see the thoughts in her head.

"You are afraid you cannot do what you have set out to do."

"I am?" she asked. Obviously, they were not thinking about the same thing.

"But you can succeed. And you must not be foolish anymore. You have your sisters to think about. If you ruin your name, you damage theirs as well."

"Oh." She did not know whether to be disappointed or relieved that this man did not really know what she was thinking.

He kissed her forehead again, this time even more chastely. Lara could not help the sad sigh that escaped her lips.

"Go, my lady, and be safe," Griff said. He lifted her and set her on her feet as if she weighed nothing.

Again, it was like something out of one of the novels Amanda could not get enough of.

And Lara was exactly like one of the heroines as she ran on shaking legs, slipped into Dryer House, and then pulled aside the drapes so that she could peek out at the man in the shadows.

God, finally her woman's heart showed itself. But, of course, it showed itself to be just as untrustworthy as a man's heart.

Chapter 4

Do not lose your heart until you have found it, dearest. Yes, a cryptic statement. But you shall understand it when it happens. Of course, then it may be too late.

The Duchess Diaries, Volume One

Lord Thomas Brayton, Viscount Rutherford, reread the article one more time before throwing the newspaper aside and contemplating the drapes. So, it seemed that this Mrs. Hastings was for real. She had piqued his interest when he had first read of the incident in Lower Tunsburrow.

Of course he knew that such things were often hyperbole. This second account, though, proved that there was something to the first story.

Thomas absently kneaded the twisted muscles of his thigh. Interestingly, both stories mentioned Griff.

It was an ugly thing to be a bitter, used-up old man when you had never really gotten through with living. But that was exactly what Thomas knew himself to be. At thirty-five, he was older than dirt. He had nothing and no one to live for; anger and bitterness were his only emotions.

The anger came when he thought about Griff—when he realized what that man had taken away from him.

The bitterness erupted when Thomas tried to walk without a limp.

And it all congealed into a horrible, ugly feeling Thomas couldn't quite name. Although Griff had lost everything as well, he still retained a bit of dignity in the fact that most of London seemed to think him some sort of fallen God.

They looked on Thomas, he knew, with pity. Thomas had come out of it all a crippled, humiliated idiot. But Griff, though he was now working as a coachman, of all things, was still just a bit larger than life.

It was amazing, really, even when Griff had been at his worst, drunk and losing money hand over fist at the gaming tables, he had a charisma that made people stand in awe of him.

That thought brought a pain to Thomas's

heart that was physical. He closed his eyes fiercely and rubbed at his temples.

Something was going on in town now that involved Griff—something strange, and possibly laced with ingredients that would give Thomas the recipe for Griff's demise. Perhaps it could be turned in such a way that Griff might finally feel a bit of Thomas's pain.

Suddenly, Thomas had reason. He had a goal: revenge. He knew, of course, that his giddiness over the thought of revenge meant he had sunk to his ultimate low. But better giddy with revenge than wallowing in the hollowness of anger and bitterness, with no way to subdue those two damaging emotions.

For the first time in seven years Thomas had a goal. And it felt damn good.

He rang the bell at his side and the ever-dutiful Sterling appeared before Thomas had even wrapped his fingers around his cane.

"Have the carriage readied, Sterling," Thomas said, shoving himself up from his chair and wobbling only slightly when he put a bit too much weight on his bad leg. "And have Egbert pack my trunks. I'm off to Town."

Sterling blinked, but to his credit did not gape or make any sound of astonishment. In fact, the man recovered marvelously, for he answered after only a few seconds of stunned silence. "Of course, my lord."

Griff rang the bell at Dryer House and then stepped back, tugging at his waistcoat as he did. He hated to admit it, but he felt completely out of place standing at the front door of his old world. He suddenly realized with a touch of what could only be melancholy that it had been seven years since he had walked through the front door of a peer's home.

A butler opened the door. "Deliveries at the back," the man said quickly.

Griff frowned, did he really look so different? With a bit of a smile, Griff caught the door before it closed and opened it in the face of the befuddled butler.

"Lord Trenton to see Lady Tattenbaum," he said quietly.

The butler bowed quickly and moved backward, allowing Griff entrance. "Excuse me, my lord, but of course."

With a snap of the butler's fingers, a maid hurried forward and took Griff's hat and coat. "Follow me, my lord," he said.

Griff sank gratefully onto an incredibly comfortable divan in a large drawing room after

Lady Tattenbaum's red-faced butler made his sixth apology and left him. With a grimace, Griff made note of his scuffed boots.

Damn.

He had not felt this bad in rather a long time. Usually, he was able to keep most of his deeper thoughts at bay, but sitting here in the opulence of Dryer house brought everything rushing back with a clarity he would rather not experience.

Not to mention the butler mistaking him for some delivery boy. Nothing like a blow to the ego a bit too early in the morning.

"Ah, Griff!"

Griff glanced up and then stood as Lady Tattenbaum advanced on him in all of her beturbaned glory. "Are we going for a fallen-woman theme today?" he asked with a wink.

Lady Tattenbaum tittered. "Do you like the scarlet?" She twirled, her bright red dress swirling around her well-fed hips. "I did feel a bit of the devil when I ordered the fabric." She leaned in close and whispered, "The woman at the shop thought I was going to make bed drapes with it." She made another turn, and Griff made a sound of admiration. "Ah, look now, you're such a charmer, Griff Hallsbury.

Come and give me a proper kiss on my old cheek, as I haven't seen you in nearly five years."

"Seven," Griff said and kissed Lady Tattenbaum's cheek.

"No, I came and saw you when you were driving the Bath coach."

Griff straightened. "That you did, Lady Tattenbaum. Shame on me for forgetting."

"Shame on you, indeed!" Lady Tattenbaum winked at him as a maid brought in tea. They made a show of talking about the weather as if it would cure all that was wrong with the world until the maid took her leave.

"Now then," Lady Tattenbaum said, "I'm sure you're wondering why I asked you to attend me."

Griff finished off a biscuit and swallowed. "Actually, I'm quite afraid I know exactly why you sent for me."

Lady Tattenbaum sighed heavily and shook her head, the scarlet feather in her turban twitching as if in pain. "I knew it. Then my fears are correct? Lara . . . ?" she let the question hang between them unsaid.

"Yes, I'm afraid so."

"Right. Well, when that second account hit

the papers I did wonder, as I've heard from the servants that she's been restless at night. I do remember, one night last week in particular she seemed rather in a hurry to get me off to bed. And Sarah, my cook, told me the next morning that she had found the back door open." Lady Tattenbaum took a large bite out of a small cucumber sandwich and chewed with great vigor. "And then the dear girl—Lara, that is—was asking all sorts of questions about you that next day." The lady glared at him, although it was a glare completely devoid of any malice.

Griff had quite forgotten how Lady Tattenbaum liked to speak in complete and long paragraphs seemingly without taking a breath. Actually, dearest Lady Tattenbaum was one of the ones he missed.

And Thomas, of course. But this morning was already hard enough without letting Thomas into his head.

"Of course, boy, you're going to have to tell me everything immediately. With the way that girl was asking about you, I'm scared to think of what has happened between you two." The glare this time was most definitely not completely devoid of malice.

Griff blinked once. *Boy*? He was no boy. He

hadn't been called *boy* in a very long time. "Nothing happened at all!" he said quickly. "What kind of things did she ask?"

And what did she know?

Suddenly the thought that Lara Darling, with her beautiful eyes and daring spirit, knew his downfall intimately made his heart feel even more hollow than usual.

"Nothing happened?" Lady Tattenbaum asked, her eyes narrowed on Griff.

He sat a bit straighter. "Lady Tattenbaum, I realize that I am no longer counted among Society, but I have not become some degenerate. I am still a gentleman."

"Well, of course you are, Griff, don't get your back up." Lady Tattenbaum made a *tsk*ing sound with her tongue.

"That's right, I'm not allowed pride anymore."

Lady Tattenbaum rolled her eyes. "As if I would ever say that to you, boy. Would you stop for a minute and remember to whom you speak? I've loved you since you were in short pants."

Griff was stunned for a moment. His throat constricted as if he might cry, or something just as strange. Cry, for God's sake.

Still, it had been forever and a day since he

had heard anyone speak of emotions, much less love, especially inferring that they felt that sentiment toward him.

"You're my cousin's son, dear boy, and, let me tell you, a son whose birth was much feted. I waited right along with your mother and father, hoping against hope that you would appear a boy, strong and healthy, to keep the title in the family."

Any tears that threatened receded completely in that moment, fortunately. Regret dried them right up. Regret he was very used to. "Ah, yes, and such a good job I've done of it," he said dryly.

"Oh well, you've tripped up, so who hasn't? Now then," Lady Tattenbaum continued, as if they'd just agreed that the hens weren't laying as they should. "Back to the business at hand. Since my suspicions are true, I am now officially worried. I am not even going to say aloud what you have just confirmed to me. But we both know, obviously, that this cannot, absolutely not, become common knowledge."

"We?"

Lady Tattenbaum narrowed her gaze at him again. "Yes, *we*. You got her into this mess, and I'm her sponsor in Town."

"I did not get that woman into any mess. She

did it completely on her own. I must tell you, Lady Tattenbaum, she's a menace."

"She's barely a woman—mostly a girl—and has the purest heart of anyone I know. She's not a menace, but a free spirit. And, let me tell you, boy, I said the same thing of you to your father on so many occasions I cannot even count them."

Oh God, his father. Griff had managed not to think of his father in at least a year, maybe two. And now the man's face came into his mind, clear as if he was sitting across from him now. He knew he should have sent a note declining Lady Tattenbaum's invitation—but of course, anyone with any mental clarity at all knew you did not decline Lady Tattenbaum anything.

"Now then, if you are the gentleman you say you are, you will help me from your side of this mess. I will do all I can to keep her away from you and this little group of boys you like to play with, and you will make sure she does not ruin herself if she slips past me. Do I make myself clear?"

"I resent that you think I am playing games with boys," Griff said.

"Clear?" Lady Tattenbaum continued, ignoring his statement out of hand.

"Clear," Griff said on a bit of a sigh.

They stared at each other in silence, and Griff knew that if silence occurred when in the presence of Lady Tattenbaum, she was very serious indeed.

"You know," he said, not a little discomfited. "I am not playing . . ."

"I know exactly what you are doing, boy, and I hope you are able to do it. I hope with all my heart. And, actually, I will once again offer my help, though I know you will not accept it."

"No, I will not."

"When you are ready to take your place in Society again, though, I will demand you accept it."

"I will not accept your money." Griff lowered his eyes and played with a bit of thread hanging out of one of the seams on the divan. "When I need your support in another way, I'll ask for it."

"Of course you will, although I'll give it even if you don't ask. I will keep my nose out of your business just so much, Griff. Right now, I think you are doing what you need to do, and, actually, I think it is a good thing. Otherwise, I would have let you know. But if you ever take a wrong turn again, I'm going to give you a good thumping."

"A good thumping?"

"Well, verbally at least, be sure of that." Lady Tattenbaum nodded and crunched into a berry tart. "Eat, boy, Sarah knows how to make tarts like no other."

Chapter 5

If you start feeling as if you keep seeing a certain man more than most and in the strangest of places, there is usually a reason. Sometimes, actually, you really aren't seeing him more often than any other, it is just that you are noticing him more than any other. On the other hand, it could also mean he's seeking you out. If both reasons are at play, it could mean something else all together. Then you'd better hope that man is eligible.

The Duchess Diaries, Volume One

She had stayed at the park too long. Usually Lara ran Goldie so early in the morning she never had to meet up with anyone at all. Today though, she had a late start and then enjoyed herself so much, she stayed too long. And had thus, as she tried to lead Goldie home, been roped into an extremely boring and much too lengthy conversation with Roddy Piperneil.

Actually, calling what had transpired between herself and Roddy a conversation was being rather generous. The boy went on for nearly an hour nonstop about Mrs. Hastings, of all people.

It seemed that all of London was abuzz—well, the young men, at least—with the idea that the Baron was actually afraid of being beaten by this Mrs. Hastings.

"You don't say?" Lara replied smugly when Roddy gave her this bit of information.

"Oh yes. You see the Baron has never been beaten. Has most probably put by a small fortune in winnings, actually," Roddy told her. He then wondered aloud for another fifteen minutes about Mrs. Hastings.

Who could she be? Was she truly a woman? For one really couldn't tell in the dark. Was she really as good as the gossips said?

And, oh, how Lara wanted to answer those questions. Especially the one about her being a woman. She actually had to picture her sisters in her mind to keep herself from doing something horrible. Perhaps arranging a race . . .

Amanda was living for her season. If Lara dared, poor Amanda would never be the belle of the ball as she so wanted.

And what of all of her sisters and their circumstances? Wouldn't it be nice to employ a staff again? Wouldn't it be nice not to have to pretend that their old housekeeper was taking in sewing when it was really the Darling sisters sitting in their shabby drawing room and doing the sewing for the people of their small town?

She was the eldest sister and ought to be the most responsible, but of course that role had always gone to Reggie. Even their father paid a bit of attention to Reggie, as she had taken on the role of mother when theirs had died. Lara had always felt her petulance coming on full force when her father mentioned Reggie's steadfastness and maturity beyond her years.

That, of course, was really awful of Lara, as it was completely true. When she was really honest with herself, she did realize that she tended to be even worse when Reggie was at her best. It was her immaturity showing through, she knew it.

But right now, in this moment, Lara realized that she could show her sisters and her father that she could be responsible too. In fact that had been her main reason for coming to Town in the first place. Yes, there was the dare Nanny L had laid at her door, but her grandmother had also laid opportunity there as well.

An opportunity to finally have her father pat *her* back and say, "Well done, Lara."

So, with a smug and self-satisfied smile, Lara

kept her mouth primly shut and listened to Roddy for what seemed like forever. With the delay added to her own late start, Lara was then forced to stop and speak with at least three other groups of people as she tried to exit the park. Poor Goldie needed a rubdown, and kept nudging at Lara's shoulder. It was a complete bother, especially as none of them were really worth her time.

Lara winced. Reggie would have given her quite an upbraiding if she had heard Lara say such a thing.

"All I mean," she said aloud, as she led Goldie toward home, "is that none of them can help me in my quest."

"And that quest would be the Holy Grail, perhaps?"

Lara screamed, but recovered herself quickly, as she was worrying Goldie. With a scowl over her shoulder at the man who had sneaked up on her, Lara quieted the horse. "Really, sir," she said primly. "You should not scare a person so."

"Where is your maid?" Griff asked as he matched her steps with his.

Lara glanced down at his scuffed boots. And then she could not help but let her gaze follow the nice, lean lines of Griff's legs, clad in rather stylish, though worn, breeches. Griff Hallsbury had lovely long legs, she thought. Fortunately, she managed to keep this thought to herself and said, "My maid does not like horses."

"You should have a footman with you, at least," Mr. Hallsbury informed her shortly.

"And aren't *you* well versed in the ways of Society?"

"You have no idea."

Lara stopped and turned on this strange man, Griff Hallsbury. "No, I don't, actually. Do educate me, please."

Griff stopped as well and looked down at her. He looked different today, dressed as he was, like a gentleman. Though the rim of his hat was worn thin and his coat was obviously owned by someone who worked for his money, Lara couldn't help but think that Griff Hallsbury had taken pains with his appearance.

She could see that he had shaved his chin recently, probably that very morning.

Lara also noticed that Mr. Hallsbury had a very nice chin. And a good throat, too. Who would have thought that one would feel fluttery about a man's throat? But fluttery was really the only word to describe her insides as her eyes caught and held on Griff's strong, tan neck.

One could tell that his neck connected to a broad and muscled chest. She wasn't exactly sure how she came to that conclusion, but she was rather sure she was right.

"You really do not know?"

Lara blinked and her gaze swept back up Griff's lovely square chin and stopped on his startlingly blue eyes. Had he just said something? She thought perhaps he had. Had it been something interesting? Couldn't be as interesting as the small lines fanning out from his eyes, white against his swarthy skin as if he spent a lot of time squinting into the sun.

Those little lines did make him look, well, manly, really. The men of her acquaintance never stayed out in the sun. They sat in fancy parlors and talked, or sat in their coaches and talked, or stood around during soirees and talked. Boring and thin and smallish, all of them.

Except for this man. But, of course, he wasn't one of them.

"Lady Lara, you should not look at a man like that."

This time Lara snapped to attention. "Excuse me? I am doing nothing wrong."

"Not wrong, per se. But, believe me, don't look at me like that. Now then, I thought Lady Tattenbaum had told you everything."

Lara furrowed her brow. "Lady Tattenbaum? Told me everything?" And then she stood straighter and stuck her finger against Griff's lovely chest. "What is there to tell, and how would you know if she told me anything at all?"

Griff laughed and Lara couldn't help but smile. She liked it when this man laughed.

"I spoke too soon," he said, wrapping his hand around her finger. Goodness, but that felt good. Lara stared for a moment where he touched her. It was amazing, actually, how very good his hand felt around hers.

She had removed her gloves, as they were dirty and she had been heated. As a result, the man in front of her now held her bare hand tightly in his.

She could feel calluses at the base of his fingers. And she could feel how warm and strong he was. Now that she thought of it, this man held her more intimately than any man before him.

She had sat upon his lap, and now her fingers had been wrapped in his bare hand.

All things that a proper young miss should find terribly upsetting. But it only made Lara yearn for more intimate caresses.

But then Griff quickly let go of her, almost as if she had burned him. "I bid you good day," he said quickly. And then he bowed and was gone.

Lara stood there with her mouth gaping, staring at her hand before a touch of anger forced her head up. "Good day?" she cried after Griff's retreating back. "Good day, my foot. Get back here and tell me what you thought Lady Tattenbaum had told me. And while you're at it, I'd like to know how you know Lady Tattenbaum at all."

The man turned but continued walking, backward. "I indulged myself, Lara Darling. When I saw you, I wanted to speak to you, and I really shouldn't. It could cause talk. Anyway, I don't need you to tell me your quest; I can guess." He winked. "And knowing you as I already do, I'm rather sure you'll find the answers to all your questions and more before the day is out. You do know how to get what you want, now, don't you?" And he turned and strode away purposefully.

Arrogant man.

He *was* arrogant and, as it turned out, wrong, Lara thought dismally later that evening. For it was nearly the end of the day and she had not received any answers to her questions. Lady Tattenbaum had fudged her off with some talk of a headache. And really, Lara could not go around asking questions about some coachman. Someone might connect her with Mrs. Hastings, after all, and that would never do.

For she had most determinedly decided not to undermine herself anymore. What Griff had told her the other night had hit a chord. Obviously, she did not mind ruining herself, but she would absolutely not damage her sisters' chances. Or her own chance at finally being the responsible sister.

So, Lara stood at the Farthing's soiree, with not one question answered and midnight just around the corner. He would never know, of course. But it did bother her that Griff had pretty much wagered on the fact that she could do something, and she had not achieved it.

Bugger it. Still, at least she had not put any money on it.

Lara let out a rather loud sigh at this thought. If she had believed that a season in Town might just foster her femininity, she was obviously hoping for too much of a miracle.

"Bored, dear?" Mrs. Braxton asked her. The circle of people Lara stood with all glared at her, brows uniformly lifted in disgust.

Lara shook her head quickly, her cheeks and ears burning. She probably looked like a stewed tomato. "Oh no, just a bit tired."

Mrs. Braxton nodded with that strange smile

she had. "How the young have fallen," she said to the group. "They would rather fix their hair than the state of affairs of this great nation."

A few of the men nodded gravely; one of the women giggled. Lara frowned. Actually, she would rather call Mrs. Braxton out. If she were a man, such a slight would have been enough for her to do so. Or at the very least give the person who voiced it a good shiner.

But, unfortunately, Lara was a young lady. And she was determined to be ladylike, even if it killed her. She actually managed to smile at Mrs. Amelia Braxton.

The woman was one of the most beautiful of the *ton*. Though her husband had no title, he was a second son of some sort of peer, and they were disgustingly wealthy. Also, the woman liked to play at supporting one politician or another, so they all vied for her attention and good will.

But for some reason, Lara could not like her wholeheartedly. There was nothing in particular, just something she felt in her heart. As when Mrs. Braxton smiled at her. They were never real, her smiles. There seemed to be some other emotion lurking behind them. And it wasn't a benign emotion, either.

Reggie had written that obviously Lara was really too bored for her own good if she were seeing malice in a woman's smiles. And, as always, Reggie made a very good point. Still, Lara knew that even Lady Tattenbaum did not relish Mrs. Braxton's company.

Not that her patron had ever said anything. But sometimes one could just feel these things. Reggie did hate it when Lara drew conclusions, using as a barometer the sensation of whether or not her skin crawled.

Her skin was most definitely crawling now. Lara had already spent nearly half an hour listening to the group argue the merits of some act of Parliament. And Mrs. Braxton had made sure they all realized that she was right and always would be. Given that most of the group needed Mrs. Braxton to approve of them for one reason or another, they all had done everything except get down on their knees and offer up sacrifices if only for the mere hint of a smile on the woman's lips in their direction.

Lara was ready to conclude, with all the nerve endings under her skin in consent, that Mrs. Braxton was at the very least an egotistical bore. Anyway, there was really just so much bowing and scraping one could watch before going mad or dropping dead on the floor from pure ennui.

"I'm just off for another glass of punch," she said quietly, though no one noticed. Which was exactly how she wanted it. She took a circuitous route to the punchbowl, her eyes peeled for a man who might meet her requirements for a husband.

Her heart was not completely in the task, though, truth be told. She had written to Reggie just that morning, after her little encounter with the arrogant Mr. Hallsbury, that she was a bit confounded by the whole process of finding a husband. How on earth did one go about finding someone who was richer than sin and wouldn't live more than maybe another year, but who was also not completely contemptible?

She was obviously going about it all wrong, for she had not found the man and she had been in Town over a fortnight already. And, truth be told, she really was not sure she could stomach much more of Town.

Actually, if she was completely honest with herself, the reason she wasn't sure she could handle Town much longer was that Lara was afraid she just might do something really terrible and ruin her family name altogether.

And then she tripped over something and went flying. No dainty little stumble for Lara Darling, oh, no. Lara fell belly first onto the floor. Belly first, because she managed to hurl her punch glass in the air and shove her palms out in front of her so that, at least, her nose was saved from a bashing against the Farthings' extremely hard wood floor.

She would have bruised hips for at least a week, she was sure of that.

"I beg your pardon, madam," a man said from above her. "I'm horribly sorry. I'm afraid I tripped you with my cane."

"Cane?" she said dumbly. *Hmmm, cane*, she thought. A cane could mean invalid, which could very well mean an older man close to death. Could God have answered her prayers so quickly?

A very strong and relatively young-looking hand wrapped around her upper arm. Damn. Lara sighed again, but kept it low enough this time to go unnoticed as she allowed the man with the cane to help her to her feet.

Lara stood and brushed at her skirts. She had ripped the ruffle at her hem nearly completely off. Lovely. And then she noticed the hush. Glancing up, Lara realized that almost every person in the Farthings' huge ballroom was staring at her. Even the ten-piece orchestra had quit playing; all twenty eyes were on her.

Actually, that was not quite true. Nineteen eyes were on her from that quarter. The flute player had lost an eye in the war.

Funnily enough, Mrs. Braxton was not looking at her at all. Rather, that grand dame was staring with obvious astonishment at the person beside her.

Be that as it may, Lara still did wish to disappear.

"I am horribly clumsy!" the deep voice said very loudly from beside her. "I cannot walk well, and my clumsy gait caused you to fall. I am so very sorry."

People glanced away. The one-eyed man with the flute hit a note. And it seemed, suddenly, that the whole room was much more embarrassed for the poor man beside Lara than her literal fall from grace.

Lara bit her lip and turned to the man. "Thank you," she said softly. Then realized that she was speaking to a button on his coat. Her eyes slid upward.

Truly, she was expecting a hunched-over man with a gouty ankle. But there was nothing hunched over about the man in front of her. And absolutely he did not have gout.

"Goodness," she breathed.

"I am sorry, er . . ."

Lara could only stare. "You look just as I've always believed Gabriel to be like." She winced then. "I mean . . ." Ah, she must have hit her head, surely. "I'm sorry." And then she just shut her mouth. She was rattled and the man in front of her was too splendid for words.

"Let me help you to the other room. You need to sit down."

She laughed, "Yes, I do. And I need to have my tongue glued to the roof of my mouth."

Her partner laughed as well, as he limped along beside her. His limp was rather pronounced. Obviously his leg injury was a serious one. Still, it did not impede their journey. And the arm he offered for her support helped her tremendously. She must have fallen harder than she realized, because as they made their way through the press of people, Lara felt as if her hips would collapse. Not to mention her stinging palms.

Her companion found her a chair and helped her into it. "I shall get you a glass of punch, miss . . . ?"

"Oh, it is Lara, my name is Lara, sorry. And you are . . . ?"

"Thomas, to be true." He rolled his eyes. "But as we must always stand on ceremony in Town you will most probably have to call me Lord Rutherford. And I will have to call you . . . ?"

"Oh, dear, of course." Lara closed her eyes for a small second. "I am Lady Lara Darling."

Her gaze flicked down to his bad leg. "And, really, you do not have to fetch me punch."

Lord Rutherford's golden eyes darkened, his brows lowering. "'Tis no trouble."

"No, I did not mean . . ." Lara stopped and drew in a long breath. "I would love some punch, thank you."

Lord Rutherford bowed slightly and smiled, and such a smile it was. He had full lips, like a cherub, and one of his front teeth was just slightly crooked. All together, it made for a very nice mouth that caused one to shiver when it smiled.

Lara watched the man as he left, tall and stately even with his limp. He seemed very nice, too. And pleasant. And he had taken all the blame for her fall, making sure others knew that his impairment had caused it, not her lack of watching where she was going.

What an interesting trait, not caring that others knew his flaws, especially in a man. Obviously, she had stumbled on a true gentleman. What a rare thing.

She bit her lip. Wouldn't it be nice if he were rich as well? But no, this Lord Rutherford would never do. He was much too young.

And then all thoughts of Lord Rutherford flew from her mind as she heard the name

"Mrs. Hastings" mentioned behind her. Lara froze.

"It had to be her, I'm sure," a male voice said.

"Why do you say that? It could have been any woman," another voice interjected.

"Come, man, even the gossip sheets have reported it to be Mrs. Hastings. Anyway, why else would the Baron be so interested in stealing her away? Obviously, the man is hellbent that no one trounce him. And he must know that this mystery woman can do just that. The story of what happened in Lower Tunsburrow is true, I tell you."

Lara tapped her knee with her fingers, looking for all the world like a bored wallflower. But, as she tapped, she surreptitiously slid back in her chair and turned her head so that she might hear better.

"No woman could outdrive the Baron."

Ha!

"Anyway," a third man said, "wouldn't it be better for him if there were someone who gave him competition? He could actually win more money, I would think. The stakes would be higher."

"He does it all for the money, you know. Could care less about his legend, just wants to find his place again."

"Lady Lara?"

Damn, just when it was getting interesting. Lara painted a smile on her face and stood, turning toward Lord Rutherford as she did. His good looks startled her for a minute, and she blinked.

"Your punch, my lady," he held out a glass of dark red liquid.

"Ah, thank you, my lord." Lara cupped the glass in her hand and took a fortifying drink, and then she sputtered. Some bored young man had obviously spiked what once had been a terribly watery concoction. It was watery no more. Lara took another, smaller sip just to be sure she had not imagined it.

Oh yes, it burned like fire going down her throat. She really ought to tell someone. At the very least, she should not drink any more of it.

Lara took another taste of her warm punch. But where would be the fun in that? She grinned up at Lord Rutherford. He wasn't drinking the punch, so he would have no idea that it was definitely the best punch in Christendom.

That thought made Lara giggle.

Lord Rutherford frowned. "Did you hit your head, Lady Lara, when you fell?"

She waved her hand in the air. "Nah," she said. And then realized she sounded very unlike a lady. "No," she corrected herself.

Lord Rutherford shifted his weight, using his cane to help. "Were you hurt in the wars, my lord?" she asked and took another long drink.

There was a pained silence and Lara gazed up into Lord Rutherford's eyes. He looked very angry for a moment, but then shook his head. "No. In *a* war, but not *the* war."

Lara frowned. "What on earth . . ."

"Rutherford!"

Lara glanced around, recognizing the voice that had just called Lord Rutherford as belonging to one of the men who had been conversing about Mrs. Hastings and Mr. Hallsbury.

Oh, goody! She really did feel the need to clap her hands in glee. Her rather boring night was taking a lovely turn, even if it had been a terrible fall that started it all.

"Goodness, man, I thought you would never return." A thin man of indistinguishable though obviously greater years slapped Lord Rutherford on the back. "It is good to see you, really it is."

Lord Rutherford nodded, but didn't seem to return the sentiment. "Cartwright."

"What brings you to Town then? Have you licked your wounds and come back to find a wife?"

Cartwright really needed to get some tact,

Lara decided, tipping her glass to her lips and frowning when she found it empty. Damn.

Rutherford cleared his throat and glared at Cartwright. "No, actually," he said shortly.

"Well, you should, man. Even with your twisted leg, you can have any woman you want. Your title and money can do that for you, at least. And you do know what's happened to Trenton, don't you?"

Lara frowned. Her stomach was turning over on itself rather frighteningly. It was the tension rolling off Rutherford, she was sure. It was palpable. And then there was the mention of Trenton.

Hadn't she heard that name before?

"You do know that Amelia married Braxton, do you not. Well, of course, you must know," Cartwright continued, seemingly oblivious to the way Rutherford's golden eyes had darkened to a shade closer in color to thick honey.

Lara's frown turned into a scowl. Mrs. Braxton had something to do with Rutherford? Yuck. No matter that Reggie would think her judgmental, Lara did not like Mrs. Braxton.

"Yes, it is amazing how differently everything turned out, isn't it?" Cartwright just refused to shut up. "Truly amazing."

Rutherford looked as if he would like to snap

Cartwright's neck in two. And probably, Lord Rutherford could do it, Lara thought as she eyed the man's broad chest.

Cartwright laughed. Now, *there* was a man who needed to lose his tongue in an unfortunate accident.

"Good God, man," Cartwright said on a chuckle. "Trenton drives a mail coach, of all things."

A muscle moved spasmodically in Rutherford's jaw.

That could not be good.

And what Cartwright had just said could *not* be a coincidence. He must be talking about Griff. But, why on earth would these people be calling Griff Hallsbury by the name "Trenton"?

It could be his middle name, perhaps? Or a title.

Surely the man was not truly a baron?

Was he?

Lara felt lightheaded with all the information she was processing. Suddenly a memory flashed in her mind. Lady Tattenbaum had asked about Griff, "Lord Trenton," when she had first arrived. That is why the name rang a bell.

And then her stomach rolled again. Oh goodness, she really did not feel well at all.

"Will you gentlemen please excuse me," she

said quietly. Obviously, it had been too quiet, though, for neither man paid her any heed.

"Can you believe it? I don't think Society has ever seen the like." Cartwright slapped Rutherford on the shoulder again. "Of course, there are those who have dabbled in trade, but to actually become a lackey." Cartwright's whoop of laughter made Lara's head spin.

She took a quick step backward and the floor beneath her seemed to lurch like the deck of a ship.

Rutherford looked at her with surprise. The man seemed to have forgotten that she attended this little conversation.

"Lady Lara," he said quickly.

But he was not allowed to finish his sentence, because Lara's stomach turned one last time. Her whole body went cold and then hot and then cold again, as she grabbed Rutherford's arm for support. And then Lara made a small sound of distress as she leaned forward and everything she had eaten that day came right back up and spewed all over the horrified Cartwright's shoes.

Once again, a hush descended. And, once again, Rutherford cut through it.

"Good job, dear," he said, with an angelic smile.

Chapter 6

Do not drink red punch while wearing a white dress. You will inevitably spill.

The Duchess Diaries, Volume One

Lady Lara had obviously come to the park very early that morning, because by the time Griff rode by, she was done exercising Lady Tattenbaum's mare.

He had found himself riding by the park in the early hours of his days off, on the chance that he might get to see Lara. He never spoke to her again as he had that day he'd met her in the park. That had been very bad of him, and he would not put her reputation in jeopardy like that again.

But he did like to watch her—though, really he should not even be doing that. Mostly because it made him feel a sadness he had not experienced in a few years. It was such an acute sadness, he did not think he had ever felt it thus. He was not exactly sure why.

No, that wasn't completely true. He *did* have an idea. He knew that Lara was the type of woman he would have liked to have courted if his life had turned out differently.

She would have been fun, really. Interesting. And refreshingly honest with her feelings. He had found himself daydreaming a few times lately of what it would be like to watch her across a crowded room. Ask her to dance at a soiree. Sit beside her at a musicale and laugh with her behind their programs at an opera.

All of these thoughts did him no good, and he had tried to banish her completely from them. But it had not worked.

And here he was again, watching her from the cover of a large oak tree. She was standing, her head cocked to the side, watching her mare crunch the dry grass at her feet. He saw her shoulders lift and then lower as if she had sighed.

She looked quite dejected, and Griff could not help but smile. Poor girl, her spirit was too large for the smaller ones around her. He wanted so badly to go and just hold her hand.

If any of the randy bucks he'd run with seven years ago could hear his thoughts now, they'd probably all keel over dead from shock. Griff Hallsbury keening away on a hill and wishing that he might hold a girl's hand.

Lara's shoulders lifted and lowered again, her head straightened, only to list over to the other side.

And Griff kicked his horse into a trot. He shouldn't, but he couldn't stay away another moment.

She glanced up as he came toward her and smiled at him.

Oh God, that smile. In that very moment, the girl in front of him could ask him to fly to the moon and he would start building wings. He was most definitely besotted.

What a horrible twist of fate. If only he could have met Lara years ago, perhaps she could have saved him. But, then, he hadn't wanted to be saved.

"I did not intentionally undermine myself this time," she said to him, tilting her head back so that she might look into his eyes. "I swear it."

Griff bit his lip and swung himself down beside her. He let go of his horse's reins, and the gelding trotted over to munch along with Lara's mare. "It certainly is a dry one this year," he said when he heard his horse's teeth crunch the grass.

"Oh, not you too," Lara groaned.

Griff glanced at her.

"Ah, it's all anyone talks about, the weather. You'd think it was actually an interesting subject, the way they go on."

"Sorry," he said with a grin. "So, what did you do this time?"

"I . . . er . . . did something very unfeminine all over Lord Cartwright's shoes."

"Excuse me?" Griff said, his mind running through possible senarios.

"I got sick on Lord Cartwright," she said, and then quickly amended: "But someone had put brandy in the punch. At least I think it was brandy. It could have been rum. Whatever it was, they put a lot of it in the punch. And I . . . well, I did not stop drinking it, as I should have, of course, but, really, it did taste rather good for a while. But then everyone was a bit tense with each other and I felt sick suddenly, and, well . . ." she lost steam then, her voice trailing off, her shoulders slumping. She turned and stared once again at her mare.

Griff watched her face for a moment. She had a lovely profile. Her nose was really rather perfect, long and straight; her lips formed a nice pout. He did so want to kiss her in that moment.

Instead he stepped up beside her and tried not to look at her anymore. He watched Lara's horse nibble at the grass. "Cartwright's company would make anyone with a brain feel sick."

Lara shrugged. "True, but I do feel rather like I am doomed to ruin myself." She glanced up at him out of the corner of her eye. "I shall do something horribly awful. I know I will. Even when I truly make an effort not to undermine myself, I, well . . . undermine myself most woefully."

"It doesn't sound like a *woeful* undermining, not by half. That sounds rather like a full-blown attempt, if you'll excuse my . . . er . . . pun."

Lara crossed her arms over her chest. "You can leave now, thank you very much. You are not helping my mood at all."

"I'm sorry, really I am." He watched the horses for a moment. "Just act like it did not happen. It's indelicate enough that most everyone will ignore it if you do."

Lara made a strangled sound and buried her face in her hands. "It *was* indelicate, horribly so," she said.

He wanted to put his arm around her. Truth be told, he wanted to put his hand on the nape of her lovely neck. She wore her thick hair wound up on her crown, and with her head bent forward as it was, Griff was rather coming undone by the delicate whiteness of Lara's nape.

Obviously, he was sick or something, because the nape of a woman's neck had never in his life caused him so much discomfort.

He stayed his hand, though, thankfully. "Lady Lara . . ." he said, quite at a loss for something to say, but wanting desperately to give her comfort. Never in his life had he really given comfort to anyone, he suddenly realized. Nor had he ever felt the need to as he did at that moment.

Strange.

"Er . . . Lara," he started again. "It will be all right. Cartwright is an idiot. I am sure most of the people there were glad for what happened. And you are a lovely woman—beautiful—and you are witty and interesting and fun. I am sure that you will have just as many suitors at your door this afternoon as you had before."

Now, why did that thought make him feel a bit like grabbing Lara and taking her to a place where no suitor could ever find her?

She sighed again. He did like it when she sighed, and it was completely selfish on his part. His view of her bosom when she sighed was enough to make him smile stupidly for a week.

Lara straightened then. "I didn't really have suitors before. Even Roddy Piperneil will probably stop calling on me."

"Roddy Piperneil couldn't care less what anyone else thinks. His intellect does not allow it, as it would be too much for him to think about. I am sure that Roddy Piperneil will continue to call on you."

Lara glanced at him and smiled. But then she frowned again. "If Roddy Piperneil is the cause of one's perkiness, one must be in a bad way," she said dourly.

That was quite true, actually, so Griff did not know what to say. They stood in silence for a while, watching the horses, and then suddenly Griff felt a feather-light touch against his fingers.

He glanced down just as Lara's hand slipped into his. He stared for a moment at their hands—his large and callused, hers quite slender with long fingers.

He should have shaken her off. It seemed she did not even realize that she had put her hand in his. She was innately looking for solace, and Griff could not pull away. He closed his fingers softly around hers and they stood silently watching the horses.

Griff realized two things in those precious moments. First of all, he very much enjoyed the idea that someone would come to him for solace. He especially liked that Lara trusted him so, even if it wasn't a conscious thing she had done.

And second, he knew that if God showed up in that moment and offered to let Griff stay on this small section of dry grass with Lara's hand in his for the rest of eternity, he would accept.

He had never felt more at peace, ever.

"How are you, Thomas?"

Thomas had been inspecting a mustard-colored vase on the purple mantelpiece when he heard Lady Tattenbaum's distinctive voice behind him. He turned, carefully keeping all of his weight on his good leg, and realized that Lady Tattenbaum was quite serious with her question, for the old woman actually waited for him to answer.

"I am well," he said.

She watched him closely, but said nothing. Yes, Lady Tattenbaum was most definitely serious.

"Why are you here?" she asked.

Thomas nearly laughed out loud at Lady Tattenbaum's bluntness. A completely mirthless laugh, but he kept it in check. His heart felt decidedly hollow at Lady Tattenbaum's cold greeting. There had been a time when this woman would have let him kiss her cheek and then spoken nonstop about how much she adored him.

Those days had come to an end.

"I came to see if Lady Lara was well. I feel at fault."

"No, I mean why are you in Town?" Lady Tattenbaum frowned then. "Why on earth would you feel at fault for Lara being sick? Did you do something to her, Thomas? I swear, boy, if you do anything to hurt that child . . ."

Well, this was a bit more like it. "I found out that someone had spiked the punch, and I am the one who got her a glass of the stuff." He looked down his nose at Lady Tattenbaum. "Of course I would not do anything on purpose, Lady Tattenbaum, I *am* still a gentleman."

That stopped her. Her eyes glittered for a moment with unshed tears, making her look so sad suddenly, that Thomas really did want to kiss her wrinkled cheek and tell her it was all fine. Of course, that was not true. So Thomas stayed on his side of the room.

"I beg your pardon, Thomas. I know you would never hurt a naïve girl like Lady Lara, and I am sorry to have questioned you so." Lady Tattenbaum came farther into the room then and sat carefully on the edge of a large divan. "Please, Lord Rutherford, do take a seat. Would you like tea?"

It was to be Lord Rutherford then? Thomas shook his head. "Thank you, no. I brought flowers for Lady Lara and wanted to make sure she is well."

"She is fine."

"Then I shall take my leave."

"But you have not answered my question, and I shall have it answered."

Thomas smoothed his hand along the front of his waistcoat, surreptitiously wiping the sweat from his palm as he took a seat across from Lady Tattenbaum.

Silence again—a strange and unsettling experience when in the presence of Lady Tattenbaum.

Thomas polished the head of his cane with the pad of his thumb. "Truly, Lady Tattenbaum, I do not think I've ever experienced such silence when in your company." Thomas laughed, hoping Lady Tattenbaum would as well.

She smiled. But it was a sad smile.

It felt odd, this silence. It felt horrible, really.

"You have finally come back to Town, Lord Rutherford. I am very interested in knowing the reason," Lady Tattenbaum prompted him again.

Thomas nodded, and then said, "I am here to find a wife." Strange that he would say that, he hadn't thought it at all, and did not ever plan to wed, actually.

But, of course, he could not tell Lady Tattenbaum why he was really in Town.

"Honestly, Thomas?" she asked in obvious surprise.

"Isn't that why most unmarried men brave the season? I am no different." The words came out before he thought about them, but as soon as they were said, he saw Lady Tattenbaum's gaze flicker to his leg and then move quickly back to his face.

Thomas pressed his lips together and gripped his cane so hard his nails cut into his palms painfully. But of course he *was* different. He would forever be different.

"You know about Amelia, of course," Lady Tattenbaum said then.

"Yes."

"You will not marry another if you still love Amelia, will you?"

"Not one to mince words, are you, Lady Tattenbaum?"

"As little as possible, dear boy."

Thomas nodded. "Right, well, never fear, Lady Tattenbaum, I do not pine after the great Amelia Braxton."

"She did not deserve you, anyway," Lady Tattenbaum told him.

With a slight shrug, Thomas slid his gaze away from Lady Tattenbaum's. He had not spoken of Amelia in seven years, not out loud, at least. And he did not like how it made him feel. It shouldn't bother him so much, not after so many years.

But it did.

"I'm not in love with her, anymore," he said truthfully. "And she never loved me." She proved that when she broke off their engagement because he was crippled. Real love didn't see a twisted leg, did it?

"I am glad, at least, that you realize that now." Lady Tattenbaum moved forward, her hand lifting as if she might touch him, but then she let it fall to her lap. "I never liked that girl, and I never thought she deserved to marry you. Truthfully, I wanted to do something terrible to her when she . . . well . . ."

"When she broke off our engagement?"

Thomas arched an eyebrow as he stared at Lady Tattenbaum. "Of course, the reason she broke it off was because of . . ." Here Thomas faltered.

"Anyway, it doesn't matter now."

"You feel as if you are ready to marry, then?" Lady Tattenbaum asked. "You have . . . healed?"

Thomas made a derisive sound, his heart beating double time as anger shot through him. "I shall never be healed, Lady Tattenbaum. I will never walk without pain. I will never be able to do half the things I could do only seven years ago. I shall never be whole."

Pity laced Lady Tattenbaum's gaze, and Thomas looked away from her.

"That is not what I meant, Thomas," she said. "I wanted to know if your soul had healed. I wanted to know if you had forgiven Griff." Lady Tattenbaum stopped and sighed. "Obviously, you have not."

Thomas could swear that he heard his heart thumping against his chest. It echoed in his ears as he tried to control himself. Healed? She wanted to know if he had healed? How did one heal after being completely physically ruined?

As to forgiving Griff, he would never.

"You know that Griff . . ."

"Stop," Thomas said softly, very happy he

had not yelled the word. He really did wish to yell, scream, throw things. Just hearing the name "Griff" out loud made Thomas feel sick to his stomach. "Don't, Lady Tattenbaum," he said, his words shaking with suppressed ire.

"But, Thomas . . ."

"No, you will never see him as I know him. My soul may be damaged beyond repair, but that man has no soul. I will not speak of him." Thomas stood quickly, too quickly. He stumbled and fell back onto the chair.

"Damn him!" he yelled. He regretted it immediately, but he did not apologize.

Instead, Thomas carefully stood. As he did, he saw a movement out of the corner of his eye and looked to see Lady Lara in the doorway. The girl's eyes were round in what could only be horror, her hands clenched in her riding habit.

Thomas couldn't help but laugh. "If this is the most horrific thing you have ever seen, Lady Lara, you have lived quite a sheltered life." He knew he sounded bitter and hated himself for it even more.

"Good day, Lady Tattenbaum." Thomas lurched toward the door.

But Lady Lara did not move away as she should have if she were any kind of gentle lady.

"You feel quite sorry for yourself, do you not, sir?" she asked, the soft brown eyes he remembered from the night before dark and hard. "I would suggest that you spend a few minutes of your day ruminating on what you have instead of what you lack. And if you ever return to this house again, you will treat Lady Tattenbaum with the respect she deserves!"

They stared at each other for a moment. Thomas, truly, could not remember being so shocked in his life. Well, perhaps the night before, when Lady Lara lost her lunch all over Cartwright rivaled this moment a bit, but not by much.

Lara tilted her chin up and crossed her arms over her chest, but did not break eye contact.

"I beg your pardon," Thomas finally said.

Lara nodded. "It is given," she said.

"And I might just take your suggestion to heart, Lady Lara."

"It might help."

"Yes."

Lady Lara moved then, so that Thomas could leave. He bowed slightly, turned, bowed to Lady Tattenbaum and limped from the room.

Chapter 7

Whatever you do, Lara dearest, do try and let men leave any encounter with their pride intact. I know this shall be just as hard for you to learn as it was for me, actually. But it does make life rather more enjoyable. Men tend to get grumpy when their pride is damaged.

The Duchess Diaries, Volume One

Two days later, something horrible happened.

When Lara wrote Reggie about the awful incident, she blamed it entirely on the scene with Lord Rutherford in Lady Tattenbaum's drawing room.

And, Lara realized later, the whole thing with Lord Rutherford is exactly what caused the problem at Lady Dorothea Johnson's garden tea.

Truly, it was.

The experience of telling such a powerful man like Lord Rutherford what to do with his obnoxious behavior had been rather thrilling.

Not to mention the fact that Lara had heard a bit of the conversation between Lady Tattenbaum and Lord Rutherford, and it all sounded deliciously interesting.

And then there had been the mention of Griff's name, which she had overheard as well.

That, actually, had caused something particularly strange to happen to Lara. She had been standing just outside the door to the drawing room, and when Lady Tattenbaum said the coachman's name, Lara's skin had prickled. Yes, prickled. That was really the only way she could describe it. And that is exactly the word she used when she wrote to Reggie about the whole experience.

She had, of course, just come from an interesting encounter with Griff, so that certainly could have had something to do with her reaction to his name. For the man had truly helped her feel very much at peace on a morning when she had woken up feeling decidedly the opposite.

Actually, her skin had prickled earlier already, when she realized that while standing in the park watching her horse, she had somehow managed to put her hand in Mr. Hallsbury's.

At least she thought she had. Perhaps he had taken hold of her? Whatever had happened, when she realized that they held hands, her skin prickled, her heart thumped and her mouth went very dry.

Very strange.

But, anyway, interesting physical experience aside, all of the other facts of the situation between Lord Rutherford and Lady Tattenbaum had gotten Lara rather excited, and when she heard the door to Lady Tattenbaum's house close behind Lord Rutherford, she turned happily toward the older woman, eager to hear the long, fun, thrilling story of scandal and intrigue which would obviously pour effusively from Lady Tattenbaum's mouth.

Much to Lara's frustration, however, the woman clammed up like she had never done before, probably in her entire lifetime.

Lady Tattenbaum then spent a few long, silent hours staring out the window of all things.

And then, nothing happened.

Lara wrote letters and entertained Roddy Piperneil.

They went to a musicale and listened to people perform who really should not have been let out in public in the first place. And they went to bed.

The next day it was more of the same.

And then the next day, Cartwright appeared

at Lady Dorothea Johnson's afternoon tea and it all just went downhill from there.

The man really did not like Lara. Which, of course, she could understand completely.

But instead of being a gentleman about it, he was extremely rude.

Lara was sitting very primly on the edge of her seat listening to Miss Sinclair talk about her family tree, generations and generations of Sinclairs, all indefatigable gardeners. A scintillating conversation, to say the least.

Lady Tattenbaum, still in a bit of a funk, had remained home, allowing Lara to attend the tea with the eldest of the Sinclair sisters. The youngest of the three was nearly eighty, so it was anyone's bet how old the eldest was.

"Miss Sinclair," Cartwright boomed, interrupting her in mid-sentence. "You are still among the living?"

Miss Sinclair frowned up at Cartwright and jabbed the man in the shin with her cane. "Don't be impertinent!" she growled at him.

He winced when the cane connected with his leg, but managed to keep an oily smile on his face as he turned to Lara. "Goodness, dear," he said. "I do think that the cut of your gown is quite out of fashion. A good ten years at least, really."

"And you are an expert on women's fashion?" Lara asked.

"Ah, yes," he lifted his eyebrows a few times. "Quite an expert, actually. I have taken many a gown off a woman."

Miss Sinclair made a choking sound.

Lara would have said something terribly glib and full of wit, but her mouth was hanging open, and she seemed to have forgotten how to use her jaw.

A few men close to them laughed, but mostly anyone within hearing distance gave Cartwright a piercing glare.

Cartwright sauntered off before Lara could commandeer the use of her tongue again.

"Well, I never," Miss Sinclair finally managed to say. "Young men do not know their place these days."

"Obviously," Lara said, patting Miss Sinclair's thin arm. "Lord Cartwright feels he must make me look bad in order to save his own reputation."

"My ears work perfectly, dear, you don't have to yell," Miss Sinclair admonished her.

But she had not spoken loudly to make sure Miss Sinclair had heard her.

Lord Cartwright stopped beside a group of men not far from Miss Sinclair and Lara. "You know," he said to them, "I visited Ashton Hall when Lord Ashton married. A shabby place, truly. Nearly uninhabitable."

The group of men just stared.

"Excuse me?" a youngish man asked.

"Lord Cartwright," Mr. Pembury said. "We are actually conversing about riding to the hounds."

"Ashton?" an older gentleman questioned Cartwright. "Lord Ashton? Goodness, haven't seen the man in a dog's age. Is he still alive?"

Lara bristled.

"Ah yes, though he lost his wife a few years back. Has a passel of daughters, poor man," Lord Saunders sputtered. Lord Saunders never said anything without spitting every time his tongue touched his teeth. Lara had realized quickly after her first introduction that it was simply better she made sure to never stand across from Lord Saunders at all.

"Isn't one of the gels here this season? Her first, I think?" Lord Saunders continued. "Not sure. I could be wrong." He clamped a pipe between his teeth.

Lara felt rather sick. She hoped that Cartwright had exacted his revenge and would now give up on humiliating her.

Idiot man.

"I'll get you some punch, Miss Sinclair," she said, taking her leave of the situation. She made her way carefully around the violinist playing by the fountain and went to the table laden with stale sandwiches. She eyed the punchbowl, realizing suddenly that she was making a habit of running off for punch to get out of bad situations.

Lara stared for a moment at the red punch glistening in the sun, and her stomach turned. No more punch, she decided. The men standing near Miss Sinclair laughed all at once, drowning out the other chattering people around her.

"I do swear," Cartwright announced, making sure his voice carried over the violinist. "I think I proved myself in Scotland summer last. I am the best shot around."

Lara rolled her eyes.

"I felled more pheasant than even you, Pembury! I could outshoot anyone here!"

And Lara made a very inelegant sound at the back of her throat. Unfortunately, at that exact moment, the violinist quit playing. And, as Lord Cartwright had been virtually yelling to everyone in the garden, the place was completely silent when Lara made the sound.

Honestly, the sound did seem to amplify and

take on a persona of its own, as it echoed in Lara's ears.

It was the same sound, actually, she had told herself she could not make under any circumstances when she reached London. Obviously, she should have listened to her own good advice.

For before she knew it, Lara was standing in the farthest reaches of the Johnson's back garden, pistol in hand, aiming at a hastily erected target.

Bugger it, she thought, as she hefted the gun. What to do now?

The entire party surrounded them. Not one person had stayed around the violinist, who had decided to begin playing again.

A bit late, thanks, Lara thought.

Miss Sinclair hadn't even tried to stop Lara's impending doom. She swayed slightly as she stood squinting out at Lara and Cartwright.

Of course, how could old Miss Sinclair control Lara? *Obviously*, Lara *can't even control Lara*, the young woman thought with a small sigh.

Still, if this were *so* bad, wouldn't someone stop her? Lara wondered as she peered down the barrel of her gun.

Where was Griff when she needed him? Actually, she did wish he would show up and save her in that moment, because she really did feel as if she were sliding down a hill and there was no stopping her. At least if no one else had heard, she could have said no to Cartwright's challenge.

But with the entire party listening, really, what was a girl to do? Especially when she knew without a doubt that she could outshoot a pompous windbag like Lord Cartwright.

Unfortunately, though, her heart was racing and her blood was pumping furiously. She felt more alive than she had felt since staring down Lord Rutherford. All this could only mean she was doing something horrible.

She was definitely not being responsible, drat it. One glance over at the smug Cartwright, though, cleared Lara's mind of any sensible thoughts whatsoever.

You idiot, she thought. So callous with your words to an obviously wounded man like Lord Rutherford, and then to add insult to injury to say hateful things of my home.

Well, take this!

And Lara squinted, aimed and fired.

"I've pricked my fingers so many times, I've bloodied all the clothes," Amanda Darling whined. "And anyway, it really is not helping this drudgery go any faster with you reading Lara's letters, Reggie."

Reggie glanced up from the page she had just read aloud. "You must be jesting, Amanda. Truly, Lara's letters read like novels, I do swear. She's gotten herself into more scrapes than I can imagine even of *her*!"

"Yes, but, it only underlines the fact that she's in London and I'm sitting here, sewing for my dinner."

"Do not be such a grump, Amanda, your turn will come," Emma told her sister as she threaded her needle for the millionth time. "You would think," she said, stabbing the thread at the small eye, "that I would get better at not pulling my thread out of my needle after all this practice."

Amanda threw down the dress she had been hemming and leaned against the back of her chair. "My turn at a season will never come. I shall be fourteen for the rest of my life."

Emma glanced over at Reggie and rolled her eyes.

"And, anyway," Amanda continued, "at the rate Lara is going, if I ever do get a turn it shall be for naught. Our family will be such a laughingstock, I shall never be able to show my face."

"She is having a difficult time of it, isn't she?"

Reggie murmured, as she glanced over Lara's letter again.

"Oh, pooh!" Emma wailed, her thread pulling out of her needle again. She scrunched up her nose. "I hate sewing."

"I do, too," Amanda agreed. "And if Lara could just do what she is supposed to, we wouldn't have to take in such dreary work anymore. Just think of it! We could have parties, and take trips to the Lake District. We could buy beautiful gowns, and I would have so many beaus, I wouldn't know which one to pick."

"And Rachel and Lissie could have a proper governess," Reggie said. "You as well, Emma."

Amanda stared at her in complete shock. No one ever agreed with Amanda. "Exactly," she finally managed to say.

"It is too bad, Reggie, that you weren't born first," Emma interjected. "You would have been able to accomplish this goal easily."

"Oh no, Emma, don't say that. Lara is a wonderful big sister. She is so much fun." Reggie admonished her little sister. "I think, actually, her absence is why we have had such a hard time of our work lately. Lara always made it easier with her stories. And, really, we must give her credit. She is in London trying to do something she absolutely does not want to do, and only to make our lives easier."

"Well, she's not doing a very good job of it," Amanda pouted.

Reggie and Emma both scowled at their sister.

"Well, she isn't," Amanda repeated.

"That's why we need to help her," Reggie said.

Silence greeted this proclamation. The three sisters stared at each other.

"But how on earth can we help her from way out here in the countryside?" Amanda asked.

Emma and Amanda both looked over at Reggie.

"Well, I don't know how," she said. "I just know we should."

Another silence ensued. Usually, Reggie knew everything. It was a bit discomfiting for her younger sisters to hear that Reggie didn't know how to do something.

After a moment, they each returned to their sewing. "I really do miss Lara." Emma sighed. "She does make us laugh, doesn't she?"

"You know," Reggie said. "I think I have a plan."

"Oh good!" Emma and Amanda cried.

"I knew you would," Emma added.

"Well, first of all, I am in complete disagreement with Lara's requirements for her husband."

"Why?" Amanda asked. "I think it's a perfect idea for her to find someone who is extremely wealthy and just about ready to stick his spoon in the wall. I especially like the wealthy part."

Reggie frowned at her sister. "Really, Amanda, do try to think of someone besides yourself for once in your life."

"I take complete exception to that," Amanda said with pursed lips.

"Actually, Reggie, we are all being selfish in wanting Lara to be married at all, since she did write that she finds the idea of marriage barely palatable." This statement came from the other side of the room where Rachel sat sewing on buttons.

The three elder sisters turned to look over at their ten-year-old sister. She just shrugged and went back to her own work. "Anyway, I'm right," she said.

"Yes, of course, dear, but we all know that Lara rarely realizes what is best for her. Don't you think I'm right, Reggie?" Emma said.

"Exactly. So, I think we do need to find her a husband. I think we need to find her a better husband than she's going to find for herself," Reggie answered.

"Of course!" Amanda snapped her fingers together. "And we are so much better positioned to find dear Lara a husband, as we have the best to choose from right here at Ashton Hall. Perhaps Yates's boy, what is his name again? Ah, that's it, Frederick. Of course, I do think he's now all of seventeen, but still and all, Lara always did like to beat him at whist."

"Sarcasm will not help, Amanda." Emma frowned at her sister.

"Oh, and you're one to talk about sarcasm."

"All right then, let's not fight. Fighting shall get us nowhere at all, and cause bad feelings besides," Reggie said sternly. "Anyway, Amanda, we shall not have to find the perfect husband for Lara. I do believe our dear sister has already found the man that will make her more happy than she could ever imagine."

Emma wrinkled her brow, completely flummoxed. "Who?"

Amanda's eyes lit up. "Of course! Lord Rutherford! He does sound absolutely divine!"

"Reggie is speaking of the coachman," Rachel offered from her little corner.

"The coachman?" Emma said.

"The coachman?" Amanda cried.

"The coachman." Reggie nodded toward Rachel. "You're exactly right, Rachel."

"Of course I am."

"Haven't you noticed how Lara speaks of the man in her letters?" Reggie asked. "How she has told us that he has saved her on more than one occasion from completely disgracing herself. And the fact that it makes her so angry that he treats her like she's an errant child. I think she's so angry about that because she'd rather he think of her as a beautiful woman." Reggie set down the letter and took up her sewing. "She is obviously smitten."

Amanda blinked, her mouth hanging agape. "You must be completely out of your mind, Regina Darling. She said the coachman is huge and obnoxious and has calluses on his hands."

"She never wrote that he was obnoxious," Emma corrected her.

"Well *I'll* say it, then!" Amanda retorted. "And I shall also remind you all that Lara spent nearly a page describing Lord Rutherford. She wrote that he put one in mind of the angel Gabriel. She called him 'the most beautiful man alive.' And she also said that he was more a gentleman than any man she has ever met be-

143

fore." Amanda stopped speaking for a moment to get her breath. She was getting rather riled up about this point.

"Just because he is gorgeous does not mean Lara will love him, Amanda," Emma said. "You do base too much on how a person looks."

Amanda gave her sister a scathing look. "I do not."

"This from a girl who spends nearly half her day in front of a mirror."

"I do not!"

"Girls," Reggie remonstrated the sisters.

"Well, I don't," Amanda said under her breath.

"Anyway, we need to be more to the point here," Reggie reminded them. "If we do not do something, Lara just might end up marrying some horrible man who will make her life miserable."

Amanda, still a bit put out by Emma, grumbled something about Lara not doing anything but digging a hole for the Darling name.

"Back to the coachman." Emma spoke pointedly over Amanda's grumbling.

"Yes, I can tell by Lara's letters that she does fancy him," Reggie said.

"But the coachman is destitute!" Amanda cried.

"Of course this is the real reason you oppose the coachman. He will not bring *you* enough *money*." Emma pointed at Amanda with her threadless needle.

Amanda looked ready to explode. "No, actually, that is not the only reason, Emma." She shook her head while she obviously dug around in her brain to find other reasons for not wanting to put the coachman forward as a candidate for her sister's troth.

"What do we really know about this coachman?" she said. "I'll tell you what we know. Nothing, that's what we know. We know nothing of the man's background," she proclaimed, her eyes glittering with triumph. "Oh, no, that's not entirely true. We *do* know that he has some horrible scandal in his past. That's a wonderful thing to have. And, oh, yes, lest we forget . . ." Here Amanda's voice rose at least ten decibels: "He's a *coachman*!"

The other sisters all blinked at Amanda.

"You do not need to raise your voice, Amanda," Reggie told her.

With a roll of her eyes, Amanda slumped back in her chair and stabbed her needle in the hem of the gown she had across her lap.

"Amanda, dearest, you raise relevant points," Reggie said.

Amanda tilted her chin and gave Emma an I-told-you-so look down her nose.

"You don't even know what *relevant* means," Emma said to her older sister.

Reggie quickly continued before the sisters could begin bickering again. "For that reason, Amanda, I think the first thing we need to do, and really the only thing we can do at this point, is meet this coachman."

"How can we possibly do that?" Emma asked.

"Lower Tunsburrow is only an hour's walk from here. If we get all of our sewing done today, we can go tomorrow and meet the mail coach with a letter for our sister."

Amanda perked up a bit at this. "Can we go shopping as well?"

"Actually, we can, I think. Lara sent us money again," Reggie answered.

"I thought you wrote and told her to stop sending us the money meant for her season," Emma said.

Reggie laughed. "I did. But 'tis Lara, dearest. She does tend to do exactly as she wishes, now, doesn't she?"

Chapter 8

Do not even consider marrying a man under the age of thirty. You will still, of course, end up training him for as long as he lives, but it is so much easier if he has learned a bit of life before you have your go at him.

The Duchess Diaries, Volume One

"I never in my life have seen so many bouquets of flowers. And you can wager that I've had quite a few years of life," Lady Tattenbaum chuckled as she wedged her body around the flowers that clogged her front hall.

"I do declare, Lara, you should write a book. *The New Way to Catch a Husband: Win a Shooting Contest.*"

Lara didn't smile at this. In fact, she frowned, as she had been all morning. So much that she was rather sure she had a permanent line now etched between her brows.

She had been pretty sure when she had returned the day before from the debacle of the Johnson's tea party that she had quite ruined any prospects she might have had.

In fact, after writing her letter to Reggie, Lara had tossed and turned all night. She was horribly angry with herself, but then again, she was a bit relieved as well, to be completely honest.

And then morning arrived, and with it the doorbell, ringing away as if it would never stop. Each time Mortimer had answered the door, there was a brand-new bunch of flowers.

The first had been from Roddy. Lara had shaken her head. What on earth was wrong with that boy? Did he not know that she was a pariah?

But then another had come, and another and another. Each one from a younger buck than the one before, until the last, which had come from a boy still at Eaton, for God's sake, who had heard of her exploit the day before, and asked her to wait for him.

"They are all from boys, Lady Tattenbaum."

"And isn't that the point?" she laughed.

Lara slumped back and glared at the handkerchief in her hand. She stuck her needle savagely through the fine linen, ripping a hole where she had meant to embroider her father's last initial. "Bloody hell."

Lady Tattenbaum made a *tsk*ing sound with her tongue.

"But don't you see, Lady Tattenbaum? I am looking for a husband who will die soon. None of these flowers are from anyone over twenty-five."

Lady Tattenbaum blinked at her.

Lara bit her bottom lip. "That did not come out right. I am not as bloodthirsty as I sound, I promise."

"You want a husband who is near death? Why, that is preposterous, child."

Lara really did feel like crying. No one understood, except her sisters, of course. Well, actually, they might not understand, but at least they knew what she meant. She missed them all dreadfully.

And in that moment, rather unexpectedly, she missed Griff Hallsbury. Strange, that. She really barely knew the man—but suddenly she just wished the whole world would go away and let her stand in the park holding Mr. Hallsbury's hand.

She had actually admitted in a letter to her sisters that standing in the park with Mr. Hallsbury had been one of the only times in her entire life that she had felt all right. And she was not at all sure what she meant by that, only that for some reason, when Mr. Hallsbury talked to her about her spirit, she felt it wasn't a bad thing. That, actually, her spirit was something good, that she was fine just the way she was.

Lara had not written the girls about the fact that she had felt that, really, she was just as good as Reggie. Different, yes, but not bad to Reggie's good.

Yes, she missed Griff Hallsbury.

Lady Tattenbaum came over and gently took the ruined handkerchief out of Lara's hands. The older woman sat down beside her and placed a warm arm around her shoulders. "Tell me, what is the matter, dear?"

Lara sighed heavily. "Well, I did have a small plan, Lady Tattenbaum. I decided that I would find a wealthy husband who was near death so that I wouldn't have to be married for very long. That way, I can take care of my sisters, but still get to do the things I want to do."

"And what is it that you want to do?"

Lara frowned. "I don't know."

"Oh."

"It's just that I know I don't want to be married."

"Ah." Lady Tattenbaum nodded.

"I have been thinking lately," Lara said

quickly. "That I might travel. I could go places and learn things and do something wonderful."

"You know, Lara," Lady Tattenbaum said, "you can travel with a husband. And you can learn things here in England. And you can do something wonderful here as well." She patted Lara's hand. "I don't mean to curtail your dreams, dearest, but it does help to know exactly what that something is that you want to do. In order to do it, I mean."

Lara shook her head and made a sound of frustration. "I know that. And I will figure it out eventually. But be that as it may, I do know one thing, and that is what I don't want to be."

"A wife, perhaps?"

"Exactly. I do not want to be a wife."

"You want to be something?"

"Yes. I want to do something extraordinary."

Lady Tattenbaum nodded as if she understood. Lara waited hopefully. Maybe if Lady Tattenbaum understood, she could explain it to Lara. Because suddenly, she really did not understand any of it herself.

"Whom do you look up to, Lara?"

Lara frowned. "Excuse me?"

"Is there someone in the world that you've admired?"

"Of course. Nanny L, I admired her very much."

"And what did she do that was extraordinary?"

Lara blinked. "Er . . ."

"You admired her. So, if you got to the end of your life, and had done all the things your Nanny L had done, would you think you had done something extraordinary?"

"Ummm . . ."

"She was a woman, a strong woman, with many friends. She was loving and kind. And she was funny. She was a loyal wife, and a mother. She was a grandmother."

Lara felt tears burn the backs of her eyes.

"Personally, I think your grandmother was more than extraordinary."

"Yes," Lara said quietly. "She was."

"Well, good." Lady Tattenbaum smiled hugely. "Now then, what on earth are we going to do with all of these flowers?"

Lara blinked. "But you have not answered my question."

"You did not ask me a question, dearest. In fact, I do believe you've just told me some interesting facts." Lady Tattenbaum held up her hand and ticked off each thing with her fingers. "You want to marry a man near death. You do not want to be a wife, and you want to do something extraordinary." She smiled at Lara. "I am right, aren't I? You told me those things. But you most definitely did not ask me a question."

Lara frowned. "But . . ." She could have sworn she was waiting for an answer to something.

Lady Tattenbaum bit her lip and reached out to tuck a loose curl of Lara's hair behind her ear. "Ah, Lara, I act sometimes like I have all the answers, don't I? And after all my years on this earth, I certainly know some of them. Not all of them, unfortunately. But I think, at least, I can tell you this. You have questions. Even though you believe you have a tidy plan and a perfect goal, somewhere deep inside there are questions. Because it's not the perfect goal for you."

Lara sighed. "But my plan lets me have what I want and still give my sisters what they need."

Lady Tattenbaum laughed. "Perhaps you don't really know what you want."

Lara really did feel the need to pout, however childish that might be. "That's exactly what I told you. I don't know what I want to be."

"And I am telling you that the one thing you have decided you shall never be may be the thing that will give you exactly what you want."

Lady Tattenbaum stood. "It's quite a circle, isn't it, Lara? A grand, confusing circle. But as with all circles, you usually end up where you started."

Lara rolled her eyes when Lady Tattenbaum turned around. The woman had not helped her at all and had, in fact, made everything much more confusing. And now, not only was she talking in circles, she was talking *about* them as well. Lovely. "I'm completely confused," Lara said.

She had not meant, actually, to say that bit out loud.

"Aren't we all, dear? Aren't we all?" Lady Tattenbaum stopped in front of a terribly large and rather inelegant bunch of flowers. "These must be from Roddy, he does tend to do everything in a much larger fashion than he should."

"Actually," Lara said, glancing up. "Those are from a boy at Eton."

Lady Tattenbaum laughed, then smiled wickedly at Lara. "Goodness, dear, you're famous."

She really *was* famous, unfortunately.

That very day, Lara read her name in the gossip sheet not once, but twice. Once, of course, was when the author found it necessary to regale the world with "Lady L——'s rather backward way of flirting with the young lads."

"I was not flirting," Lara said to no one, as Lady Tattenbaum had gone to visit the Sinclair sisters. "No one with a brain would flirt with such a complete idiot like Cartwright."

Once again, no one answered her. She sighed and read on—only to stand quickly and speak to the room again.

"Oh no! Well, goodness. Oh for the love of . . . Oh no."

It seems that Mrs. Hastings had made the paper as well. Someone had taken out an ad asking the woman to reveal herself.

"This is not good," Lara said.

Lara felt rather like running away and hiding. Instead, she trudged upstairs to ready herself for Almack's. It was Wednesday night after all, and if she were going to find some rich old goat on the edge of death, the perfect place to do that was Almack's.

Actually, most of the people at Almack's were already dead, or at least they seemed that way.

And that night was even worse, because each circle of people Lara approached seemed to dissolve before she was able to make her hellos.

"Goodness," Lady Tattenbaum said, "I do think you've done yourself a disservice with your shooting contest." To make matters worse, she did seem rather worried about it all.

"This is just a small glitch in my plan, isn't it?" Lara asked. "They will all forget about this soon, won't they?"

Lady Tattenbaum shook her head, the silver feathers quivering in her piled wig. "The *ton* rarely forgets anything, dear."

Of course, Lara was still asked to dance. Roddy escorted her to the dance floor twice. He asked for a third, but Lara just scowled at him.

"Right, then. Didn't think I could get away with three dances, anyway, but thought I'd try." Roddy grinned. "Did you hear about the person looking for Mrs. Hastings? I wonder who it is. Almost answered the ad myself, just to see who placed it. I do hope she comes forward, don't you?"

"Why does someone want Mrs. Hastings, I wonder?" Lara said, catching the eye of Amelia Braxton. The woman raised an eyebrow, and then went back to telling her little group of friends something that was obviously extremely hilarious.

Lara turned so that she couldn't see the woman anymore. Nothing like watching Amelia

Braxton and her scary smile to make a really dreary experience even worse.

"Not sure, really. Though, I've got to think it has something to do with her driving ability. I'd wager that someone is eager for a person who might be able to beat the baron in a race."

"Really?" Lara asked, all of her attention now centered on Roddy, of all people.

"Of course, it is rather hard to believe anyone could beat the baron."

Lara knew exactly what Roddy was going to say next, and she grimaced even before he said it.

"Especially a woman."

This was the reason she was standing at Almack's being completely ignored by everyone of consequence. Because right at that moment, she felt like telling Roddy Piperneil exactly what she thought about Mrs. Hastings's ability to win a driving race against a man.

She closed her eyes for a minute. She had to control herself; look at what had happened with Cartwright and the shooting debacle.

Obviously, she had whittled down the number of prospective husbands considerably, now that at least half of them would not even be seen in her presence. She absolutely could not afford to do anything to make it worse.

Her extremely logical brain knew that, of course. But, oh, how she wanted to dare Roddy Piperneil to a footrace across the dance floor.

She opened her eyes and glared at the way the material of Roddy's waistcoat pulled between the buttons.

Oh, yes, she would leave Roddy wheezing and writhing on the floor before they passed the punchbowl.

Oh Lord, Lara thought, these were not good things to be thinking about.

And then she saw someone who looked incredibly familiar. Roddy was still talking, of course, but Lara was trying desperately not to hear him. She squinted at the young man standing near the door. He seemed to be looking for someone.

They made eye contact then, and as the man's eyes' narrowed, Lara's grew wide. "Oh dear," she said.

"Are you all right, Lady Lara?" Roddy asked.

"It's the man from the coach," she said.

"Excuse me?" Roddy frowned at her.

But Lara was not paying any heed to Roddy. She watched as Mr. Whitehead said something to the man next to him. Lara's eyes moved to the young man's companion. Though his back was to her, she immediately recognized Lord Rutherford.

"Oh no," she said.

And then Mr. Whitehead grinned, and his hand came up, his pointer finger extended.

It was as if the next few seconds happened very slowly. Or at least that is how Lara described them to her sisters.

First, Lara realized that Mr. Whitehead was actually pointing at her, and then Lord Rutherford started to turn.

Lara grabbed Roddy, spinning him so that he stood directly between the two men and herself.

"Lady . . . er . . ."

"Shh!" Lara silenced him.

Unfortunately, Roddy Piperneil was a good half foot shorter than she was. Still holding the man in front of her like a shield, Lara crouched behind him.

"What on earth . . . ?" Roddy cried.

Obviously, Roddy was just going to make this all worse. Lara glanced around. A young woman was just walking past her, and Lara said a quick prayer of forgiveness as she stuck out her foot.

The young woman went flying. At least three young men went to her aid, and everyone else in the room looked over to see what was happening. . . .

And Lara scuttled out the other way. She dodged through the people trying to get into the ballroom, and with a surge of relief found the doors that would take her outside. She slipped quietly through them, not even bothering to stop for her coat.

And then she was outside, with nowhere to go.

"Bugger it," she said out loud.

"Get in," a voice said from the street. Lara blinked at the dark form on the box seat of the coach that sat at the curb.

"Griff?" she said, amazed. "Are you my guardian angel?" she asked. Just then a commotion at the door behind her spurred Lara forward. She lunged toward the coach, pulled herself quickly up beside Griff and ordered him to be off.

"No, get inside the coach, Lara," he said.

"If you don't drive now, I will," Lara said. "Go!"

And with a crack of the whip, they were off. Lara grabbed the edge of the seat behind her and placed her feet far enough apart so that she would not fall.

"What on earth are you doing here, Griff?" she asked.

"It doesn't matter," he said.

Lara wanted to protest, but there was something about the tone of his voice that made her stop. Griff Hallsbury sounded "bone-deep sad," as Emma would say.

"Why don't you tell me why you came hurtling out of Almack's like the hounds of hell were snapping at your heels?" he asked, slowing his team to a walk.

Lara scrunched up her nose. She really did not want to talk about this with Griff. "It doesn't matter," she said, echoing his own words.

He chuckled.

Lara grinned. And then Griff laughed some more, and Lara did too, and pretty soon, Griff could barely drive.

"I do swear, woman, you make me laugh about things I never thought were funny."

Lara laughed some more. "Yes, my sisters say the same thing."

"Now, tell me what happened."

"Ah, it was just that man on the mail coach. You remember, that Mr. Whitehead person who rode with us from Lower Tunsburrow? He was at Almack's tonight. He saw me."

Griff stilled. Lara could not see his face in the dark, but she was rather sure he was not laughing anymore. "Did he recognize you?" Griff asked.

"No, I was running out the door because I couldn't stand the thought of drinking another cup of punch."

"Well now, Lara Darling, that would be sarcasm I hear in your voice, I think."

She laughed again. "Yes, it is, and yes, he obviously recognized me." She sat a bit straighter. "Still, I must tell you, Mr. Hallsbury, I did a lovely job of dodging Mr. Whitehead."

Griff glanced at her out of the corner of his eye, and she grinned up at him.

"I am very afraid to know what just happened in Almack's," Griff said.

"I created a lovely diversion and ran out when Mr. Whitehead was looking the other way."

"Still, he saw you."

"Yes, but Lord Rutherford did not."

Griff cleared his throat harshly, and Lara bit at her bottom lip. She did not understand what was between Griff and Lord Rutherford, but she knew from what Lord Rutherford had said to Lady Tattenbaum that there was something. And it was not good.

"What does Lord Rutherford have to do with it?" Griff asked softly, his voice cracking when he said the other man's title.

"Mr. Whitehead was with Lord Rutherford." Lara suddenly realized something. "Actually, Mr. Whitehead started to point me out to Lord Rutherford. I wonder if Lord Rutherford is the one who placed the ad asking that Mrs. Hastings reveal herself. Probably, he is."

Griff shook his head slowly. "Holy hell."

Lara sighed. She truly did not want to waste her time with Griff Hallsbury speaking of Mr. Whitehead and Lord Rutherford. No, she would much rather sit next to Griff and breathe in the lovely night air as they trotted about town on the box of a coach and four.

She hooked her arm through his. "No need to worry, he did not see me. It is such a beautiful night, is it not?" she asked.

Griff's arm stiffened beneath hers, and she prayed he would not take it away. She knew, of course, that she was probably in a bit of trouble. Well, not a bit, but a lot, given that she had already gotten herself into quite a quagmire. But she absolutely did not want to think about it.

Not now, at least.

She wanted to laugh again with Griff. That had been really lovely. She wanted to enjoy herself. And she realized in that moment that the only times she had truly enjoyed herself since she had gotten to London had been when she was in the company of the man beside her.

Lara scooted a little closer to Griff. She had forgotten to retrieve her coat, after all. He glanced down at her then.

"Are you cold?" he asked.

"I am perfect," she said.

He chuckled. "Yes, you are," he said.

Lara was rather sure that she glowed then. Truly, she felt as if she could light up a dark room. Griff Hallsbury thought she was perfect. And he had not sounded in the least bit like he was teasing.

"We are enjoying incredible weather," Lara gushed.

"I was just thinking the same thing," Griff answered her. "There's a nice breeze, and a nice smell to the air. I will bet we have rain sometime this week."

"Oh shush," she said.

Griff laughed again.

"You were sitting out in front of Almack's on top of your coach thinking that rain is coming?" Lara asked.

"Ah, no, I didn't have a single thought of rain until I saw you run pell mell out of there."

Lara frowned. "I do not run pell mell."

"I beg to differ."

"I am a very good runner," she told him with a sniff.

"I'll just bet you are," he said. And she knew that he was grinning from ear to ear.

"Do not use the word *bet*, or I might just make you stop this carriage and challenge you to a footrace," she told him.

"But I'm a gentleman, so of course I would let you win."

"So, you are a gentleman, then?" she asked.

He drew a deep breath and they rode quietly for a moment. "I was on my way home tonight, and I realized it was Wednesday, so I went by Almack's." Griff stopped suddenly. "I mean . . ." he said, but still did not continue his sentence.

"Why?" she asked softly. "Why would you stop and wait outside Almack's?" And she really wanted to know. She wanted to know everything about Griff Hallsbury.

"It doesn't matter," he said. "I didn't mean to say that."

"But you did," she prompted him. "Do you sit outside Almack's every Wednesday night?"

Griff took a moment to turn their conveyance down a side street. "No," he said then.

"Just tonight?" she asked.

"I have been remembering things lately, and I was driving close by and remembered that everyone would be at Almack's tonight."

Lara shivered. Had he, perhaps, wanted to see her? That thought made her feel as if she could fly. She very nearly giggled, of all things.

"I was just sitting there, thinking," he said with a teasing tone in his voice. "And suddenly the doors cracked open and of all people, Lara Darling came skittering down the stairs as if she were a cat that had just gotten her tail stepped on."

"Lovely imagery, thank you very much."

"You're welcome."

"So, what were you thinking about, Griff Hallsbury?" Lara asked quietly. She did not think he would answer her, but she rather hoped he would. What did this man think about in the dark of night? What had made his voice so sad when he told her it didn't matter, when obviously it did, very much.

"Girls in pretty dresses, mammas with a gleam in their eye, men pretending to be bored," Griff told her.

She smiled in the night. "Goodness, I do think you are a poet, Griff."

"Those things used to be everyday occurrences in my life. All of this used to be something I did every day. I thought it dull. I thought it boring. And now, I would do anything in the world to have it back again."

Lara swallowed, hard. And she felt horribly ashamed.

"Well, actually, I'd do anything to have another chance to do it again, and not hurt so many people this time."

"Griff," she asked. "Who are you?"

He laughed, but this time, there was no humor in the sound at all. "That's a good question, Lara Darling. But here you are safe," he said, pulling his team to a stop.

Lara looked up. They sat in front of Dryer House. Once again, Griff had rescued her and brought her home.

Why then, did she not want to take her arm from his and leave? It felt rather more like home right here on the box seat of a coach, as long as Griff Hallsbury was there with her.

"Griff," she said suddenly. "There is nothing for which you can't say you're sorry. Especially when you mean it so much in your heart."

He sat very still for a moment. "Perhaps. At least I'm trying to say I'm sorry in my own way."

"What is that way?" she asked.

"I lost a fortune, and I'm going to make it back."

Lara nodded. She was pretty sure, though, that this wasn't all about money. She looked up into Griff's shadowed face. She did feel a need to kiss his cheek, put her hand against his face, something. She simply wanted to touch this man and make him whole.

Save him, like he kept saving her.

"Go on, before someone sees you," he said roughly.

Lara sighed. She really didn't want to go, but she pushed herself up from the seat and then clambered down. "Thank you," she said, but Griff had already cracked his whip and left her.

Chapter 9

Don't take everything men say to heart, dearest. Most of the time they have no idea how to say what they really mean. And when they finally figure it out, they inevitably say it all wrong anyway.

The Duchess Diaries, Volume One

The morning started out gray and only got grayer. It had not rained in forever, it seemed, but obviously the weather had decided to make up for it all in one day.

Still, though he was sure the rain would start at any moment, Griff went riding. He had little time to indulge in any type of leisure activity, so he was not going to let a bit of mist spoil his morning off.

And, of course, he ended up at the park. Possibly, he had lost his mind. He had to quit finding her the way he did. It was not good for either of them. One of these times, someone would see them, and then Lara's tenuous hold on respectability would be forever broken.

Yes, he had most definitely lost his mind, but he could not stop thinking about Lady Lara Darling. He had even started reading the gossip sheets to see how she was getting on.

He had taken quite an ego-beating when one of the mail guards had caught him with the gossip rag. The other coachmen and ostlers had not let up on him for a week.

Still, today he did not think Lara would be out. He knew she had been up very late the night before. He had watched to make sure she entered Dryer House safely.

And then he had circled back. He watched as a light went on in a window and surmised that it was hers. And that light had burned through the night and into the early morning hours.

Griff had been unable to force himself to go home to his small, ugly room. He had spent the night with his mind in places it had not been for a very long time. Regret made his heart feel so hollow as to be gone completely.

Yes, as Lara had said, he could say he was sorry. He could work as a coachman and race against the young bucks in Town to make back the fortune he had lost. He could retrieve what his father, grandfather and great grandfather had once owned.

But they had all passed on. His father had died knowing that Griff had turned out to be a bounder and a rake with a penchant for gambling . . . and losing.

He could never apologize to his father. He couldn't make it all right now, not really. Because, of course, there was also Thomas.

A drop of water pelted Griff's greatcoat. And then another and another. Yes, there was a downpour in the works, surely.

The first of it fell out of the sky like a curtain dropping on the last scene of a play. Griff had just crested a hill when it hit, and he had just seen that Lara *had* decided to ride. She was at a full gallop, in fact, and did not even flinch as the water came down in sheets.

Griff frowned. She really ought to slow down.

But it was as if the danger of the rain just goaded Lara to go faster. She was truly a lunatic.

Even with that thought, Griff had to smile. But his smile quickly disintegrated as Lara's horse slid on the wet grass. It looked as if the beast had possibly thrown a shoe.

Whatever happened, Lara kept her seat as

her horse slid and then bucked. Griff held his breath. And then, just as he felt she might actually get through unscathed, the horse lost her footing completely and went down on her side.

Lara was thrown about fifteen feet. Griff didn't see anything else, because he had dug his heels into his own horse's sides and put his head down. He reached her in seconds, jumping from his seat quickly.

"Are you all right?" he asked. "Lara, can you hear me?"

She blinked up at him, her face covered in mud. "Where on earth did you come from?"

"Are you hurt? Does anything hurt?" he asked.

She struggled to sit up, but Griff held her down. "Don't."

"I'm fine! And, anyway, lying here as I am, I'm sure to drown."

Griff helped her sit up. "Did you hurt anything?"

"My pride is absolutely tattered. I didn't realize anyone was watching or I'd have done a double flip as I fell."

Griff couldn't help grinning. "Well," he said, "your mouth seems to be in perfect working order."

"Yes, but I was serious about the drowning."

The rain had not let up at all, and a rather large puddle was forming around Lady Lara. Griff helped her to stand. "Can you put your weight on your legs?" he asked. "Is there anything broken?"

"I'm fine, I think," she said.

"Good, here," he took off his great coat and draped it around her shoulders. "Shall we find shelter?"

"There's a lovely tree just down the path," Lara said. "It's so thick and huge, I'm sure it'll keep most of the water off until this rain recedes."

Griff grabbed the reins of Lara's horse as well as his own and followed Lara to a huge oak tree. Beneath it was relatively dry.

Lara laughed as she glanced down at herself. "I'm sure I look a mess."

Griff stepped closer to her and pulled a clump of grass from her sodden hair. "A mess, yes. But, I must say you make a beautiful mess."

A blush stained her cheeks pink.

"Lara Darling blushes," Griff teased. "I never thought I'd see the day."

"Oh, do be quiet." Lara swatted at him, before turning away and wiping at her face with the sleeve of his coat. It came away streaked with mud.

"Oh goodness," she said. "I've ruined your coat. My face must be covered in mud."

Griff handed her his handkerchief. "The coat has seen worse, believe me. The handkerchief is a bit wet, but it might help."

"Thank you," she said, glancing up at him quickly, and then away as she mopped at her face.

He nodded. He had not been teasing her, she was absolutely beautiful. Soaked to the bone, her hair tangled and muddy, she was gorgeous.

She looked around again, and Griff noticed that there was a scratch on her forehead. Obviously, it had been covered by the mud, so he had not noticed it. Now he took a step forward and cradled her chin, tipping her face up.

"You are hurt," he said.

"Am I?"

"Do you feel faint at all? You've hit your head."

Lara reached up and felt the bump that was now forming. "Oh, 'tis nothing. A scratch. It's not even bleeding."

"Still, even without blood, if you've hit your head hard enough, the damage can be fatal."

"Oh, I'm fine. I can't even feel it." She grinned. "Do you whine so much when you hit your own head, Griff?"

The sound of his name on her lips gave him pause, and Griff stood very still for a moment, realizing with a bit of shock that he stood very near Lara. The skin of her jaw was smooth against his fingers.

He stroked her chin with the pad of his thumb. "I never whine, dearest girl." He gave her his most wicked smile. "I am a very strong and capable man."

She laughed. "Right. I have yet to see any man not cry mightily when hurt or sick."

Griff frowned. "I have been hurt many times, and I will tell you now, I have never cried."

"*When* you were hurt," she stabbed his chest with her pointer finger. "I will put money down to say that you curled up and cried like an infant once you were alone in your bed. When my father had the headache you would think he was dying of dysentery."

Griff touched the spot where Lara had poked him with her finger. "Ouch."

"I rest my point." She laughed again.

He wanted to kiss her.

"Come now, Griff, tell me true. If there was a

woman about, to rub your feet and bring you soup, did you not cry? Or at the very least moan, and perhaps go on as if you had been broken in two when it was just a splinter or some such thing?"

He smiled. "Oh, see, you did not tell me there was a woman around. If there is someone there to make it all better, of course, I take advantage of that."

Lara rolled her eyes. "I told you. But I am fine." She pushed his hands away so that he did not hold her chin any longer.

Oh how he wanted to keep touching her. He glanced around, the rain was not letting up; in fact he could not see a foot beyond their little spot beneath the tree.

It was as if they inhabited a world unto themselves.

"Are you sure, though, that your head does not hurt?" he asked.

"Very sure, thank you."

"You know that running your horse that fast in the rain is really not the smartest thing to do."

Lara's grin turned down and she narrowed her gaze. "Are you telling me that you have never run your horse in the rain?"

"Err . . . um, well, yes, I have, but . . ."

"Then perhaps you should not tell me what to do."

"I was not telling you what to do. I was just telling you that—"

"I know, I know, you were trying to remind the poor little girl that she might hurt herself. Might I—"

"Stop." Griff put his hand over Lara's mouth. It had been an impulse, but he immediately realized that it was a bad idea. He could feel her lips and teeth against his palm, and it made him soft-kneed but hard somewhere just a bit higher than that.

Damn, the woman was making him absolutely randy.

"I . . ." he faltered. "I am just worried you might hurt yourself. You are an incredible rider, and you could outdrive most of the young bucks in this town. I would never dream of belittling your abilities."

Her eyes were very large above his hand. He took his hand away reluctantly, and they stared at each other for a long moment of silence.

The rain beat endlessly about them, as Lara breathed heavily, the wet bodice of her riding habit rising and falling.

Damn.

He felt an intense need to touch her. That was very bad.

They were too alone.

"I hear as well," Griff said, trying to bring a bit of levity back into their situation, "that you can outgun them. Cartwright, anyway."

Her gaze, which had been somewhat dreamy, blast it, turned to one of surprise. "How on earth did you hear that?"

"I read about it."

She sighed, and her face seemed to crumple. All the spirit in her eyes was doused and gone. He hated that.

"I really did try not to, but the man just . . ."

"Ah, and isn't he an idiot?" Griff said. "I'm amazed you didn't turn the gun on him."

"I didn't have to. I have a feeling someone will, soon enough. He has no tact whatsoever, and he is stupid enough that I'm sure he'll say the wrong thing to the wrong person one of these days."

"Well then, Cartwright hasn't changed in the last seven years."

Lara Darling turned those incredibly soft brown eyes on him, her delicate eyebrows arched just so, her beautiful pink lips pursed in such a way that he wanted to smooth them with his own.

That thought made him feel like an excited young buck, there was nothing else to it. He glanced again at the sheets of rain.

He needed to be away from this woman as soon as possible. Lady Tattenbaum would kill him. And he'd never forgive himself.

At the very least he figured they would not be seen. No one with half a brain would be out in this. He frowned. Probably, he did have only half a brain. Look at where it had gotten him.

He glanced back at the beautiful wet creature in front of him.

"How do you know Cartwright?" she asked. "And why did I hear Lord Rutherford call you Trenton?"

Lord Rutherford. Griff's throat tightened.

"When did he call me that?"

"Well, actually, I think it was Cartwright." Lara nodded. "Yes, it was Cartwright. Lord Rutherford didn't say much at all, if I remember correctly."

No he wouldn't.

"Anyway, who are you?" Lara asked.

Who was he? A good question. One that this woman kept asking of him. And one that made him feel hollow inside. Still, it was not as if he was new to this experience. Whenever he remembered or thought about what he had done, he felt exactly this way.

Of course, at those times he was usually alone, not staring into the eyes of some fey creature who made him shiver at the touch of her hand.

"I am a coachman," he said finally.

"Don't," she said. "Already you have told me more than that."

"But Lady Tattenbaum has not told you everything, then?"

Lara furrowed her perfect brow. "No. She mentioned your name once, but actually, she goes completely mute when I ask anything now. Especially since she spoke with Lord Rutherford about you."

It was as if a dagger had been thrust into a hole in his chest. Griff tried to breathe.

"It does not matter," he said.

"You said that before, Griff, but I can see in your eyes that it isn't true."

"It's all done and finished."

"*What* is done and finished?" Lara actually stamped her foot.

"Nothing."

"Ooooh!" Lara Darling picked up her sodden dirty skirt in one muddy hand and took a threatening step toward him. "It isn't nothing.

Last night you seemed on the verge of crying, I do swear. And Lord Rutherford got very upset when Lady Tattenbaum spoke of you. And I want to know exactly what this is all about!"

"Why? It is none of your business."

"Of course it is!"

"And how do you think it is?"

"Because it has to do with you, and I lo—" She stopped, her eyes rounding in obvious horror. She blinked then, her fingers going to her mouth.

Griff watched her but did not move. He felt as if he could not move, truly, or his entire being might shatter into a thousand different pieces.

"Oh no," she said quietly and took a step away from him. His coat, which had been precariously draped about her shoulders, softly dropped to the ground in a heap at her feet, but she paid it no heed.

Griff pressed his lips together. He knew exactly what she had been about to say. He clenched his hands into fists when he realized that he was actually trembling. He felt sick suddenly.

If he had been what his father had wanted, this would be his life now. If he had not lost everything, he would have what he had been daydreaming about lately. He would be sitting beside Lady Lara Darling at Vauxhaul Gardens, watching her eyes dance as she took in the fireworks, wondering if perhaps she wasn't the one he would make his wife.

She could have been a potential Lady Trenton. Oh, most definitely, this was the sort of woman who would make his life complete.

Except that he did not have that life anymore.

Griff swallowed, bile rising in his throat.

"Dear God," Lara said.

The tone of her voice made all of the ache in his heart turn to a burning anger. He wasn't sure what exactly made him feel like throwing something, the fact that Lady Lara thought she loved him, or that she found such horror at the idea.

"I am very used to this, Lady Lara, do not worry," Griff said with a forced smile. "There are many women, who think themselves above my station, who find some sort of excitement in the idea of loving me."

Lara frowned. "I do not love you. Don't be ridiculous, I don't even know you."

Truth be told, that hurt more than anything else.

"I just . . ." Lara shook her head. "Well, all right then, I . . ." she stopped and looked away from him. "You're such a gentleman, sir. And you have worried about me and tried to help me when anyone else would have let me get into my little scrapes and let it be done."

She looked at him, then. "Do you know that when I was shooting against that horrid Cartwright, I just kept thinking, if only Griff were here, he'd save me."

"I am most definitely not your savior."

"Well, you've certainly done it more than once."

"And I am not a gentleman," he said quietly.

"You're more a gentleman than Cartwright."

Later he could not explain what had driven him in that moment. He thought perhaps it was the same devil that had pursued him when he was a young buck of the *ton* and had gambled away his life, drank away his self-respect and kept company with the kind of woman who assured his ruination.

Whatever it was, Griff knew that he had to show Lady Lara Darling that she was absolutely wrong about him.

He could not have this young girl thinking she loved him. He did not deserve it, and he did not want it from her. Ironically, his damnable pride, which had goaded him on for the last seven years to make up what he had done wrong, now made him want to make sure this woman knew that he was exactly the opposite of a gentleman. He always had been.

He grabbed her around the waist, lifted her to him, and kissed her.

It was not a light fluttery thing, either, but a deep, dark taking. He opened his mouth over hers and took her with his tongue.

Her body was rigid against his for a moment, and then she melted. It was the only word for it. Her body became a part of his, her lovely breasts soft against him, her thigh sliding between his.

Her gown's condition made it so that he could feel her intimately. His hand spanned her ribcage, and he felt it heave beneath his fingers. He trailed them up to the underside of one of her breasts, and lightly ran his thumb over its crest. Her nipple went rigid beneath his touch.

She moaned, her mouth opening even more.

He pressed her to him tightly and delved into the soft heat of her mouth.

And she let him.

The heat was like something he'd never experienced in his life, burning through him like a fire that he could not control. And in a deep, dark part of his mind, he realized that he and Lara Darling fit perfectly against each other. She was exactly the right height so that he did not have to bend too far down to keep her curved exactly against his body.

That thought frightened him more than any other, actually. For in that moment, he knew he had found the woman who had been destined for him. But he could not have her.

It would be his penance.

He pushed her away quickly.

"There," he said darkly. "Am I such the gentleman now?" He grabbed his horse's reins.

"You are not going to be another mistake," he said darkly. "I have too many of them in my life." Griff grabbed his horse's reins and marched out into the pouring rain.

It was only after he was soaked through to the skin and colder than he'd ever been in his life that he realized he had left his coat behind.

Your coat and your heart, left under a tree in the rain with a woman, his mind said quietly. But Griff gritted his teeth and didn't listen to his feelings. He was very good at doing that after so many years of practice.

It was all overrated. All of it. The season in general, the balls and soirees, and the men.

Especially the men.

Lara had just about had enough of them all. Her father had been bad enough, ignoring them all to such perfection that he did not even go to her mother when she cried into her pillow at night.

If Lara had heard her, why on earth had her father not been able to?

Of course, she understood it a little more now. They were all a bunch of pea-brained shites, men. And they completely deserved her language, she said to herself, as her mind's voice indulged shamelessly in stable talk.

Here she sat, ignored by any man possessing even the slightest hint of any of her prerequisites—and all because she had dared to shoot better than one of them.

And then the one man who had seemed to be her savior, and had actually kissed her in such a way that made her reconsider her poor impression of men, had called her a mistake.

A mistake!

Ha!

Lara stalked across the dark room. The rain had not let up and even Lady Tattenbaum's bright pink front room seemed rather like a tomb. There was a fire burning, but it didn't seem to brighten the room at all. She glared at the fire. Perhaps she should throw Hallsbury's coat on it. That would bring some life to the room, surely.

Stupid coat. She had thrown it into the darker recesses of her wardrobe that morning. And it seemed to have taken on a personality of its own. She knew it was in there. She hated that it was. But then she would suddenly feel a burning sense of rightness that it was there, that a part of Griff was with her in her room.

It was all so incredibly inane as to be maddening. She was doomed for bedlam, surely.

Lara grabbed a wilting daisy out of one of the bouquets that still crowded Lady Tattenbaum's front room and started to pluck off its petals, one by one.

"Lord Rutherford to see you, my lady," a maid announced.

Lara glanced up from the daisy with a sigh. "Fine, send him in."

She did not want to see Lord Rutherford, or any Lord for that matter. She wanted . . . What did she want? She really had no idea.

Lara sat carefully, though, arranging her dress across her knees and sniffled a bit. She had been soaked through that morning when she finally made it back to Lady Tattenbaum, and now she had a bit of a stuffy nose.

It wasn't Griff Hallsbury's fault, of course, but she blamed him anyway.

Stupid man.

"Lady Lara," Lord Rutherford said as he entered the drawing room. "And how are you today?"

"Lord Rutherford," she smiled as he bowed. "I am tolerable. Surprised, really, that you are talking to me. Don't you know that I am to be ignored at all costs?"

With a slight chuckle, Lord Rutherford limped closer and sat across from her. "Only because you've scared the women, my dear. The men are enthralled. Well, perhaps Cartwright isn't, but most of the others are. 'Tis their wives that have decided you're to be ignored."

Lara sniffed. She had quite ruined everything, and she suddenly wished to cry. How on earth was she ever to find a man that would take care of her sisters now?

Unless, of course, she married some young bloke just out of shortpants. And that would absolutely ruin her life.

"Are you playing 'Does he love me'?" Lord Rutherford asked, and Lara blinked up at him.

He gestured to the daisy petals on the floor.

"Oh," she said. She glanced down at the sad-looking flower in her hand. "No." But she didn't elaborate. She couldn't really. *Does he love me* kept ringing in her ears.

Does he love me?

Does it matter?

Why do I feel so awful?

"Ashton Hall is out near Bedford, isn't it?" Lord Rutherford asked then.

Lara nodded, her thoughts elsewhere.

"So, might you go through Lower Tunsburrow, Lady Lara, on your way into London?"

Lower Tunsburrow? Lara glanced at the man before her and blinked. She felt a slight shiver of dread run up her spine. Lord Rutherford had been the man with Mr. Whitehead the other night.

Oh dear.

Lara stood quickly. "I am not well, Lord Rutherford. I got caught in the rain while riding, and I do believe I have a cold." She sniffed again, loudly.

Lord Rutherford did not move.

"Perhaps, Lady Lara, you saw this infamous Mrs. Hastings when you were making your way to London? It seems the two of you arrived around the same time."

Lara realized that she had crumpled the white daisy she held. The rest of the petals fell about her feet as she relaxed her hand. "No, actually. I would never have taken the mail coach, of course."

"Of course."

Lara's head pounded. "I do not feel well, Lord Rutherford."

"I am sorry, Lady Lara." The man stood then, and Lara felt a rush of relief.

"If, by chance, you remember later that you did meet this lady, and that perhaps you know how to contact her—"

"Of course I do not."

"I just thought that you might give her a message for me." Lord Rutherford limped forward. "I am sponsoring a race."

Lara bit her lip. "A race? I do not know much about races, my lord." Her voice came out rather high and thready. "You mean a footrace, perhaps? Or a race to finish a bit of needlework?" Oh yes, she sounded positively idiotic.

"It's a special race with coaches and four."

"Oh, yes, a coach and four. That would be a carriage, right? Like the kind that the mail is taken about on?" Lara had to admit that she felt rather proud of herself. She had never sounded so inane in her life.

"Exactly." Lord Rutherford moved away from her and stared into the fire for a moment. "I am quite a gambling man, Lady Lara." He turned and glanced at her, his golden eyes shadowed. "At least I once was. But, I must admit a good wager can still stir my blood. And I have decided that I am bored. A race is exactly what this town needs right now. A good race between two very good drivers."

"Really?" she said, her voice quiet in the pink, cavernous room.

"Yes. This Mrs. Hastings has piqued my curiosity. And I do think that she might be just the one to give London exactly what it needs. A good race."

Lara worried her lip with her teeth. This was bad. She could feel her blood stirring and her nerves jumping. This was all very very bad.

"I'm also enough of an enthusiast, that I'm going to make this race even more exciting."

"More exciting?"

"I am putting up a small fortune to the winner."

Lara frowned. "A what?"

"A fortune, Lady Lara." He turned toward her fully and cocked his head to the side as if he were pondering a thought of great magnitude. "Enough money, say, as to give five girls at least thirty seasons each, actually. And fix up an old crumbling manor, perhaps, as well as provide old retainers enough to set them up for life."

Lara stared at Lord Rutherford.

"You will let me know if you speak to Mrs. Hastings, then?" Without waiting for her answer, he said, "I thought you would." And he bowed slightly, smiled and left the room.

Lara stood without moving for at least a minute.

"Oh dear," she finally said to the empty room.

Chapter 10

Never underestimate the soothing qualities of a good day of shopping.
　　　　The Duchess Diaries, Volume One

The three Darling sisters who witnessed Mr. Hallsbury's daring feat that next day did not find it quite as thrilling as Lara had.

"He's a show-off," Emma announced.

"He obviously isn't very careful about his passengers, is he?" said Reggie.

"He does look rather nice, though, doesn't he," Amanda said, eyeing the coachman as he jumped from his seat, handed the reins to an ostler and stalked into the inn.

Emma wrinkled her nose. "But he's probably going to have a nip before he's off again. I've always found that most unsavory in a coachman.

You'd think they would know that they really ought to keep their minds clear for their job."

"Did you see the way he walks?" Amanda asked. "He's rather manly."

"Is that a good thing?" Reggie asked with a small smile.

"Well, of course, it is!" Amanda said indignantly. "A man should be manly, it makes him more of a man."

Emma made a loud sound of disgust.

"Anyway, let's go in and speak to this manly man," Reggie said.

"What then, are we just going to surround him and ask him for his credentials? 'Are you good enough for our sister, because I don't think you are?' " Emma queried her sisters.

"Oh, I'll get him to talk." Amanda sashayed forward, but Reggie caught hold of her shawl, nearly choking her.

"Really Amanda," Reggie admonished. "You're fourteen, not twenty-four."

Amanda's face darkened stormily.

Emma shook her head and held up the letter they had written to Lara. "Come on then. Make it purely about business, and he won't suspect a thing."

Reggie and Amanda hurried to follow her.

The inn was dark compared to the outside, and they had to stop on the threshold and squint. But there was no missing the coachman sitting in the public house of the inn. Even hunched over the trestle table, he was obviously the tallest man in the room. Not to mention the most gorgeous man any of them had ever seen.

"He's beautiful," Amanda said.

"He's awfully tall," Emma said.

"All well and good," Reggie said. "But we really must get to know him better than just the fact that he is tall and good-looking." With a deep breath, she strode forward.

"Mr. Hallsbury?" Reggie asked when she reached his side.

The man before them glanced up from his supper. "Yes?" he asked.

"We need you to deliver this for us," Reggie said, holding up a piece of folded paper.

The man gave them all such a grin that even Reggie blushed. "I'm just the coachman, ma'am," he said. "You'll need to see the postmaster for that."

"But our sister has spoken so highly of you, we thought you'd deliver it to her yourself." This was from Amanda, and both Reggie and Emma just stared at her for a moment. Her words literally dripped with honey. And she had started batting her lashes as if she were trying to shoo flies away with them.

She glanced around, saw her sisters staring and her syrupy gaze turned rather murderous.

The stewed lamb that sat upon Mr. Hallsbury's spoon hovered halfway to his mouth.

"Your sister?" he asked.

"Lady Lara Darling," they all said in unison.

The lamb plopped back onto the coachman's plate. "Oh good lord," he said.

"We were wondering if you could take her this letter." Reggie waved the paper under his nose again while Amanda took a seat across from him. "You're much taller than she made you seem," she said sweetly.

"I . . ."

"We're ever so worried about Lara, Mr. Hallsbury," Reggie said, sitting beside her sister.

Emma took a step closer to the coachman, but stayed standing, effectively cutting off his escape, just in case he decided he'd rather not be a part of this conversation.

"I'm not sure I know . . ."

"Oh, of course you do!" Amanda interrupted him. "She's the one who drove your coach through the inn's entrance. Really, though, I'm not sure I understand what all the fuss is about."

Griff frowned. "It's a difficult task. . . . I mean, that was not your sister. No, definitely, it wasn't." He glowered at them. "You're going to cause more harm than good if you go in that direction," he said quietly.

Reggie smiled. "Of course, sir, we did not mean to speak of that." She placed the letter on his crumpled serviette. "We knew that you would not mind putting this directly in our sister's hands for us."

The man stared at the paper as if it were liable to burst into flames at any moment. "Couldn't you just use the post?" he asked without looking away from the letter.

"Oh, we trust you completely," Amanda said.

"Our sister has written of you often," Reggie informed him.

"Lovely."

"Are you really a peer, then?" Emma asked.

Amanda glared at her.

Mr. Hallsbury took up the letter finally and tucked it inside his thick coat. "Do you always listen to stories?" he asked with a bit of a smile.

Amanda sighed, and Reggie surreptitiously smacked her leg under the table.

"Tsk," Amanda said.

"The townspeople seem to think that you really are a baron, Mr. Hallsbury," Reggie said.

"If I were, do you think I'd be driving a coach and answering to 'Mister'?" he asked, laughing.

"You speak well," Emma commented.

"Where were you born?" Reggie asked.

"Don't mind them, sir, they have atrocious manners sometimes," Amanda said.

"Ah well, I don't mind." He winked.

Even Emma blinked at that. The coachman had the most beautiful blue eyes any of them had ever seen. And lashes a man should not have: so thick and dark and curled up at the ends. And he did make one's heart beat just a tiny bit faster with those winks of his, not to mention the wicked grins, like the one he was giving them now.

"It's been said, actually, tha' I 'as born on the kitchen table. Me ma got just that far 'afore she broke her fast and felt me a comin'."

Reggie frowned at him. All three of them then turned and glanced at one another. They all, of course, noticed how his accent went from cultured to country awfully quickly.

"G'day, ladies," he said, standing.

All three of them stared at him knowingly as

he grabbed his hat, tossed some coins on the table and left.

"Well," said Amanda, "he's definitely manly."

"That's for sure. He's lying through his teeth, isn't he?" Emma said. "And men are all very good liars, I reckon."

"He took the letter, though," Reggie reminded them. "Now let us see if he delivers it."

"Why on earth would that matter?" Amanda asked.

"Well, for one, he'd be doing something he really didn't need to do just because we asked him to."

Emma nodded. "I guess that says something for him."

"Right, and, more importantly, it means he's looking for any reason he can find to see our sister."

"How romantic," Amanda sighed.

"But what if he truly is a bounder?" asked Emma.

Amanda frowned suddenly. "And what if something does happen between them? Our prospects would be cut in half, surely—probably worse."

"Really, Amanda," Emma admonished. "You can be so selfish."

"Well, 'tis true. Not only would we be back to one season each, still sewing away to make ends meet, but our sister would have run off with a coachman. The Darling sisters will become laughingstocks. Probably, we would not even get into Almack's, much less find husbands of any worth at all." Amanda's pouty lips pouted even more.

"You're thinking much too far in the future, Amanda. I suggest we take a moment and find out who this coachman really is before we go even an inch farther," Reggie said.

"Right." Emma nodded, and then frowned. "How?"

Silence answered her.

"We could pay a visit to Mrs. Richards," Amanda suggested.

Her two sisters nodded.

"We never did thank her appropriately for the dancing lessons she gave Lara," Emma said.

"And she does live between here and home," Reggie nodded.

Amanda twirled a perfect blonde ringlet around her finger. "If I remember correctly, Mrs. Richards had a few seasons in Town. She's married to the younger son of a baron, or something like that. She might know something."

Reggie and Emma nodded.

"Yes," Reggie said then. "A peer should know the story. Very good, Amanda."

Amanda straightened on the hard wood bench. "I do have a brain, you know." She preened a bit. "I am not *just* a beauty."

"Oh do spare us," Emma said.

"You know, Father might know something as well," Reggie said, ignoring her sisters' minor squabbling.

Emma laughed. "Right. Father wouldn't notice if a group of raging rhinos crashed through the library wall and trampled through the house. I'm sure he couldn't even tell us which of us is older than the other."

Amanda rolled her eyes and Reggie looked particularly pained. "Yes, I do believe you're right, Emma."

"Well, then, let us find a nice gooseberry pie and take it to Mrs. Richards, then," Amanda said, glancing about at her two sisters.

Emma scrunched up her nose. "I am rather starting to feel like I belong in Scotland Yard or some such. What with interrogating witnesses and everything."

Reggie laughed. "Right, I'm sure the lads at Scotland Yard often sugar up their witnesses with gooseberry pie."

Emma shrugged. "If they don't, they should. It is a very good idea, I think."

"Yes, but they are all men," Amanda said. "I do think women handle bribery better. We have more subtlety. We know how to slip the right word in, all dainty-like and guileless, and then twist it perfectly to get what we want."

Emma and Reggie could only stare at their sister.

"What?" Amanda said.

"You know, Amanda, sometimes you really do scare me," Emma told her.

"I cannot believe how much fun I am having," Lara said to Lady Tattenbaum. "Honestly, when you told me we were going shopping, I could barely suppress the need to crawl under a rock, and now here I am, having the best time trying to find slippers that match a purple bejeweled turban. Who would have thought?" Lara smiled largely.

"Oh, you have no idea." Lady Tattenbaum patted Lara's arm. "Just you wait. It is even more fun when you are out using up huge amounts of your husband's money after he has done something so manlike as to be downright shocking."

This thought took a bit of the shine off Lara's

smile. "Yes, well, look at these," she picked up a pair of slippers the color of an evening sky. "They don't match the turban, but they are beautiful, aren't they?"

"Ooooh yes, I love them. We shall have to buy them and find a matching gown. In fact, you *need* to buy these slippers, for I saw a wrap in the other store that will match them so perfectly I'm sure it is God's will we were to find these shoes."

Lara giggled. "Surely that is quite sacrilegious, Lady Tattenbaum."

Lady Tattenbaum shook her head mightily. "No, no child. God is good. We know that to be truth. Thus He smiles heartily upon shopping."

Lara laughed outright.

"Now then, let us go and pay for them, and make them yours."

"Oh no," Lara said on a sigh. "It is fun, but I really couldn't possibly. I do not have the money for a new gown, and I do not have anything to wear these shoes with."

"Oh bother." Lady Tattenbaum frowned at her. "You do have a bit of money, I know you do. Spend it on yourself for once, and don't worry so about your sisters. They aren't starving, for goodness sake."

Lara bit her lip. "But . . ."

"If you buy those slippers, I'll pay for the gown," she said.

"Oh no, I couldn't."

"Of course you can. Come now, you're ruining my fun."

Lara laughed again. "Oh, all right." She took the slippers to the proprietor and watched as the man wrapped the beautiful dark blue silk shoes in paper.

She couldn't help but grin as she picked up the parcel and felt the slippers through the paper. Perhaps she would take Amanda shopping here someday. Amanda would be in heaven, and suddenly Lara realized that she and her sisters could have a lot of fun shopping together in London.

That, of course, brought thoughts of Lord Rutherford's race. Which completely took all of the fun right out of the day.

She could not think straight, she was so confused. The thought of entering this race of Lord Rutherford's brought up all those feelings that arose whenever she knew she was doing something terrible. The exhilaration, of course, felt very very good, but it did tend to bring about circumstances that were very very bad.

Life could be extremely difficult sometimes.

And there really were one too many reasons

to refuse to enter Lord Rutherford's race. First, she might just lose. (And then she would have ruined not only her own chances of marrying, which in truth did not bother her, but her sisters' as well. And that *did* bother her.)

And second, even if she did win, she would probably still suffer the cut direct from even more people than she did now. And then her sisters would have an even worse time of it.

Ah, but if she did win, she'd be free, wouldn't she? No marriage needed. Enough money to finally give her sisters what they deserved.

And a lot of good it would do them, too, with their name completely ruined.

Lara took a deep breath and followed Lady Tattenbaum out of the shop. Ah, she needed to quit thinking about it for the moment, and shop.

It was a beautiful day, the kind of day that only came after a long, hard spring soaking. The sky was a clear blue that reminded her of Griff's eyes.

Lara quickly put a stop to that line of thinking. No, she did not want to think of Griff or Lord Rutherford. She just wanted to gaze upon beautiful things through shiny windows.

She spied a lovely purple fabric in the shop across the road and immediately realized that it would perfectly match Lady Tattenbaum's favorite gown. She'd buy it for her as a present.

"Lady Tattenbaum," she said nonchalantly. "Do go on, I'm just going to pop across the street for a moment. I'll meet you."

"Yes, of course, dear," Lady Tattenbaum said, charging forward, for she had just seen Mrs. Selfton. Mrs. Selfton always knew everything about everyone—always a good person to chat up.

Lara watched as Lady Tattenbaum became immediately embroiled in an intimate conversation with Mrs. Selfton, and then turned to negotiate her way across the street.

It took every ounce of her concentration to make it across without being killed, and as a result, she walked right into the back of a man standing just outside the window of the shop she was heading for.

"Pardon me," she said quickly, her head down so that she noticed the man's scuffed boots first.

They looked awfully familiar.

"Always," a deep voice said that made every nerve in her body tingle.

Lara glanced quickly up into the eyes of Mr. Hallsbury. And the only thing that she could think of was his kiss. Her face burned, and she swallowed audibly.

"Mr. Hallsbury," she said, her voice so soft and feathery as to sound like a caress.

The man's eyes darkened and a muscle in his jaw jumped.

"You do turn up in the strangest places, do you not?" she asked with a bit of a smile.

And then she remembered his last words to her, and she quickly stuck her chin in the air. "Pardon me," she said. "Mistakes have a rather irritating way of trodding on your feet, don't they?" She moved around him, but he caught her arm.

"Don't," he said.

She glared down at his hand on her arm, and he let her go.

"I'm sorry," he said. "I should not have said or done what I did."

For some reason that just made Lara angrier. So the kiss had been a mistake. That wonderful experience had been all wrong. How come anything that made her feel alive was wrong, bad, a mistake?

It was enough to make a person crazy.

"Pardon me," she said, and headed toward the shop, but her heart was no longer in it.

"Lara," he said softly from behind her.

All right, so he could make her name sound like a poem, so what? She stopped, feeling the distinct need to thrash somebody.

"I have a letter from your sisters."

Lara whirled around, her gaze catching on a piece of folded paper Griff held out to her.

"My sisters?" she asked, grabbing the letter. "How do you know my sisters?"

"They made my acquaintance, actually, at the inn in Lower Tunsburrow." He stopped quickly and glanced around.

She was sure, though, that no one was sparing them a bit of attention.

They probably looked like a lady and her footman having a touch of a spat. Though, Griff Hallsbury was surely the tallest, nicest-looking footman Lara had ever seen.

And his kisses were like something from heaven.

Or perhaps hell.

"They made your acquaintance?" she prompted darkly.

"Three of them," he told her. He looked as if he wanted to smile. "They scared the hell out of me."

Lara couldn't help but laugh.

"Anyway, I was just on my way to deliver

the letter to Dryer House when you bumped into me."

Lara glanced down at the paper in her hand. "Well, thank you."

"Do you tell them everything?" he asked.

Lara glanced quickly back up at him. "Excuse me?"

"Your sisters. They seem to know everything that has happened."

Lara shrugged. "They are my best friends."

Griff nodded shortly. "Well, I hope they are not as naïve as they seemed. Do they know that they must keep your intimacies confidential?"

Lara did not like Griff's tone at all. "My sisters wouldn't tell anyone something they shouldn't."

"I surely hope not."

She frowned.

"Good day," he said and walked away from her.

She hated when he did that. Lara pounded down the pavement after him. "Mr. Hallsbury!"

At least five people turned at the loudness of her voice. Fortunately, Griff was one of them. He glared at her.

"I am sick to death of you just saying your last words and taking off as if I haven't the right to end our conversations."

A few people around them laughed, but continued on their way.

"Lady Darling, you should not do this. It is too public a place."

She rolled her eyes. "You're the one who started this conversation in such a public place."

"Once again, I should not have, truly. But I . . ."

She watched him, wondering if he might feel something of what she felt for him. For certainly what goaded her to stop him wasn't just that she found him completely frustrating. In truth, she did not wish him to leave.

Life was such that she might never see him again. And her heart ached at that thought.

But it shouldn't. And since she really could do nothing about it, she ought to turn around and leave this man.

"Anyway, I beg your pardon if I upset you, my lady."

"Actually, you have," she said.

Two days before, under a tree, in the pouring rain, Lara had almost shouted that she loved this man. She had ruminated on that fact ever since.

She certainly did not love him. How could she? She barely knew him.

But, what *was* this feeling then, the one that

held her feet to the ground so that she could not turn away?

Why did she want to brush away the curl of dark hair that was sitting above one of his sky blue eyes?

Why did she balk at the idea of allowing this man to walk away from her? Why did the thought of never seeing him again hurt so?

And why on earth did she want to take him to get his boots polished, for goodness' sake? It was madness, surely.

Not love.

"Tell me," she said. "Please tell me who you are."

He frowned. "You sound like your sisters."

"They asked you who you are?"

He rolled his eyes. "Among other things."

Lara could only imagine what her sisters had said to this man. Especially Amanda, who probably batted her lashes and swooned.

And why were they so interested in the Bloody Baron anyway? Oh, it did feel good to call him the Bloody Baron in her thoughts, at least.

It made her remember exactly what this man was: a frustrating arrogant fool.

Again, "fool" would actually be a more appropriate moniker to place upon the person who allowed this man to kiss her and then practically begged him on a public street not to leave her.

"It is not a huge secret, everyone knows it," the Baron was saying. "I am a man who has made enough mistakes as to be no longer welcome among the Society I was born to."

Lara winced when he used the word *mistakes*.

He noticed, obviously, because he took a step toward her and lowered his voice. "You are not a mistake. The kiss was not a mistake. I am sorry I ever said that."

Lara swallowed loudly. It was much easier dealing with Griff when he made her angry. Right now, with his soft apology hanging between them, she felt rather like throwing her arms around him and burrowing her head into his chest.

That would never do.

"You *are* a baron, then?" Lara said quickly, stepping away from him.

"I am Griff Hallsbury, tenth Baron of Trenton, Lara Darling. But that doesn't matter when there is nothing to the title but the title itself, does it?"

She didn't answer, but kept staring at him. She could see such pain in Griff's eyes in that moment, she had to fight a strange primal instinct to touch him, soothe him.

Oh yes, she was most definitely a complete fool.

The Baron did not move as he asked softly, "Do you wish to say something else, my lady? I do not want to leave if there is anything you wish to say to me."

She wondered if he mocked her. "No, I have nothing else to say," she said crisply. And then she shook her head. She could not stand the pain in his eyes. "Except that there is always something left if a man has dignity. And you have yours, my lord. You are still a gentleman."

He took a deep, quick breath and then let it out slowly. "But, as you have already said, you don't know me."

She did feel like slapping him then. "I know enough, my lord. Don't be a ninny about it. You made mistakes, and you have not run away from them. That, I would say, makes you a very good man. Hence, a gentleman."

He watched her silently, and then one corner of his mouth twitched up into a grin. Lara blinked and looked away quickly, for that smile was rather devastating to a young girl's breathing. She did want to kiss him again.

Again. Good lord, she had kissed him! And more than anything else, in that moment, she wanted to again.

That did not mean she loved him, did it?

No, no, that is not what it meant.

"Oh lord," she said.

"Excuse me?" he said.

She looked up into his beautiful face, her own surely looking completely perplexed. "Why do I always want things I am not supposed to want?" she asked.

His breath caught in his throat.

"Trenton!"

Griff's eyes darkened threateningly as he took a quick step away from Lara, and then glanced up and behind her. "Amelia," he said.

Lara had to take a moment, her hand against her chest. She had completely forgotten that they stood on a busy street. Surely, they had been standing so close as to be nearly touching just a moment ago.

With a heavy sigh, Lara turned on this new intruder. Mrs. Braxton was bearing down on them, her dress a pale pink that perfectly complemented her still-dewy complexion. Her dark brown hair was coiled around her head in an extravagant arrangement that made her hair seem that much richer and shinier.

She was an incredibly beautiful woman. The only thing wrong with her was that smile. It was downright sinister.

"Goodness, man," Mrs. Braxton said, that smile of hers in full glory. "What on earth are you doing here? And with our dear Lady Lara, of all people?"

Our Lady Lara? Lara wrinkled her nose at this statement.

"Hello, Mrs. Braxton," Griff said.

"I say," she said. "I don't believe I've seen you in nearly seven years, darling. Much too long, I think."

"Or not long enough, depending on how you look at it," he said.

"Oh come, now, Griff, darling, no hard feelings after so many years, right?"

Lara shivered. Griff looked as if he might like to strangle Mrs. Braxton. Even Lara would have backed down if someone had glared at her like that.

"So, Lara, I see you've found someone to help with that boredom problem?" She laughed.

"Leave it, Amelia," Griff said.

"Oh come, Griff, I am all for a bit of a slap and tickle from the convenient lackey."

Lara's mouth dropped open, and before she

knew what she was doing, she had pulled back her hand and landed a blinding slap to Mrs. Braxton's cheek.

Surely the entire country went silent for a few very long seconds.

Whoops. Lara bit her bottom lip. Really, it would be nice if she could have been born with Reggie's sensibilities. Life must be much easier for Reggie.

"Well, I never!" Mrs. Braxton cried, her fingers going up to gingerly touch where Lara's red handprint was now brightening her cheek.

Griff had not moved an inch. He looked, actually, like he thought he had dreamed what he had just seen.

"Ah, there you are, Lara." Lara heard Lady Tattenbaum's voice from behind her. The woman came up quickly and took Lara's arm. "Mrs. Braxton," she said with a nod of her head. "Lord Trenton." She smiled warmly at Griff.

"Lady Tattenbaum," Amelia said through gritted teeth, "you need to keep a better eye on your charge. She hasn't done well enough in Society that she can stand in Oxford Street speaking with someone of Hallsbury's character."

Lady Tattenbaum arched her eyebrows so high they disappeared under the green turban on her head. "Ah, I think she's done well enough, if the bouquets of flowers that sit on every single available space in my house have anything to say about it."

Amelia Braxton narrowed her eyes. It was truly not the best look for her. "Be that as it may," she said, spit hurling from her mouth and hitting Lara's cheek, "she has just sealed her fate today. I don't think you can expect any more flowers, much less suitors, if I have my way." She stuck her nose in the air then. "I do not need to stand here and take any more abuse. Especially when I am forced to stand in the company of some idiot lackey." She glared at Griff then and stalked off.

Griff looked as if he wouldn't mind mopping the ground with Amelia's face.

"Griff," Lady Tattenbaum said. And he glanced at her and quickly bowed.

"I'm off," he said. He turned and walked away quickly.

"He's good at that," Lara murmured. "Running off, I mean."

Lady Tattenbaum stood staring at her for a moment. "Actually, he doesn't run off. He always does what he can to make everything right."

Lara turned her gaze on Lady Tattenbaum

then. "What exactly happened to him? I have gotten bits and pieces, and dearly would like to hear the entire story."

"He just did exactly what most of these young bucks do, only it really caught up with Griff. He gambled and played, and he lost everything, including his father's respect and his best friend's trust. His father died, and his friend will not speak to him. But instead of trying to live off someone else or run off to France, Lord Trenton has spent the last seven years trying to make it all up again." Lady Tattenbaum glanced down the road, and Lara followed her gaze. They could still see Griff's broad back as he made his way through the people that clogged the street.

"A better man you'll never know," she said.

Lara watched him until he disappeared. And she knew in that moment that she *did* love Griff Hallsbury.

Chapter 11

The most viperous people in the world are women with old jealousies. Of course, if they have old jealousies preying on their minds, they tend to let themselves be pulled into new ones very easily. Do stay out of their way, dearest, or something very bad might happen.

       The Duchess Diaries, Volume One

Reggie could not help laughing as she read her sister's letter. "Here it all is, then. Everything we found out from Mrs. Richards is right here in Lara's letter."

"Still, we did get a few more small details that Lara does not mention," Amanda said. "We know about the accident he caused that made Lord Rutherford an invalid."

Emma made a sound of disgust. "Oh, really, he did not cause it. Not really. They were both drunken louts. And they both got onto that coach knowing they should not be driving."

"Anyway, we should probably write to her

about that. And about Mrs. Braxton being engaged to Rutherford and breaking it off when he was hurt," Reggie said.

"I don't think Lara is very happy that we went to meet Mr. Hallsbury," Emma told them all dourly.

"Really, we ought to call him Lord Trenton now, I think," Amanda said.

"He does not want to be called that, obviously. So we call him what he wishes," Reggie said.

Emma sighed. "Anyway, we lost an entire day of sewing to sit in Mrs. Richards's drawing room and hear about the color of every single dress she ever owned, exactly which parties she wore them to, and who saw her in them."

"Yes, a bit of a bother, really," Reggie said.

Amanda frowned at her sister. "I admire Mrs. Richards's ability to remember every single one of her gowns."

Emma blinked. "Surely you jest."

"Probably she doesn't," Reggie said with a little laugh. "Be that as it may," she said quickly to cut off Amanda's retort, "what should we do next?"

Both Amanda and Emma looked over at Reggie expectantly. "Yes, what?" they asked.

Reggie pursed her lips, as it could get rather

bothersome having everyone always thinking you could do anything and everything.

"Well, if you *do* decide she should marry the coachman, don't tell Lara, whatever you do," Rachel said from her place next to the fire. She had been reading a book, and the elder three sisters could have sworn she had not been listening.

They looked over at their younger sister as if surprised to see her there.

Rachel shrugged. "Make sure she thinks it is her idea," she said, and went back to her book.

"And, really, shouldn't we know for sure it is the best thing? What if there is another man who will do just as well?" Amanda asked.

"You are just worried about yourself," Emma said.

"Well, and shouldn't somebody?" Amanda glared at her sister. "And anyway, I don't think I'm being selfish when I point out that the coachman seems to have been very much a rake and a scoundrel at one time. Is that really what we want for Lara?"

"It does not matter what we want. It matters what Lara wants," Emma told her sister.

"Right, and she wants a wealthy man near death. The coachman is a virile, penniless man. Goodness, Emma, that does fit!"

"Oh shush," Emma said. "Lara really has no idea what she wants."

"Oh, that's right, you are sooooo much more mature at twelve years of age, are you not?"

"I am twelve and three quarters, I will have you know," Emma snapped.

"This would all be very much easier if we were in London with Lara," Reggie said, ignoring her sisters completely.

Amanda sighed. "That would be so lovely, wouldn't it? And do think, sisters. If Lara marries a wealthy man instead of the coachman, you can all come to Town with me for my season. We could shop together and, Reggie, you could go with me to the balls and soirees."

"I'm sure that thrills her to no end," Emma said.

"And what fun would such things be, Amanda, if Lara were completely miserable, married to some man whom she did not even love?" Reggie reminded her. "Suffice it to say, this would all be easier if we were with our sister in London."

Surely providence was looking over the girls, for in that very moment their father burst into the room. They all stared at him as if he might be a ghost.

"That's it then, girls. We're off to London," he

said matter-of-factly. And he started out of the room again.

The girls all stared at each other for a moment. Rachel even put down her book.

"Wait!" Reggie cried after her father.

The man stopped and turned around, and then shook his head and continued out the door.

"Father!" Emma said.

But he was gone.

Reggie surged from her seat and ran after him. The other girls let her go. If anyone could get anything out of their father, it was Reggie.

"Father!" she said, running up to him and grabbing his arm.

He glanced at her as if he couldn't quite place who she was.

"Father," she said, her voice a bit softer. "Whatever are you talking about, going to London?"

He nodded. "I've done it. I've finally figured it all out, and it's off to London for us." He stopped. "Actually, I can go by myself, I guess."

"Oh no," she said quickly. "We should all go."

"Yes, yes."

"Except Rachel and Lissie, I think. They can stay with Yates and Mrs. Thornbury."

"Of course," he said, his face showing he wasn't exactly sure who Mrs. Thornbury was, even though their housekeeper had been with him since before Lara was born.

Reggie carefully shook her father's arm. "But, what are you talking about, Father? You have figured out what?"

"My invention, silly girl! It shall change everything, I promise you! I shall give your mother the life she's always dreamed of."

Reggie stilled. She knew, of course, that her father was a bit absent-minded, but surely he had not lost his mind altogether.

"Make ready. I have a bit more work to do, but I shall be ready Monday next, I should think," he said then, and seemed to skip as he left her.

Reggie watched him, afraid to go after him. He was talking such nonsense. Give her mother a good life?

Emma and Amanda tiptoed up to her.

"What on earth was that about?" Amanda asked.

Emma put her arm around Reggie's waist. "We were watching through the keyhole, Reggie. We heard what he said about mother. Is Father all right?"

Reggie glanced down at her little sister. "I don't know." She did not want to scare her sisters, but she said softly, "It *is* Father we talk about, of course, and so we must remember that he isn't quite normal. But he really did not sound right in the head just now."

"An invention? What invention? Someone needs to find out what he is talking about," Amanda said.

They looked at each other hopefully.

Rachel came out of the drawing room then, her book tucked under her arm. She walked right past the three elder Darling sisters.

"Not to worry. Father is fine, I'm sure. I'll find out what this is all about," she said without slowing down. "And I do think we should not write to Lara about any of this. It will just worry her, and you know how she gets when she is worried."

The three elder sisters looked at one another. None of them, it seemed, knew how Lara got when she was worried.

Rachel had stopped, fortunately. She looked at them all and then shook her head. "She runs or swims, drives or shoots. Quite frankly, I do not think it's a good idea she do any of those things in Town."

The three elder sisters nodded their agreement.

"Anyway," Rachel said, turning on her heel and continuing after their father. "I shall get to the bottom of all this."

Reggie and Emma just looked after their younger sister.

Amanda nodded. "I actually think Rachel can do it."

"Of course I can," the girl said as she rounded the corner.

Having Cartwright as an enemy had been bad. Having Mrs. Amelia Braxton as an enemy was downright horrible. Lara's invites had dwindled until, one morning a week later, there was absolutely nothing on the silver salver in the front hall when she came in from running Goldie.

She stared at the empty salver for a full minute, and then she turned right around and ordered that a carriage be brought about.

The butler hesitated for just a second, and then did as Lara asked.

She did not change, which was terribly gauche. And she did not bother to take her maid, a footman or Lady Tattenbaum with her, which was against all measure of propriety. But, really, she had hit bottom. Surely, nothing else could make it any worse.

And anyway, it was still early. Most of London had not even left their beds.

Which, it seemed, included Lord Rutherford, for it took him forever to come to her in his rather dark drawing room.

"Lady Lara, such a welcome surprise," he said when he finally entered.

She nodded at him, not even deigning to smile.

"Shall I ring for tea?" Lord Rutherford asked.

"No." She stood and pressed her hands against her stomach. Now that she stood here in front of Lord Rutherford, she suddenly wavered in her course. But she could not. She had no choice, really. And she was pretty sure that she had thought of a good way to make this all work out for everyone involved. "I think you know why I've come."

Lord Rutherford remained silent, but his eyes burned golden. He rather reminded Lara in that moment of a tiger.

"I . . . that is, Mrs. Hastings has agreed to this race of yours. But she needs to have your promise that her identity shall remain a secret."

Lord Rutherford stilled, and then nodded. But he said, "That might be difficult, impossible even."

"Then I have wasted your time, my lord." She turned to leave.

"But it might be arranged," he said hastily.

Lara stopped and turned back to the man.

"And do not forget, Lady Lara," he said. "*I* know who you are. That could be disastrous in and of itself."

Lara just stared at him for a long moment. "You would blackmail me, then, Lord Rutherford? You would use your knowledge to ruin me completely because I will not do what you want?" She shook her head and made a sound of disgust. "You're all horrible, do you know that? All of you. Why on earth does Society believe itself above others? I have known farm animals with better morals."

Lord Rutherford just shrugged. " 'Tis the way of things, Lady Lara. Welcome to life."

He sounded immensely bitter, and Lara truly did not like him in that moment. Yet there was a small part of her that felt sorry for him.

The man limped past her and sank into one of the tall-backed blue chairs before the grand fireplace. He propped his cane beside him and began rubbing at his thigh.

Silence thundered in the small room.

Without getting up or looking at Lara, Lord Rutherford said in the soothing voice of a parent to a child, "Shall we just continue with the idea that you might do what I want? We can both win here, you know."

Lara shivered. She realized suddenly that she was probably in over her head with this man. Still, he was offering her a fortune—if she won, of course. Another shiver tingled down her spine, but it was not one of dread at all. Rather, Lara, again, felt the thrill of the race.

She stepped up beside Lord Rutherford's chair. "This race is to occur at Hampstead Heath, right?" she asked. "During the next full moon, like the other races?"

"Actually"—Lord Rutherford glanced up at her—"I had thought about making this race different. A bit more exciting, if you will."

Lara tensed. Yes, she *was* in over her head. "More exciting?" she asked. "And how exactly would you go about making the race more exciting?"

"You must admit, Lady Lara, Hampstead Heath doesn't make for that exciting of a race, and having it at night makes it hard for others to watch, don't you think?"

Lara felt as if she might cry. She rather liked that about Hampstead Heath in the dead of night. "I don't think this is going to work, Lord

Rutherford," she said then, amazed at the relief she actually felt.

"Don't say no just yet."

Lara sighed. She felt rather like Daniel must have felt in the lion's den. Except, of course, that she really did not think God cared much about her little coach race.

She lowered herself into the chair opposite Lord Rutherford. " 'Tis not me, remember, but Mrs. Hastings," she reminded him.

"Of course, I meant Mrs. Hastings. And I think it will work. People see what they want to. If Mrs. Hastings wears something to make her look different, taller maybe, or something to give her more girth—that, along with a good mask—then no one will be the wiser."

"Do you really think so?" Lara asked.

"Of course, have you not been to a masque yet, dear?" he asked. "It is terribly difficult to tell who is who, I promise you."

Lara nodded slowly.

"Now then," he said quickly. "I was thinking of having a race during the day, right through the middle of London."

Lara blinked. "You cannot be serious."

"Oh, but I am."

She stood. "Right through the middle of London? Why, that could be terribly dangerous."

"Not if everyone knows about it."

"And horribly difficult."

Lord Rutherford smiled, "Oh yes."

Lara bit her lip. "It would be incredibly exciting."

He grinned. "As I said."

She turned away from him. Her hands shook as she clasped them together in front of her.

"I wonder, though, Lady Lara, if you could meet me?"

She turned to frown at him.

"As Mrs. Hastings, I mean. I have heard, of course, of her exploits, but I would like to see how well she drives." He shrugged. "Perhaps even give her the opportunity to practice?"

Lara took a moment to answer him as she pondered what he had said. "Yes, I see your point," she said. "I will have to think about it, though."

"Fine, fine," Lord Rutherford said.

"I have just one more question, my lord."

"Yes?"

"When you said before that you wish Mrs. Hastings to race the best driver in London, you did not say exactly who that would be. I am assuming that you mean Lord Trenton."

Rutherford closed his eyes when she said

Griff's name. But he opened them quickly and nodded. "Yes, of course."

"I must tell you, my lord. He knows who Mrs. Hastings is, and I fear that he might not race against her."

"Oh, I think I could persuade him," Lord Rutherford said. "Mrs. Hastings doesn't need to worry about anything else now, except to race well. I will take care of everything."

Lara nodded, but the excitement she had felt before had dulled a little. "And you want this because you are a gambling man?"

"Yes," Lord Rutherford said quickly.

She watched him for a moment. "I know there is more. I know that you and Griff have differences, though you were best friends once."

Lord Rutherford did not allow any emotion to show on his face, but Lara knew that there was much happening beneath his calm demeanor.

"Mrs. Hastings has another thing she wants you to promise her."

"Anything."

"Promise her that Lord Trenton will not be hurt in any way."

"I promise."

"As a gentleman," Lara prodded.

"As a gentleman."

She watched him closely. There had been a moment there when she had suddenly wondered if Lord Rutherford weren't doing this just so he could rig Griff's coach and cause him injury.

But, really, if the man wanted to do that, he could do it tomorrow morning to the mail coach. She sighed and decided to trust Lord Rutherford. She had to, really. He was the key to her freedom, after all.

And as Lara walked out into the bright sunshine of another beautiful day, she figured that she had done a good day's work.

Lord Rutherford would worry about all the details. All she needed to do was find a very good mask, wear a few layers of clothing and drive better than she had ever driven before.

And she would make enough money to make her sisters happy and keep her name as unsullied as she could, given that it was already a bit tattered around the edges.

Anyway, if anyone could clear their family name, it was Reggie. And she would have time enough for that when Lara won them enough money for Reggie to enjoy a dozen seasons at least.

Lara smiled brightly as she started down the street. Yes, all was right with the world.

And she felt that way, right up until a man woke her in the middle of the night with his hand over her mouth.

Chapter 12

*Ah, dear child, I'm thinking as I write this that
I wish God would give me just a few more years
so that I might be there with you right now. But
I know that he won't, old goat, so just remember, Lara dearest, that I'll be there with you in
spirit. And always remember that I love you.*
The Duchess Diaries, Volume One

"**A**re you some kind of fecking idjit?"

Lara blinked into the darkness, her
heart thumping so hard she could barely breathe.

"Don't you dare scream, whatever you do,"
the man said. "I'm going to uncover your
mouth."

He did and Lara immediately sat up in bed.
"Are you absolutely mad?" she asked her intruder. "You are, aren't you?" she said. "You're
completely bonkers."

"Oh, yes, you're one to talk," Griff Hallsbury
whispered. "That's right, I'm crazy, but you're a
fecking Bedlamite."

Lara wanted to slap him, really, she did. "Would you watch your damn language!" she said.

"Fine, if you'll watch the level of your voice. If you speak any louder we shall be found out, and then where will you be?"

She could only stare at him in the gloom. "Where shall I be?" She made a sound of disgust. "Well, I know where you'll be. In Newgate Prison, you ingrate."

"I'm a peer, remember. Even as far as I've fallen, they'll take my word over yours and figure that I'm coming to your bed at your invitation."

Lara could only shake her head.

"And of course you'll have not a leg to stand on, since you've completely ruined your name. Lord above, you're like a dog with a bone, aren't you?"

"What the devil are you talking about?"

Griff was sitting on the edge of her bed, and he leaned in very close to her when he said, "Is it a race you want then, Mrs. Hastings?"

Lara frowned, his breath had a touch of the brandy to it. "You're pissed."

"I'm not, actually. Had a drink with my dinner, but that was mostly to calm my nerves. If I'd come in here without it, I'd probably have thrown you out the window I just crawled through."

"You crawled though my window?"

"Could we stay on subject, here? What the hell is your problem?"

Lara did not like Griff's subject at all. "I've just fixed all my problems, that's all. But you'll have a very large problem when I drive past you to the finish line."

"God," Griff said between gritted teeth, as he launched himself up to pace about her room. "You are seriously some kind of unholy nuisance."

Lara bit her lip. "I am not. And how dare you come into my room in the middle of the night, scare me near unto death and then berate me like this. Who do you think you are?"

"I have no idea," he said as he made another turn about her room. "I shouldn't even care, should I? You've given me the opportunity I've been waiting for since this whole mess happened. I take up Thomas's dare, and I'll have it all back, and more."

Lara simply sat and watched him move. He was incredibly graceful, like the dark panther she'd seen at the menagerie last week: sleek and powerful, moving about her room and making her fearful and excited all at once.

"You're so sure you'll win, then?" she asked, her bravado ringing false even to her own ears.

Griff just stopped in the middle of her room and turned toward her. "You have no idea what you're doing, do you?" He took a step closer to her bedside.

"You don't know what you play with. I was right where you are once. I was young and rather sure I could do absolutely anything I wanted."

"I don't think I can do anything I want."

"I was so sure of myself that I gambled everything, and lost so completely I can never bring it back."

Lara swallowed hard. "What do you mean?"

Griff sat again on the side of her bed, the mattress dipping with his weight. "I thought I was indestructible. Thomas did, too. We ravaged this town. Hopping from bed to bed and from one gambling hell to another."

Lara pressed her fingers against her mouth. She did not like to think of Griff jumping into beds that were not hers.

"I lost everything I owned, including my father's respect. And when he died, a sad, broken man whose only son had turned out to be a complete waste, I lost my entire inheritance as well. And then I entered a race. Thomas and I were to be partners, and although he thought it a good idea to go to bed early the night before, I dragged him around town. We drank and gambled the night through."

He thumbed his chest. "I could do anything I wanted, after all. I was indestructible. And the next morning, I toppled our phaeton within minutes of the start of the race. My very best friend nearly died."

Griff shook his head, his voice softening. "He has not spoken to me since. Until he came to me tonight with this scheme of his."

Griff leaned his elbows on his knees and buried his face in his hands. He looked forlorn and broken. And Lara hated it.

She reached out carefully and put her hand over his. And then she leaned into him and put both of her arms around his body, her lips finding his neck and then his chin and finally his mouth.

He resisted for only a second, and then he plowed his hands into her hair and pressed her face to his. He kissed her again, and it was just as thrilling as the kiss they had shared beneath the tree in the rain.

He held her so tightly, she felt like she had become a part of him as he took her mouth, his tongue, tasting of brandy, sweeping along her teeth.

She really liked this. Of course, she knew that it was wrong. It had to be wrong, didn't it? What with the way her heart beat faster and her skin tingled, just as when she had sat atop the box waiting to drive her team up Tisney Cob.

Oh yes, this was very wrong.

But it felt so damn good. And she wanted it so badly.

And who would ever know?

Lara decided to banish her logical thinking completely. She really was horrible at it anyway—might as well throw it to the birds. She smiled against Griff's mouth and leaned backward so that he was forced to follow.

He groaned low in his throat, but she felt him pull away a little.

With a small sound of protest, Lara tightened her arms around him.

Probably, the very same thoughts that had just run through her mind tripped across his as well. He balked for all of a second, and then, with a low moan, he sank into her.

He kept one arm bent, staying on his elbow so that his weight did not crush her, and he kissed her.

And kissed her.

And kissed her.

She felt as if she could kiss Griff Hallsbury

forever. She touched her tongue to his, tasting him, breathing in his scent.

He tasted like brandy and smelled like mint mixed with cigars and musk. Lara took everything she could from the man on top of her, his smell, his mouth. She threaded her fingers through his hair. It curled around her hands, tickling her palms.

Every part of her body was alive. She felt suddenly as if she could fly, or at the very least run faster than she had ever run in her life.

She yanked at Griff's shirt with one hand, pulling it free from his breeches. He moaned as her fingers traveled across the flat of his bare stomach.

"We shouldn't," he said against her mouth.

"No, we shouldn't," she said, dipping a finger in his navel, and then reaching up and tracing the muscles of his chest.

His mouth trailed down her neck, his tongue dipping into the hollow of her collar bone.

"Oh." She sighed.

Griff tugged at the neck of her nightrail. And then she gasped when she felt his fingers against her skin. He slipped the now-loose yoke of her gown away from her shoulders, his mouth following the material.

Her breathing was ragged as she closed her

eyes and gave herself completely up to Griff's touch.

He stripped her, slipping her gown to her waist, and then pulling it all the way down. She was naked against him, her body alive, every touch of Griff's fingers and mouth making her writhe.

He left her, but came back quickly, the hair of his chest rough against her, her nipples aching at the touch.

"You're so beautiful," he said, kissing her stomach. Lara breathed deeply, her fingers tangling in Griff's hair.

He kissed her thigh and then pushed her knees up so that she felt exposed and vulnerable.

She heard herself protest, but Griff's fingers touched her lips and she took one into her mouth.

He made a strange sound.

Lara was not sure exactly why she had done that, but it felt right. It felt good.

She sucked on Griff's finger. It was strong and long and she wrapped her tongue around it, taking it as far into her mouth as she could.

And then Lara felt her lover's tongue touch her intimately.

She shuddered.

He touched her again and again, flicking a

part of her where, surely, every single nerve ending in her body was centered.

He left her again; she felt his body lean away from her and she opened her eyes, making an impatient sound.

"Shh," he said, his form dark above her. Lara opened her knees, and his body pressed intimately against her.

Her head fell back as Griff nipped at her neck and then kissed the tops of her breasts, his manhood hard against her. He slipped it into her slightly, and she shuddered again, grabbing at his shoulders.

His mouth found her nipple, taking it and sucking at it. There was pain as he entered her completely, but it did not last and it was so barely noticeable that she spent only a moment digging her fingers into Griff's back.

He slid out of her and then returned, his mouth on her breast.

Lara moaned, her head back and her body moving against Griff's in some rhythm that it knew without her ever having learned it.

"God, yes," he said, his voice deep and needing. It made her even more excited. She cradled his head in her hands, holding him against her as a feeling of intense need welled in her, spiraling through her and then, like the breaking of the sun through rain clouds, bathing her in glorious heat.

Her body convulsed around Griff again and again, and Lara curled her fingers in his hair and her toes into the sheets and felt it all the way to her soul.

With a short, stifled moan, Griff's body bucked on top of her, and she felt a coolness against her belly when he pulled quickly out of her.

He collapsed on top of her, his entire weight across her chest. And it did not bother her at all. She felt as if she would like for him to stay on top of her forever.

The darkness and silence was punctuated only by their ragged breathing for a long moment.

"You're pulling my hair," he said finally.

And Lara laughed as she let go of his silky curls. "I rather like your hair," she said. "I never really noticed it before, but it does make a good anchor of sorts."

Griff balanced his weight on one arm and looked down at her. She could just make his face out in the grainy darkness. Dark hair, eyes like round black stones, his nose and then his mouth, bruised from their kissing.

"Is that it, then?" she asked. "Can't we do it again?"

His mouth spread into a grin. "I've created a monster."

"Oh, I take complete exception to that statement. You have not created a thing. I am exactly as I've always been."

"Ah yes, 'tis true. And I do believe you are perfect."

Lara smiled. "No exception there." She reached down and cupped Griff's bottom. "But couldn't we do it again, please?"

He sighed. "Perhaps. But we shall have to wait."

"Truly? How long?" She reached up and kissed Griff's mouth, her tongue exploring his. She pressed up with her hips.

"Not long, if you keep doing that, I tell you," he said with a laugh. "But at least let's get you cleaned up, shall we?" He sat up, and Lara realized that he had spilled his seed on her stomach.

"Don't move." Griff went to the basin on the sideboard and then came back with a wet towel. "It's a bit cold," he warned. "I'll try to warm it with my hands, though."

He pressed the towel just below her belly and she gasped. "You didn't get it very warm, I'll tell you that, Griff Hallsbury."

"Sorry," he said, and cleaned her quickly.

She lay silent, her mind suddenly grasping what she had just done.

"If that had gone inside of me, we might make a baby," she said. Though, she had not meant to say it aloud, actually.

"Yes," he said and left to wring out the linen.

He returned and sat beside her. "It's never happened to me, but I've known others."

Lara quickly covered Griff's mouth with her hand. "It's not romantic to be talking about your numerous conquests when you're with another," she said shortly.

He nipped at her fingers. "You're not a conquest, Lara." He kissed her then, his mouth warm against hers. She closed her eyes and kissed him back, reaching up to wrap her arms around his neck.

"God, you feel good," he said, rolling next to her onto the bed.

"You feel good, too," she said with a smile.

"Will you be after marrying me, then, Lara Darling?" Griff said with a put-on accent.

But Lara could only blink in the dark at her lover. "Marry?" she said.

Griff said nothing for a moment. And then he kissed her mouth quickly. "Of course, I wouldn't do something like this and not marry you."

"So," she pushed away from him and sat up. "I'm a duty, then?"

Griff sat up as well. "Of course not."

"Still, if I remember correctly, I am a mistake."

Griff shook his head. "No, I told you I was sorry for saying that, Lara. Truly, I did not mean anything of it. It's just that . . ."

"Oh, it's quite all right," Lara said quickly. She reached out and smoothed a finger along Griff's square jaw. "I understand now, of course. You've made all of these mistakes in your life and you did not want me to be another one."

"No."

"You did not want to do anything to ruin my chances. You are now, finally, living up to your father's expectations?"

"Well, yes, but . . ."

Lara let her fingers trail down Griff's neck and linger on his chest. She had been right that time when she'd deduced that his chest was wide and strong.

It was lovely.

"Oh, don't worry, darling. I'm not going to marry you," she said.

"What?" he cried.

"Shhhh!"

"What do you mean you're not going to marry me?" he said, his voice lowered to a harsh whisper.

"Come now, Griff. I am not your mistake or

your duty." She looked around the darkened bed chamber. "Do you see anyone else here? Who will know of this but us?"

"That's preposterous."

"It is not," she said. "I am right, no one will know."

"Of course, but . . . well, there is a principle here which you are flagrantly disregarding."

Lara blinked. "Right. Anyway, you said you would do it again. Can we now, Griff?" She snuggled closer to him.

"No," he said in complete disbelief. "Absolutely not. You are seriously deranged if you think we are just going to keep doing this as if everything hasn't changed."

"Well, of course, things have changed." She slipped her hand around his warm neck. "I have been introduced to a lovely pastime I like very much, which I can do without anyone being the wiser."

"And which will ruin you completely," Griff said harshly. "Lord, woman."

"Exactly," Lara said.

"What on earth does that mean? You want to be ruined?"

"No, of course not. But the only reason you want to marry me is because you have taken my maidenhead, and you now think it is your duty to marry me," Lara told him.

Griff closed his eyes for a moment. "I will give you the best life I can, Lara. And it is truth. You will not be able to marry now. You *are* ruined." His eyes opened, dark in the night, staring into her soul.

"Fustian," she said. "No one will know, as I said."

Griff ground his teeth together. Lara could hear the grating, she could see his jaw clench.

"I will tell you a secret," she said. She stopped and took a deep breath. "I do this knowing that you will honor my confidence."

"Of course," Griff told her.

"I overheard my parents once, when I was young. They were arguing. It was strange, actually. Usually, they ignored each other completely. Well, my father ignored my mother, at least. He spent most of his time out in his workshop. He likes to putter and work with cogs and wheels and little bits of coil and wire. Making something, or fixing something, who knows. He never really talks much."

"Lara . . ."

"No, shh . . ." she said, pulling her hand away from Griff's neck and moving to put space between them. "Anyway, when I heard them yelling at each other, I was seriously flummoxed for a moment. I truly did not know what the sounds were I was hearing. I went to the door of their chamber, thinking that perhaps someone was dying. And I heard things that children should not know."

Griff made a dark sound at the back of his throat. "I think I can guess where this is going."

"Yes. My parents started just like this, Griff. I begged for more information from my Nanny L, and she did try to make it sound a little better than it probably was. She told me that my father courted my mother, and they were very much in love. Obviously, they could not stay away from each other. But my father did not offer marriage until his hand was forced by the fact that I was on the way."

"This is nothing like that," Griff said, moving toward her.

Lara scooted back. "No, it isn't. You haven't courted me."

"Lara!"

"No, listen, Griff." Lara dragged her hand through her hair. "I will not be my mother. She obviously loved my father very much, but he ignored her. She was miserable. I heard her cry so often. And I knew what she felt. I tried to grab my father's attention, too. I couldn't. I don't want to be ignored, Griff. And do you know something?" Lara swallowed hard; something that had always bothered her had suddenly become clear to her.

"My sister Amanda talks about marriage and beaus all the time. Even Reggie accepts that of course she will marry someday. But when they would talk about those things, I never wanted to think about it. Somewhere in my heart I just thought that I could go on living at Ashton Hall my entire life, fishing in the pond with my skirts tucked into my waistband, driving my father's old coach and four hell for leather along the deserted roads on my father's estate, shooting geese for dinner. That is all I have ever wanted. I don't want to marry. I never have. And I'm not going to marry you."

"But you are here for a season with the intent to marry, am I wrong?"

"Oh, I'll marry someone who does not matter," Lara said softly, "if I have to." She did not say what her heart had just understood completely. She absolutely was not going to marry someone who mattered to her. She did not know one person who lived in a marriage of love. Even those who had started out with love never ended up with it. Her Nanny L had nearly danced on her grandfather's grave.

But her mother had been heartbroken, because she had adored Lara's father. It had broken her, Lara knew that. She could remember when her mother died after giving birth to Lissie. Lara could remember sitting in her mother's sickroom, her father nowhere in sight. Lady Ashton had asked for her husband, but he never came. And the last time her mother had opened her eyes, and then closed them forever, Lara knew that she had died because she could not live with the rejection anymore.

No, that was not how Lara was going to live. If she must marry, it would be to someone she did not care about, at the very least. Her heart was not going to be broken beyond recognition.

"That makes no sense at all," Griff said, honest confusion in his voice.

Lara sighed. "Griff, I am not going to marry you. Especially now."

"Especially now?"

"Now I would forever be the wife you had to marry. I would be your next project. You would spend years trying to make this one mistake right again. It would fester and grow until you hated me, and then you would ignore me completely as you'd take mistresses to your bed." She shook her head. "No, dearest, I would much rather be a mistress than a wife."

"Come again?"

"And what of me, Griff? What of my life?"

"That's exactly what I *am* worried of here!"

"My sisters are the main reason that I'm here. Marrying you would not help their plight in the least."

"Aha," Griff said darkly. He leaped from the bed. Lara heard the rustle of clothing and could see in the shadows that her lover was dressing.

"Griff," she said.

"I understand now, my lady," he said as he yanked on his breeches. "A quick toss with the coachman is all you wanted. Before you set your sights on richer gains."

"Griff."

"Fine then, I hope you enjoyed yourself." He slid his waistcoat over his unbuttoned shirt. "I aim to please, you know. Fast on the roads, slow in bed."

"Griff, please."

"By the way, dearest, if you're so hellbent on making sure your sisters have the life they deserve, might I suggest something?"

Lara felt bereft sitting alone in the nest of sheets where she had just had the most wonderful experience of her life. "Please don't, Griff. I lo . . ." But she stopped.

"Right." He moved close to her and she could smell their lovemaking on his skin. "Don't say anything so horrible as that, Lady Lara. Anyway, let me just warn you. Do not enter the race. You'll be found out."

Lara's heart beat a little faster and her hands started to shake. "Is that a threat, Mr. Hallsbury?"

"More a promise, my lady." He turned and disappeared so quickly out the window Lara thought for a moment that he had surely jumped.

She leaped from her bed and ran to the open window. But Griff was nimbly using the trellis to make his way to the ground. She wanted to say something but knew that she was now on dangerous ground.

Because, truly, it was a very bad idea to scream out her window as her lover climbed down the trellis.

Well she had had a lover, at least. Somehow she did not feel that Griff would be climbing up to her bedchamber again anytime soon.

Lara launched herself onto her bed and curled into the sheets. His smell was all around her, and her heart felt hollow and used. "Damn him, anyway," she said aloud.

But she did not mean it, not really.

"I quite bungled that," she said softly.

That, she meant.

Chapter 13

*Never just put a period at the end of your con-
clusion of someone's character. I have learned after many years that people will always surprise
you. Even people you have completely despised
for long periods of time can suddenly do something incredibly stunning, and you realize that
you really just misunderstood them. Or you did
not really know them at all. Of course, that said,
dear, there are others who are complete wastes of
humanity and always shall be. It's the discerning
between the two that makes one wise, I think.*

> *The Duchess Diaries*, Volume One

Reggie, Amanda and Emma stared at their
younger sister, shock and awe mingled
on their faces.

"How did you find this out?" Emma asked.

"Yes, dear, did you actually speak to Father?"

"And did he answer you?" Amanda could
not help but sound completely incredulous.

Rachel rolled her eyes. Her sisters did tend to

make everything much harder than it really needed to be. All one had to do was use one's brain power, and, really, everything fit into place, did it not?

"He has invented a gadget that will make the handling of carriages much easier than it has been before. Our father has been working on this project since before Lara was born, in the hopes of bettering the family's situation, as the title was completely destitute when he received it from his father," Rachel said. "Our paternal grandfather, if any of you have read the family histories, was quite the philanderer. A horrible man, actually." She wrinkled her nose. "He spent all his money on women and wine and did not invest a jot. He is completely the reason we are in such dire straits."

"Really?" Amanda asked.

Rachel pursed her lips in disgust. "Reading is a very good way of finding out things that are already known, sister dear. Anyway, Father has this gadget which he feels is now perfected. Of course, the whole reason he began the project was to make Mother's life better. Being a man, he, of course, did not realize that simply loving her would have made her life better. But, be that as it may, I don't think he has really come to the point where he realizes that he's a bit late."

Rachel shook her head and frowned. "I hate to think when that will happen, or what he will do when he realizes. Being Father, as he is, he will probably sink into quite a funk, because it took him so long to get the thing done that he will feel as if he has ruined all of our lives and let Mother down completely. He might even think that he wants to end his own life."

"What?" Reggie cried.

"I'm sure he will not. He doesn't have the ability to deal with the guilt," Rachel said.

Emma glanced at her older sisters and then back at her younger sister. "How on earth do you know all this?"

Rachel just sighed. "Oh, honestly, I use my brain." She stood. "There you go, then. If you need any more help, just let me know."

Reggie, Amanda and Emma stared after the elfin creature that was their sister as she sauntered out of the room, the perpetual book under her arm.

"You know, I am amazed," Reggie said. "Here we have lived with Father all of this time, and I did not even know that he was inventing something at all."

"Yes, I know what you mean." Emma nodded.

"I thought he was fixing something," Amanda said.

"Do you really think this thing could change our lives?" Emma asked.

Her other two sisters just shrugged.

"I guess it wouldn't harm anything to try and market it," Reggie said. They thought quietly a moment.

"If it is an important invention, the best thing to do is get it into the right hands, I'd think," Emma said.

Amanda blinked. "What on earth do you mean?"

"Well," Reggie took over for her sister. "What I think you're saying, Emma—and I completely concur—is that we must find someone who can test this gadget and prove that it is a good invention."

"Yes, exactly," said Emma, who had not actually thought that far ahead.

"I think we need to know exactly what this thing is." Amanda assumed a very intelligent pose, head nodding, lips pursed.

"Well, it's something to do with carriages. What if we were to take it to the coachman?" Emma asked.

Reggie bit her lip. "We really don't know the man. Can he be trusted? He might take it and say it was his own invention."

"And even if we do all of this, there is still Father to consider. I wonder if he is going to be all right," Emma said.

They all nodded at each other, but turned as one when the door creaked open.

Rachel stuck her head back in the room. "Just a thought," she said. "Our father has a rather limited concentration span, the obvious exception being when he's fiddling with his contraption, which he's been quite fixated on for nearly twenty years. Given that fact, I would surmise that when he does realize that he's a bit late in perfecting this design, it would be helpful if you all got him excited about his invention again. He might, then, quite forget that he is depressed. That would take care of that problem." She nodded at them succinctly. "Carry on, men," she said, and she was gone.

"You know, I never realized that Rachel was so smart," Emma said.

"Yes," Reggie agreed. "Quite amazing little head she has, really."

Amanda's delicate brow was furrowed deeply. "She is decidedly strange, I think."

"Anyway, what do we do now?" Emma asked. And, of course she and Amanda looked directly at Reggie.

Reggie smoothed the front of her gown with her hands and glanced surreptitiously at the door. Maybe Rachel would enlighten them all once again.

But the door remained closed.

"Right." Reggie hooked her fingers together, trying to think.

"Let's just take the thing to the coachman. I'm sure he's very trustworthy. He has such beautiful eyes." Amanda punctuated this statement with a sigh.

The door opened. "Patent it before you do anything else," Rachel said before closing the door again.

Amanda frowned.

"How do we 'patent' it?" Emma asked.

Reggie grinned. "Something tells me that Rachel will know."

"Of course I do." This statement drifted through the closed door, and each of the elder sisters giggled.

Lara was incredibly proud of herself. She had been so good, so completely boring and regular that she had managed to get herself back on the invite list of many of the *ton*.

It helped, of course, that Cartwright had managed to get himself shot in a duel. He had not died, more's the pity. But he had been seen about Town with his arm tied in a large, white sling.

The *ton* immediately started mumbling about Cartwright's insufferable ego and horrible aim. And Lara had seen a few invitations hit the silver salver in the hall.

There was still Mrs. Braxton, of course. There would always be Mrs. Braxton. And with the fact that Mrs. Braxton did not like her, Lara was rather sure there would never be a bevy of invitations on the tray.

But honestly, that did mean, now, that she wasn't obliged to sit through quite so many dull evenings. It was amazing, really, how many times one could yawn in the space of an hour. It was a decided plus that she did not have to spend so many evenings with Roddy Piperneil.

Lara adjusted her mask and snuggled deeper against the leather squabs of the darkened coach in which she sat. She was waiting for Lord Rutherford at their usual meeting place, just outside of London on a dirt road that seemed to lead to nowhere.

They had met now three times. The first to test Lara's ability, which the man obviously found very pleasing. And the other two to give Lara some time to practice.

He was even nice enough to send an unmarked coach for her. Of course, she had to meet it a block away from Lady Tattenbaum's after climbing down the trellis, but it was still very nice of him.

It was also very nice to know that she had done so well as to give herself options. She had started this whole season with only one way of making life good for her sisters, and that was through marriage. She now had this lovely race that could possibly bring her a fortune, with none the wiser, so that her name was not completely ruined.

Of course, if she won the race and didn't marry, it did mean she lost Nanny L's bet, but the race seemed rather more urgent at the moment.

All in all, Lara felt terribly proud of herself.

"I hope you're proud of yourself!" The door to her cozy world opened on a rather brisk breeze and Griff Hallsbury glared at her.

She blinked at him in surprise, and he stared at her in equal surprise.

"Lara?"

Her mouth fell open. She did have a mask on, after all.

"How did you . . . ?"

"It doesn't matter, but if I knew you, don't you think others will as well?"

Lara shrugged. "No," she said. "I haven't been intimate with others."

"Shh!"

She rolled her eyes. "Do not shush me, Lord Trenton."

"Lord Trenton, what a nice surprise," Lara heard Lord Rutherford say from behind Griff. The Baron stiffened, and Lara suddenly felt sorry for him.

She wished she could hold his hand as he turned to face his friend.

"Grifford. Oh, so sorry, I remember how you hate that name."

Lara grimaced. Grifford? No wonder he hated it. She did prefer "Griff."

"I hope you are proud of yourself," Griff said to Thomas. Obviously he had thought Thomas was sitting in the carriage when he burst in.

"Quite, actually."

"You will ruin her, you know. Doesn't that matter to you?"

Lara pushed her way out of the carriage. If they were going to talk about her, she intended to be present. She jumped to the ground and then pulled her wrap tighter about herself. It was absolutely freezing.

Of course, it had been rather cold in Town,

but it was even more so here. A bit of wind kicked up and the boughs of the tree above them clacked together.

"You are a fine one to talk, Trenton."

"Put our differences aside here, Rutherford. You are playing with a young girl's life."

Rutherford shifted his weight slightly.

"Excuse me?" Lara said. "I do not like being spoken of as if I'm not even here."

Griff turned on her. "You've got to see reason, Lara."

"Lara is safe at home in bed, thank you very much. I am Mrs. Hastings. And I am well acquainted with reason."

"Right."

Lara glared at Griff. "This is not your business."

"This man made it my business when he challenged me to this race," Griff said, pointing at Ruthford.

"So back down," Lord Rutherford stated matter-of-factly.

Griff's jaw clenched as he shook his head. There wasn't much he could say. Lord Rutherford was right.

Griff stalked away from them and then returned. "You knew I couldn't say no to this, Thomas. You made the pot too much for me to say no to."

"I haven't done anything to force you, though, have I, Griff? Just say no."

"Damn you," Griff said.

This was all sounding rather familiar.

"You already have, Griff. To a long, lonely, painful life, thank you."

Griff made a sound of disgust. "Oh, do get over it, Rutherford. I did not force *you* into that carriage that day."

"You were arrogant enough to defy my warnings though, weren't you, Griff?"

Griff seemed to crumple then, and he turned away from Lord Rutherford. Lara saw his eyes shining in the light of the moon.

Lara swallowed hard. Did he love her, perhaps? Is that why he was so upset? She suddenly wanted to back down and leave this dark, cold place. There was too much hurt here.

"Please, Thomas, not her. There has got to be someone else to pit me against. Young Reynolds is turning out to be a fine driver. He has nearly beat me on many occasions."

Lara frowned, and then she shook her head. No, he did not care about her. He wanted to win the race. And he knew she had a chance at taking that away from him. Arrogant man.

"You have beaten Reynolds a hundred times. Face it, Griff. You have not been beaten yet.

New blood is exactly what is needed to get a bit of excitement in this city."

"I don't understand you, Thomas. What more do you want? I'm a coachman, for God's sake. How much further do you want me to fall?"

"Hell would be nice."

"I'm going there, I promise."

Lara really did feel like protesting, but they continued before she could say anything. And anyway, her lips felt like they were frozen to her teeth. She shivered.

"Listen, Griff, you have no idea what you did to me that day. Did you know that Amelia wanted you? She never wanted me. She said yes to me in order to make you jealous. I was always just one step behind, wasn't I? You were always the hero, always the one that everyone loved."

"Thomas, that's not true."

"Even as a ruined man, you've managed to be a hero. Your exploits are written about in papers everywhere. Well, let's see what happens when you have a real race on your hands."

Griff advanced on Rutherford. "And you're willing to let another person go through the same hell you've been through to see this race? An innocent like Lara?"

"No one will ever know the hell I've been through."

"But she will be ruined."

"Fine then!" Rutherford yelled. "I shall promise you now that if she is found out, I will marry her. She will not be ruined if she has my name to protect her."

That took the fuel away from Griff's anger. He bowed his head. "Fine," he said.

"Excuse me?" Lara said, her anger running as hot as the night was cold.

The two men continued their bickering as if they were four-year-olds fighting over a toy.

Lara made a loud sound of disgust. "I do hate to interrupt," she yelled.

"Hello," she said sweetly when the two men finally turned to her, looking shocked that she still stood there.

"I'm very glad you two have decided on my future as if I'm some sort of thing to be used as you please. Or maybe you think of me as a child? Right. Well, you can both just shove your wonderful ideas right back where they came from." She glanced pointedly at Lord Rutherford's buttocks.

"I am a woman, and I know what I'm doing. I will not marry either of you, thank you very much. And I'm sick to death of you both proclaiming such a thing as if it is a fact you can just state, and it will happen."

"You asked her to marry you?" Rutherford asked Trenton.

"That is none of your business," Griff said.

"You say you worry of her reputation, and then you ask her to marry you? A coachman? Oh, yes, *that* will help her reputation." Rutherford laughed darkly.

"You know nothing about it, Thomas. So, really you should just keep quiet on the subject."

"Once again the conversation continues without my input," interjected Lara. "That is going to drive me mad. And so, because you both seem unable to stop this frustrating habit, I am leaving."

"Lara . . ."

"*Mrs. Hastings*," Lord Rutherford cut in. "Really, I am only trying to look out for your own good."

Lara just laughed.

"That is rubbish," Griff said.

And they were off yelling at each other again.

Honestly, it was much too cold to do any driving anyway, Lara decided. She was all for thrilling experiences, but if they also included being uncomfortable, Lara honestly could not see the point.

She drew her wrap tighter about herself and jumped thankfully back into the carriage. She thumped the ceiling, and they were off.

She could get used to opulence, Lara decided as she pulled the fur blanket Lord Rutherford had provided over her lap. Especially if she could provide it for herself, no marriage needed.

But most definitely, she would not be marrying Lord Rutherford or Griff. What a couple of ninnies.

Thomas and Griff watched the coach drive away into the cold night. Then they looked at each other.

"I know exactly what you want," Griff said.

"You were always the smart one, Griff."

"You want me to be humiliated, don't you? I have never been beaten, and now I will be beaten by a woman."

Thomas raised his brows. "I am impressed."

"If I had said that while she was here, she would not go through with this race."

Thomas made a small sound of disbelief. "Really? She is so besotted with you, then? It doesn't seem like it to me."

"It is not that, Thomas. She is a good person. If she knew that you were staging this race with the sole purpose of humiliating me, she would not do it."

"But you could win, couldn't you, Griff?"

"Lara Darling is the only person who could possibly beat me," Griff said. "I know that, and you do, too. And you have always been a gambling man, haven't you?"

A muscle in Thomas's jaw ticked. He nodded, but there was such irony in his movements, Griff suddenly felt very tired. Defeated, really.

"You love her, don't you?" Thomas said. "You asked her to marry you because you love her."

Griff just shook his head. "Don't, Thomas."

Thomas sighed. "It is all wrong. This life." He turned and limped toward his carriage, which waited on the hard, packed ground behind them. His footman automatically opened the door. But Thomas stopped before he got there and turned around. "You lost all your money, Griff. I still have mine. You would think it was even, wouldn't you?"

"No," Griff said. And, truly, in that moment, he felt like crying. Sobbing, screaming at the sky. No, it wasn't even. "It will never be even. I am sorry, Thomas. I hate myself for getting on that carriage that day. I was not fit to drive."

"I am not ever without pain, Grifford."

Griff clenched his teeth together. He could feel tears threatening. "I'm sorry," he said again. But he knew it wasn't enough. It would never be enough.

Mistakes. So many mistakes in his life. He couldn't stand them all.

And here he was on the brink of another one. Another innocent: tumbled, tossed and spit out.

"I am not going to do it, Thomas," he heard himself say. "I will not race." There went his fortune. It would take him another ten years to make what he needed to buy back his father's childhood home. And then perhaps another ten years to put it all to rights. Probably more, really.

Ah, Lara, were you a mistake? But, no, he could never think that. He would not give up even what little time they had shared to get his fortune. And he would not jeopardize her innocence to get that fortune either.

Peace settled in his heart. "No, Thomas. I won't race." Griff stared at the man who used to be his closest friend.

"I will tell the world who she is," Thomas said quickly, as if he had known what Griff was going to say.

"No, you won't."

Thomas made a frustrated sound.

"She will still race," he said then. "She has what you used to have, Griff. She does it because she loves it. If I give her a race, she'll do it."

"Don't."

"You would have me take away the prize, then? It's what she wants."

"She will be found out, Thomas." Griff took a step toward the man he had known since childhood. The only man he had ever really trusted. "Please, don't do this."

Thomas just stared at him for a long moment. And then without saying another word, he turned away and got into his carriage.

Chapter 14

*There is nothing like family to make a mess
even messier. Of course, they also make it all
worthwhile and a bloody hell of a good time. I'll
bet you have always wondered why you swear
so much, haven't you, Lara dear? 'Tis in your
blood.*

The Duchess Diaries, Volume One

They decided to take Rachel along on their
expedition this time, as the girl was proving to come up with the perfect idea at the perfect time.

A very good person to have around.

The Darling sisters stood waiting for the
coachman when he rushed into the inn's posting yard and the villagers flowed in after him.

"Impressive," Rachel murmured.

"Really?" Emma said with a smirk. "It seems
to me that he's just showing off."

"Well, yes, of course he is. But it isn't anyone
that can take a coach and four at that speed

273

through that small of a space. So, I'd say he quite deserves to show off."

Emma rolled her eyes as Amanda sighed.

"Really, Amanda," Reggie admonished her sister. "If you continue to sigh so, you will most probably faint."

Emma laughed.

But the coachman jumped from his seat then, so there was no time for a good, protracted sisterly row.

"Mr. Hallsbury," Reggie called.

"Shouldn't we call him Lord Trenton?" Amanda asked.

"No, you shouldn't," Griff Hallsbury informed them. "Hello, girls, fancy meeting you here." He tipped his hat at them and continued toward the inn's public room.

"Er, Mr. Hallsbury," Reggie called after him. "We have a matter we wish to discuss with you. It's rather a delicate subject."

"We need privacy," Rachel informed him.

He turned to look down at Rachel. "You're a new one."

She nodded. "I'm Rachel."

"Yes, and I'm Reggie, Amanda has the ringlets and this is Emma. We did not really introduce ourselves before, sorry."

"Well hello to you all once more." Mr. Hallsbury frowned. "And you wish to discuss a delicate subject? Perhaps that subject isn't as delicate as you all think?"

The girls glanced around at one another trying to decipher the Baron's remark.

"I am just guessing it's about your sister Lara," the man said.

"No, actually," Reggie informed him. "We are here on business."

"Ah," he said as if four young girls waiting to speak with him about business was an everyday occurrence. "Right then, follow me."

They all trudged into the inn and made their way to the back of the public rooms where they were most definitely beyond earshot of anyone else.

A small girl came over to their table. "The regular, Amy," the Baron said to the girl, and then turned his attention to the Darling sisters when she left.

"So, business?"

"Right," Reggie cleared her throat. "We have this invention, you see."

"It's our father's, actually," Amanda interjected.

"Stunning, that," Emma said sarcastically.

"Patent pending, mind you," Rachel informed him. "The specifications have been stamped by three out of the seven offices."

"And we wanted you to take a look at it," Reggie said.

"Me?" he asked.

"You," they all said at once.

Reggie leaned away from the table and pulled something from her pocket, and then placed it on the table with a soft *clunk*.

"What is it?" he asked.

"We don't know, really," Reggie answered.

"Just that it is supposed to make it easier to drive a carriage," Amanda explained, feeling rather as smart as her sisters in that moment.

Mr. Hallsbury cocked a dark eyebrow as he took up the small metal piece. He examined it from every angle. And then he examined it again.

The girls looked around the table at each other as he did.

"Well," he finally said. "I'll be damned. Excuse my language."

"Of course," they chorused.

"This is truly interesting."

"Is it?" Emma asked.

"Yes, it is."

"Remember we've already begun the patent process," Rachel reminded him.

He squinted at her. "Of course." He went back to his examination.

"We were hoping you would allow our father to install this in your mail coach," Reggie said.

The sisters all stared at her, even Rachel, for they had not spoken of this idea at all.

"Well done," Emma said, slapping her sister on the back.

"Well, not that well done, I'm afraid," Mr. Hallsbury informed them. "I really cannot do anything to the mail coach, as it's not mine to tinker with."

The girls sighed.

"But I think I may have an idea."

They brightened.

"Has your sister informed you of the races that occur on the night of the full moon?" He asked, a hint of wariness in his tone.

"Yes," they said in unison.

"Good," he said, and then stopped suddenly. "Er . . . has she told you of the *other* race?"

"There is another race?" Reggie asked.

"Well, there was going to be, but not anymore. She did not tell you?"

Amanda looked perplexed.

Emma looked rather peeved.

Reggie looked decidedly wary, and Rachel kept all of her emotions carefully hidden.

"Listen, the coach I use for the monthly races is a private one. It is not mine, but I am sure the owner would not mind if we used this contraption in his coach."

"You will tell him of the patent, of course," Rachel said.

Mr. Hallsbury glanced down at her. "You are terribly excited about this whole patent thing, aren't you?"

Rachel grinned, her left front tooth only halfway grown in and a bit crooked as well. "You have no idea."

Mr. Hallsbury laughed. "Right, I'll tell him about the patent."

"Good," Rachel said.

Mr. Hallsbury smiled at her. "You are much easier to please than your sister."

"Excuse me?" Reggie said.

"Well, I never," Amanda cried.

And Emma just chuckled.

"I meant Lady Lara."

"Oh, of course," said Reggie. "She can be a touch stubborn."

"Like you would not believe," Mr. Hallsbury said.

"Oh, believe me, we do," Amanda told him.

"Actually, since we're on the subject," Hallsbury said, glancing around at the sisters. "I want you to promise me something."

"Yes?" Reggie said.

"Do not tell Lara of your father's invention. At least, not yet."

The girls gave the coachman very critical looks.

He sighed. "There was a race set up between her and me."

The girls made sounds of astonishment.

"But it would ruin her," he said.

"Oh no," Amanda cried. "She is going to ruin herself, isn't she?"

"I have backed out of the race, though," he said. "And I am pretty sure that it will not happen. But, believe me, if Lara hears of this invention, she will find some way to make the race happen. I think we should just keep it to ourselves for the moment."

"I think you are exactly right," Amanda said.

"We'll have to think about it," Emma said.

"Why did you back out of the race?" Reggie asked.

Rachel snickered. "I'd think that's obvious."

The elder sisters turned dark looks on their little sister. "Well," she said with a shrug. "It is."

"Actually," Reggie turned back to Hallsbury. "We need to talk to you about something else, come to think about it."

"Oh yes, that's right." Amanda smiled, and tapped Mr. Hallsbury's hand with the fan that she had insisted on bringing along.

"We were wondering what your intentions are toward our sister," Emma said.

"Emma!" Amanda blinked at her sister. "Goodness, you could have found a more discreet way of putting that, dearest." She batted her eyes at the Baron. "Mr. Hallsbury is a gentleman, after all."

"Still, that is exactly what we were wondering," Reggie said. "Mr. Hallsbury?" She glared at him down her thin, long nose. Reggie could give quite scary looks when the time called for them.

The young girl brought the Baron's food then, and they had to pause the conversation. The girls all kept Hallsbury pinned beneath rather uncomfortable stares, though.

He picked up his spoon, looked up at them, glanced back at his food, and put the spoon back against the plate.

The girls exchanged glances, obviously wondering if they might just have to get physical with Mr. Hallsbury. Rachel could give a mean kick to the shins and Amanda's ability to pull hair out by the roots was truly legendary.

"Has something happened between you and my sister?" Reggie asked, her look just this side of terrifying.

Mr. Hallsbury examined his tankard for a minute. "I sure wish there was some strong ale in this cup right now."

Amanda peered over the lip of the vessel. "Are you drinking water?" she asked.

"Never anything stronger when I drive."

Another exchange of glances among the girls: They approved of that, at least.

"Has your sister told you anything?" he asked.

The girls' faces went from faintly approving to darkly dangerous.

"What exactly does she need to tell us?" Reggie asked.

"Right." Mr. Hallsbury pushed his food away. "I did ask her to marry me. She refused me."

Amanda gasped and flapped her hand in front of her face.

"When did this happen?" Emma asked.

"She did not write of this," Reggie reminded them.

"I am rather sure she has skipped a few things in her letters home," Rachel said sagely.

"She refused you, though?" Amanda asked, her voice a mix of relief and disappointment.

Emma glared at her.

"What!" Amanda said peevishly.

"Lara really does have a hard time realizing what is best for her," Reggie informed the Baron.

"She's truly stubborn most of the time," Amanda said.

"Oh, and you're the picture of sweetness," Emma said to her sister.

"Girls!" Reggie gave them a look.

Mr. Hallsbury furrowed his brow, obviously confused. "Wait. You wouldn't mind if your sister married me?"

They all glanced over him, from the top of his thick, dark hair to what they could see of his chest.

"Will you take care of her?" Reggie asked.

"Will you be nice to her even when she drives you mad?" Amanda asked.

"Will you let her drive?" Emma asked.

"And shoot?" Rachel added.

Mr. Hallsbury blinked. "Well, yes."

"Then we approve," Reggie told him.

"But what about you? Lara seems to think you all need her to make a splendid match so that you will be wealthy and your name will be treated with respect."

"It would have been nice," Amanda told him wistfully.

"Of course, that would have helped us," Emma agreed.

"But most important, we want our sister to be happy," Reggie said.

Mr. Hallsbury tapped his finger against the table and then sighed deeply. "All well and good, my friends. But I'm not at all sure your sister knows what is going to make her happy."

They nodded their agreement, but Rachel said, "We do, though. So she's not completely lost yet."

"And we'll be there to help her very soon," Reggie said. She carefully palmed her father's invention and put it back in her pocket. "We'll be seeing you in London then, Mr. Hallsbury. My father will be able to put this little gadget in your coach."

"And collect his patent," Rachel reminded them.

"Right, and collect his patent," Reggie said.

Mr. Hallsbury seemed nonplussed. "Erm, so you are all coming to London?"

"Yes," they chorused.

Reggie frowned at Rachel. "Except for you, dearest."

Rachel curled her lips into a pout.

"Well, then, I shall await you there. And we will not shake hands on this until you arrive."

"Why ever not?" Emma asked, alarmed.

"Just in case you all change your mind," Mr. Hallsbury said, a dark and foreboding note to his voice.

"That was a bit strange at the end, don't you think?" Emma asked as they watched the Baron leave.

Amanda shrugged. "I think the coachman is lovely."

Emma made a sound of disgust. "That's not the subject here, Amanda. Really, all you care about is if a man's eyes make you swoon."

"Oh, and his do, I must say."

Reggie, Emma and Rachel all rolled their eyes at each other. However, if the truth were told, they all felt exactly the same way.

Goldie looked as if she might expire at any moment. Lara had run the poor mare for over an hour. Finally, she let the horse slow down to a trot, then pulled her to a halt and dismounted, wishing desperately that she were home.

At Ashton Hall she might swim in the pond or go running, to calm the fluttery feeling she had in her stomach. A feeling that made it nearly impossible to sit around drinking tea.

Well, all right, the feeling made it completely impossible.

Lara walked Goldie along the paths, going as fast as she could and kicking up dust as she went. It was cold again, but today Lara barely felt it.

A thought was niggling at the back of her mind, and she could not make it go away. As she had ridden away from Rutherford and Hallsbury, the other night, it had suddenly occurred to Lara what Rutherford's true intentions were.

He wanted to humiliate Griff. He wanted the one person to beat him to be a woman.

It had struck her because she had not known, until Rutherford said it, that Griff had never been beaten by anyone. With that kind of reputation, being beaten by a woman would be incredibly humiliating.

She had asked Roddy about it the next morning, and he had agreed completely. They were the first words out of his mouth, actually, when Lara said that she had heard there was to be a race between Mrs. Hastings and Mr. Hallsbury.

"Goodness, if she wins, he will never be able to show his face again," Roddy said.

And Lara had really wanted to cry.

She could not do it. Of course, there was always the possibility that Griff might win. But if *she* did, Griff would completely lose his opportunity to make back his fortune.

She could not do it.

"Lady Lara Darling, what a lovely surprise."

Lara glanced up to see Lord Rutherford sitting on a bench under a tree. He had a blanket—the same blanket Lara had used the other night, actually—over his lap, and a footman standing terribly erect behind him.

"My lord," she said.

"Do come and keep me company," Lord Rutherford said.

Lara sighed. She would absolutely never be able to sit on a bench for long. Especially a cold bench on a very cold morning. Especially with the churning of her thoughts.

But of course, all she had to do was refuse to race, and it would all be over.

She dropped Goldie's reins so the mare could

munch on grass and went to sit beside Lord Rutherford.

"You're quite energetic this morning," Lord Rutherford said. "So much exercise so early in the morning seems to do you well, though."

Lara frowned. "Do not flatter me, my lord. I will not marry you."

He arched one eyebrow over a golden eye. "Goodness, have I taken to saying things and not remembering them? I do swear, Lady Lara, I don't recall ever having asked you to marry me."

Lara bit her lip. Of course. Lord Rutherford had asked Mrs. Hastings to marry him. Or rather, the man had announced that he would do the deed whether it pleased her or not.

Anyway, it was getting rather difficult to keep the two women straight in her mind.

"Since we are on the subject, though, might I offer my humblest apologies for any upset I might have caused you or any of your many friends the other night?"

Lara laughed a little. She looked up at Lord Rutherford through her lashes. "Thank you. But my friends still don't want to marry you."

"Of course they do not."

Lara frowned. "I did not mean . . ."

"Of course you did not."

Lara frowned even deeper.

"Now then, Lady Lara, I found it very interesting that you or your friend, or whomever we're speaking of now, had already been asked to marry?"

She rolled her eyes. "It does not matter."

Lord Rutherford nodded. "Actually, I've heard rumblings from some gossipmongers that Roddy Piperneil will probably ask for your hand as well. Good work."

"Yes." Lara toed the hard, cold ground with her riding boot.

"You don't sound as if you agree."

"'Tis nothing, really." She smiled at him, but then slouched back against the bench. "Anyway, I need to ask you something, Lord Rutherford."

"Goodness, this sounds terribly serious."

"What are your intentions with this race? There is more than what you told me, I knew that. I just wasn't exactly sure what it was. I want to know from your lips."

He glanced at her, but Lara kept her gaze firmly on Goldie's legs. They were much more toned since Lara had first set eyes on the mare.

Lord Rutherford pulled one of the edges of his blanket from between them and laid it over Lara's legs. "So you won't be cold," he said.

"Thank you," Lara said.

He nodded but stayed silent.

"You want to humiliate him, don't you. You want to make it impossible for him to live in this Town anymore."

Rutherford did not say anything.

"I will not race," she said.

Rutherford took in a long, deep breath. "Yes, you will."

Lara blinked and then turned toward Rutherford. "Excuse me?" she asked very slowly.

"If you do not, I will find someone who will. As Griff said the other night. He will gladly race another. And I will make sure the race is his last."

Lara's heart felt like ice in her chest. "What are you saying?" she asked.

But Rutherford refused to speak.

"You disgust me," she said finally. She hated him, truly. And then she shrugged suddenly. "I'll lose."

"You will win. I know you can, I have watched you drive. You are at least as good as Griff ever was."

"It is a race!" Lara cried. "You can't know for sure that I will win."

"If you do not, I will tell the *ton* who Mrs. Hastings is."

Lara pressed her fingertips to her temples. "You wouldn't."

"I would."

She sat up straight then and glared at him. "If I lose, I am ruined."

"Yes."

Lara nodded. She was an idiot. She had known when she accepted this man's offer that she was in over her head. If only she had never jumped in.

Without another word, Lara stood abruptly and, letting Goldie follow, she ran.

Lord Rutherford was actually very happy that Lady Lara left in such a hurry. Better they not speak again until this was all over.

He stared after her, his head aching, his thigh burning and his heart empty. Who was he? This man who could manipulate the people around him with such callous disregard for their feelings?

It scared the hell out of him.

Thomas rubbed at the head of his cane and closed his eyes against the gray day around him. It had just come, suddenly. He had felt so desperate to have revenge, he had threatened something he absolutely could never go through with.

But he knew that Lady Lara thought he could, so he used that against her. Used her innocence. Used her goodness.

"Damn," he said softly.

If he continued on this course, he could very well become someone he despised. With that thought, Thomas made a small, ugly sound in the back of his throat. "I already hate myself," he said under his breath.

He stood suddenly. "I am leaving," he announced. The footman behind him came forward.

"I shall have the carriage brought," the boy said quickly.

Thomas looked at the young man, his breath a ghost of frost in the chilled air, and shook his head. "No, I'm leaving the country. I'm done."

Chapter 15

Never, ever speak out loud about something that needs to stay completely private. The only time you might be able to do such a thing is if you are alone in the privy. Even then, be careful.

The Duchess Diaries, Volume One

"**D**arling, it has been too long."

Thomas blinked at Amelia. That she stood like this in his drawing room seemed a dream. He had nearly reached out and touched her when he first came in, just to make sure it wasn't.

He was suddenly twenty again, strong and whole, and the woman in front of him had just agreed to be his wife.

"I have meant to call on you since you came to Town," Amelia said with a smile.

God, she was beautiful. Still, she was beautiful. And she personified his youth. He wanted to weep.

"Amelia," he finally said. The name sounded foreign to his ears. He had used that name a million times in the past, but it had not crossed his lips for a very long time.

Though, of course, she had pervaded his mind always.

"We should not stand on ceremony, Thomas," she said, coming toward him. She took his hands in hers, looked up into his eyes, and then slid her arms around his neck.

Thomas stood paralyzed for a moment. He could feel her body against his, and he wanted her just as he had ten years before, when they first met.

He breathed in her scent. Lavender and mint, just as it always had been.

She stepped back from him then, but did not stop touching him. Her hands rested on the crooks of his elbows. "You have been naughty," she said, and winked.

"Excuse me?" he said.

Always, this woman had turned his tongue to glue. He had never known what to say, he had adored her so. She was intelligent and interesting, and he had wanted to spend a long life with her. He had known that waking up with this woman every morning would make his life worthwhile.

And it had all gone horribly wrong.

"It turns out, darling, that one of your footmen is second cousin to my lady's maid." She lifted her eyebrows, and then pulled away from him completely and went to take a seat.

"Come, Thomas, sit with me."

He tried desperately not to limp as he took a chair opposite Amelia. "Shall I ring for tea?" he asked, suddenly remembering his manners.

She smiled, but it did not brighten her face at all. "I am not here for tea, darling." She looked away and concentrated on the task of pulling off her gloves as she said, "Now then, I wish you had told me of this race!"

Thomas felt as if he had been punched in the stomach.

Amelia laid her pristine white gloves over her knee. "Well, actually, I've known for a while. I intend to make a killing on it, really."

"You have known?" Thomas asked.

Amelia blinked up at him. "Well, yes, Thomas. I told you. My lady's maid is related to one of your footmen."

Thomas rubbed his thumb against the head

of his cane, seeking the calmness that action always brought to him. "It is not happening anymore," Thomas said finally.

"That is not what my lady's maid told me," Amelia said with a grin. "She said that your footman told her that you have been quite ruthless in your dealings."

That footman is sacked as of ten minutes from now, Thomas thought to himself.

"Ruthless!" She pretended to shiver. "I have never seen you be ruthless, I don't think, Thomas. I am very much interested in this new facet of your personality."

Thomas quietly rubbed at the head of his cane. She was beautiful, this woman. Perfect, really. Tall and slender, her hands like a choreographed ballet as they slid against her thigh one moment, and then brushed at her hair which was never out of place.

Perfect, everything about her. But suddenly Thomas realized that perfection was not always pure. Amelia's perfection, in that instant, seemed tainted. As if perhaps her perfection had come from some other source than God.

"I do hope that you can continue in this new vein, darling. I always knew that you were stronger than you acted. And, really, such ingenuity!" she clapped her hands with pure glee. "This race. It is a lovely idea. I wish I had had it!"

"But you didn't," Thomas said.

Amelia batted her lashes. "No, I didn't. But I am going to make a lot of money on it. One can never have enough, can one?"

Thomas nodded. He rather thought that Amelia did not have enough at all. From what he had heard, Mr. Braxton had made a few bad investments lately.

"You know, Thomas," she said softly, "I must tell you." She leaned toward him. "I had a moment of true regret when my lady's maid spoke of how you have manipulated Griff."

"Regret?" he asked, his mind shying away from the accusation. *Manipulation.* Ugly word, ugly deed. And, yes, he had very much done exactly that.

She reached out and touched his hand with her bare one. "I should never have broken off our engagement. We could be together now, if only. I would be the Lady Rutherford to your lordship. I would have made you happier than you ever dreamed." She traced her fingernail along his knuckles, and then slipped her index finger beneath the cuff of his jacket.

"I could still make you happy," she said.

Just a few minutes before, Thomas had felt his body respond to this woman's nearness, but as Thomas watched her slender white hand caress him, his heart was like lead in his chest.

"Now?" he asked, still staring at her thin, white fingers, "you say you regret your decision to leave me when I needed you most. And I find I have to wonder why you have decided to tell me now?"

Amelia laughed, but it sounded very strained. She shifted closer to him so that he could feel her breath fan his chin. "Darling," she said. "I find you incredibly attractive."

"No, Amelia, you don't." Thomas pulled his hand away from her and sat back against his chair, putting some much-needed space between them. "I don't matter in the least. You see a way to get what you want, you don't see me at all. People don't matter to you—only what you want and need."

Amelia shook her head.

"The race isn't happening, Amelia," he said. "And I must take my leave now. I have a horrible headache." Thomas stood. He did have a terrible ache in his head, but he also felt lighter and more agile than he had in years. Truly, he felt like he could run across the floor as he had before the accident. Amelia did not sit at the back of his mind any longer, a shadowed hurt of what he could have had.

No, she sat before him, in bright sunlight, a small and pitiful woman.

She stood then, also. "I knew it," Amelia said, her eyes turning feral before Thomas's gaze. "I knew you could not do it. I knew that you would not go through with this on your own."

"Wait," Thomas said with a chuckle. "Do you despise me, or want me? I am getting very confused."

Amelia took in a deep breath, her full lips curling and turning unbecomingly thin.

This is exactly where he was headed with his bitterness and revenge. If he continued, he would be just like Amelia. She had not been so bad when they were younger, no, or he could not have loved her then. But he did remember that she had that potential. The small, mean remarks she liked to make about people.

It was sad, actually. She was an intelligent woman, and he did remember rightly that she used to have such a wit that he was always entertained in her presence.

But that wit had turned acrid—her intelligence used for ugliness. She did rather make one feel as if the prince of darkness might arrive at any moment and shake hands with her.

And he had been very close to following in her wake.

He knew in that moment that he could not. He glanced around his home and knew that he had to leave. He needed to get away from England—London, especially. There were painful memories in this place.

He needed to create new memories that did not make him recoil and try desperately to shut his mind to them.

"You started this, Thomas, and it will happen. I will not allow you to back away," Amelia said.

First, of course, he had to deal with the mess he had made. He waited without speaking, for he knew that Amelia had more to say. And he rather knew what was coming next. And, really, he deserved it, for what he had done in the past few weeks.

"I am going to make a fortune on this race, darling Thomas. I have put my best diamonds up as collateral on a wager. And you are going to make sure it all happens."

"I won't," he said.

"Then I'm going to make sure everyone knows that Lady Lara Darling is Mrs. Hastings. And I'll also make sure they all know that you are the one who revealed her identity. Just to put a bit of icing on the cake, you might say."

Thomas nodded quietly. Of course, he had seen that coming in the last minute. He knew, rather, how her mind worked now, for his had worked very much the same lately.

A part of him wished to laugh. Of late, he had been reading a good deal, alone in his room. His readings had introduced him to a religious belief in India called Karma, and he now believed in it.

"I will see you in hell," he said to Amelia.

"Won't that be fun." She winked at him.

Griff had taken a very small room just off Haymarket. It was a bit dark and dingy, but it was cheap and, with his work, he was not there very often anyway. At the moment, he was, though.

He lay on the lumpy bed, throwing a hard leather tennis ball up in the air just above his head, and then catching it just before it beaned him right between the eyes.

He probably could have found a safer way to think. He threw the ball and grabbed it again, just in time.

He had heard from one of the young bucks

that the race was already on the betting books. His name was written down right alongside Mrs. Hastings'. He had backed down, but no one had listened.

And now his name was in the books. If he backed down now, he would never reach his goal, that was assured. No one would take him seriously again.

Still, he knew that it was the right thing to do.

But would his sacrifice really be worth it? It did seem that Lady Lara was determined to make her life absolutely miserable. He could keep trying to save her, but one of these times, she'd achieve her goal.

Why not just let her go ahead with it now? And come away with something for the trouble?

And now there was the contraption that he had gone up to Ashton Hall and spoken to Lord Ashton about. He had tried it out on an ancient carriage that the old groom, Tumley, had brought out for him.

Tumley had commented that his mistress Lara had learned on the old rig. The small bit of metal with rotors that went just behind the back axel *had* made the coach much easier to handle.

Griff was extremely excited about it.

Thomas had no idea that he had given Griff

the perfect opportunity to show what Lord Ashton's new invention could do.

Of course, Lara didn't know about it either.

Lara.

Her name went through his mind, and then images followed.

Lara, wet and beautiful, kissing him like no one had ever kissed him before. Her eyes, alive and burning when she came beneath him. That same look as she took up the reins of his coach.

The look in her eyes when she almost told him she loved him.

Damn.

If only everything could happen backward. If only he had met Lara after he had fixed his world. If only he had never ruined it. If only he had never been young and stupid, and had gone straight from shortpants to being old and stupid.

Damn. He threw the ball again, but had to roll quickly when he did not catch it in time. It bounced off his mattress, hit the floor with a thud and rolled beneath his bed.

Well, it was gone forever now. He had always thought of himself as a courageous man, but there was no way he was going to stick his hand under the bed. He had not found it important enough to have a cleaning woman. There were scary things alive under there.

Another thumping sound had Griff frowning.

It sounded again. Someone was at his door. He walked over and carefully opened it a crack.

Thomas.

Griff opened the door. "Well, if it isn't the devil himself," he said. At the same time, though, he felt as if he had lost his best friend again. Thomas was no longer Thomas. And it was all Griff's fault.

"You have to race," Thomas said.

Griff shook his head and turned away from his friend. "I know. It's on the books already. But that doesn't mean I have to race."

"You don't understand."

Griff turned in the dreary room. There was something different about his friend's voice.

"Amelia knows. She's the one who put the race on the books."

Griff just shook his head. "You are going to blame Amelia now?"

"No, I'm going to tell you that Amelia knows everything. She knows who Mrs. Hastings is."

Griff closed the distance between himself and Thomas with one stride. He grabbed his friend's cravat and curled it around his fist.

"You told Amelia? You are even more stupid than I thought."

"Get your hands off me," Thomas said through gritted teeth.

Griff stared at him for a moment without moving, and then pushed away from him. "You're not worth it."

"Her lady's maid is related to one of my footmen—although he is not my footman any longer."

Griff turned to stare out his grimy window.

"If you don't race, Amelia will expose Lara."

Griff laughed in disgust and shook his head.

"She's still got you right where she wants you, doesn't she?" he asked. "Can't you see she's not worth it?"

"Yes," Thomas said shortly.

Griff frowned. And then he turned around.

The two men stood silently watching each other until Thomas broke eye contact and glanced around the room. He laughed. "Looks a bit like some of the places we used to frequent."

Griff did not smile.

Thomas closed his eyes and pushed his fingers against the bridge of his nose. "I wish I had never come to Town," he said. "But what is done is done. Are you going to race?"

Griff shook his head and looked away from

his old friend. "I don't know." He sighed. "Yes. I think I will have to. If Amelia is involved, it will get ugly. She's going to do anything to ruin Lara."

"She has baited the hook. There *is* definitely a hook beneath it all," Thomas said.

"Finally, you realize what she really is."

"I knew. I probably always knew," Thomas said.

Griff just nodded.

"The fortune is there to be won," Thomas said. "But I am not in this anymore. I will stay and try to cushion whatever Amelia decides to do, but then I am going away."

Griff glanced at Thomas's leg.

"I am not that much of an invalid. I can travel."

"I didn't say you couldn't." Griff shook his head. "What a mess."

"They used to be much more fun, didn't they. Our messes, I mean," Thomas said.

Griff ran his hand through his hair. Had they been? He could barely remember most of them. He had usually been so drunk that he lost weeks at a time. Mostly he remembered the constant ache that traveled with him in his heart. The knowledge that he could never really be what his father wanted, so he might as well be the exact opposite.

He had tried when he was young. For many years, he had tried to do well in school, find joy in the estate—running it, organizing others' lives. But he had never done well at it.

His father just kept telling him to try harder—until finally, Griff tried very hard to show his father that he was completely worthless.

He had done a very good job at that.

"There really weren't that many fun messes that I remember," Griff said then, smiling slightly at Thomas. "Except perhaps when we would ride or hunt together. I always did enjoy any time spent with you, Thomas. You are a good man."

A muscle moved in Thomas's jaw.

"I was a bad influence," Griff said.

"No, you weren't." Thomas looked at Griff's bed, and then at the dark window. "I am proud of you. You did not run away. You could have just gone to France. Your father would be proud. He is proud, I'm sure."

Griff stared down at his scuffed boots. "I'm sorry, Thomas." He glanced back up at his friend.

Thomas squinted at the window for a moment more, and then he nodded. "I know."

Chapter 16

If you find yourself feeling very differently about a subject that you have always felt the same about, dearest, you will know that you have changed. It is called maturity, really. Or getting old. You suddenly understand a bit more, make better decisions. Believe in yourself. That is the maturity part, and it is really lovely. The getting old part isn't so much.

The Duchess Diaries, Volume One

The Darling sisters were helping old Tumley get Reggie and Lord Ashton's trunks loaded on the back of the carriage that Lady Tattenbaum had sent them.

Well, they were all helping except for Amanda. She was sulking.

And Lissie. At eight, she was more in the way than anything else, so they had sent her off to help Mrs. Thornbury make a food basket.

Lord Ashton was nowhere to be seen. He had spent the last week sitting in the library and staring at the wall as if trying to peer through a fog, and then suddenly he would make a sound, jump to his feet and make his way out to the old barn.

There he would tinker with the invention he had said was finished, but seemed to need perfecting on a regular basis.

Actually, he was acting as he had the entirety of the Darling sisters' existence. So they were rather relieved, though continually a bit breathless as they waited for Lord Ashton to finally remember that he would not be making Lady Ashton's life any better with his invention.

"Now then," Emma said as she strapped down the trunks on the back of the carriage. "You must be careful, Reggie. I know that you are always quite competent, but really, the job before you is rife with difficulties."

Amanda glanced up from sulking on the front steps of Ashton hall. "Do speak in English, Emma. Such big words. And you, only twelve."

"Thirteen in three months time, thank you very much. And I do speak English, dear. You would know that if you deigned to open a book."

"Girls," Reggie said.

Amanda just rolled her eyes.

"I shall have Lady Tattenbaum's help," Reggie said, turning to Emma. "I just wish you all could come."

"So do I," Amanda wailed.

"Lady Tattenbaum has invited only Reggie and father," Emma reminded her. "Anyway, we don't need to be there. Reggie and Lady Tattenbaum can do this."

Reggie nodded, but her hands were shaking as she retied her bonnet strings for the tenth time in as many minutes.

"Do not forget the last signature for the patent," Rachel said. Her words were muffled, though. She had her head under the carriage, and she was meticulously studying the way the axle worked.

Reggie glanced at her, and then up at Emma, and they both just shook their heads.

"*She* is Father's daughter," Amanda said.

And they all silently agreed.

Emma sighed then. "I must say, I am a bit put out that Mr. Hallsbury forgot to inform us that this Great London Race, as they are calling it, is actually going to happen."

Reggie finally threaded her fingers together and pressed them against her stomach so that she would not touch her bonnet again.

"I am just put out," Amanda said flopping back against the step behind her.

Reggie sighed. "Listen, dears, you do realize what Mr. . . . Lord Trenton was ready to give up for our sister, do you not?"

"A fortune!" Amanda said. "Imagine it, so romantic." She finally smiled for the first time that day. "And so much money."

"I dare say we all know that Lara is, as always, not thinking right. She has turned Lord Trenton's proposal down when he is exactly right for her."

"He does love her, obviously," Emma said.

"He will make her very happy," Reggie agreed.

"We will have a coachman in the family tree," Amanda said dourly.

"If all goes well, dearest," Reggie reminded her young sister, "that coachman will have a fortune."

Amanda nodded. "Well yes, there is that."

"And, really, what could go wrong?" Reggie said with a smile. "With Lady Tattenbaum's knowledge, we are ahead of everyone involved."

"I cannot believe that she would make some gossipmonger an underbutler," Emma said with a twist of her mouth. "Really, the man is obviously not to be trusted. He told this Mrs.

312

Braxton person everything she needed to know to put our Lara in a most precarious position."

"Lara has put *herself* in that position, truth be told," Rachel piped up. "And Lady Tattenbaum obviously wants to keep this line of gossip to the horrid Mrs. Braxton close to home. Smart woman," she said, but did not come out from under the carriage.

Emma blinked down at the carriage wheel. "How old are you, again, Rachel, because you rather sound ancient."

"Now," said Reggie clapping her hands. "Just to go over it all one more time . . ."

"Again?" Amanda wailed. "How many times will we do this?"

"If it were your dilemma we were speaking of, I would wager that you would not mind us talking about it ad nauseum," Emma said to her sister.

"You will not wager on anything," Reggie frowned at Emma. "Now, do help me here, girls. As Emma said, the task before me is tricky and involves the fate of so many people, I rather feel sick."

Emma and Amanda fell silent. They were not used to seeing Reggie nervous.

Rachel appeared then, her dark hair more out of the plait Amanda had fixed that morning than in it, a large swipe of black grease running from one ear to the end of her nose. "Just remember your final goals. Get Lara through this race, name intact, and then marry her off to Trenton. And, more important: Get that last patent signature."

"If you mention the patent again, I will thrash you, I swear," Amanda said darkly.

Rachel just smiled. "Good luck, Reggie." And she skipped off like the girl of ten she was.

"Oh dear," Reggie said. "I do hate just jumping into things, you know. I'd rather have a plan."

"We *do* have a plan," Emma protested.

"A better plan," Reggie clarified.

Amanda stood then and fluffed out her dress. "Oh really, plans change. They always do. And, anyway, the hardest part is over, I think. Lara will marry this man—how could she not? When she finds out about how he placed Father's invention in her carriage without her knowledge so that she would win the race." She shrugged. "Who would not marry him?"

"That's not true," Reggie said on a sigh. "To get Lara married to the right man, there will have to be more. She is stubborn, remember. And it really has nothing to do with Lord Trenton at all, and everything to do with the fears she keeps close to her heart. The more the man woos, the more afraid she will be, I tell you."

"Afraid?" Amanda asked. "What on earth would she have to be afraid of? She'll have a lovely husband and buckets of money."

"She is afraid to love, Amanda. We've already discussed this. Do you ever remember anything that does not directly influence you?" Emma chided her older sister.

"Of course I do!" Amanda cried. "It's just . . . *did* we talk of this? I don't remember. And I certainly did not realize that you all have figured out our Lara's strange ways. I don't understand our oldest sister in the least."

Emma rolled her eyes.

"Emma," Reggie admonished her sister. "Amanda wasn't there last night when Rachel pointed out that Lara is probably afraid to love someone."

"Ha!" Amanda stuck her nose up at Emma. But then she frowned. "Rachel? Rachel has figured out Lara's eccentricities? Goodness. Perhaps I should start reading more. It seems to be doing that little one a world of good."

"I am going to refrain from saying anything in hopes that God will shower blessings upon my head," Emma said dryly.

Amanda stuck her tongue out at Emma.

"Anyway, Rachel just pointed out that Lara never joined in when we would all talk about what we wanted our future husbands to be like," Reggie said.

Amanda sighed dreamily. "I do miss doing that. We haven't played that game in ever so long. It is my favorite."

"We know," Emma said.

"Be that as it may," Reggie said quickly. "Last night Rachel deduced that our Lara, our sister who always lamented Father's way of ignoring Mother, is afraid that if she loves someone and then marries that person, she will be hurt."

"Nonsense," Amanda said. "She will not be hurt if that man loves her as well."

"Father loved Mother, we know that especially now," Emma said.

"And Mother was very hurt," Reggie said.

The sisters stared at the ground in silence.

"Poor, dear Mother," Emma said softly.

"Don't." Amanda bit her lip and turned away.

"Yes," Reggie said. "We have work to do. No time for regrets and tears."

Amanda took a few steps away from them, breathed in deeply and turned around.

"Well, then," she said. "Just worry about getting Lara through this dratted mess without raking our family name through the mud any more than my sister marrying a coachman will." She sighed, her delicate shoulders lifting and dropping prettily. And then she walked over to Reggie, looked into her eyes and said, "Ah, you will do just fine," and she gave her older sister a hug.

"Thank you, Amanda."

"Just make sure you bring me home a treat. I may never speak to you again if you don't," she said, but smiled to soften her words.

Emma stepped forward then. "It will be all right, I know it will," she said. "Lady Tattenbaum will help you. Just remember to tell Lara about the invention. Offer to put it in her carriage, like we decided."

Reggie smiled. "When she hears about the invention, she will refuse to put it in her carriage; as it will give her an unfair advantage, but she will also know that it must go in someone's coach so that Father can receive recognition."

"And she will place it surreptitiously in Lord Trenton's coach." Emma nodded.

"And then we shall, at the very least, have an equal race," Reggie concluded.

"And Father will be acknowledged, surely, for this will be the fastest race London has ever seen." Emma clapped her hands.

Amanda *tsk*ed. "Who knew that two people in love could be such trouble?"

"I do worry, though," Emma said. "If Lara does win the race, it could make our job of getting her to marry nearly impossible."

"Yes," Reggie agreed. "A fortune in Lara's hands could be a very bad thing."

Amanda pretended to swoon then and made a sound like a sob. "And, really, that is just tragic. How could a fortune ever be construed as a bad thing? If I had that fortune, I would make sure it was never a bad thing."

"You would probably cause a shortage in the silk industry, actually," Emma said.

"Yes? And since all the silk would then be swathed about my body in beautiful gowns, why on earth would that be bad?" She stuck her nose in the air and pranced about their graveled drive. "Ah, you there," she pointed at an overgrown shrub. "Do bring my carriage around, I am off to the shops. And you," she pointed to a chipped planter. "I shall then need a bath, but instead of water, I would like to bathe in pearls as soft as a baby's bottom."

Reggie and Emma giggled.

Amanda laughed and whirled around. "And you!" she pointed to Old Tumley who had just emerged from around the side of the house with grain sacks for the horses. Take two diamonds to each of my sisters—they need to learn how to appreciate the finer things."

Old Tumley did not even glance away from his task as he strapped the feedbags to the horses. When one had been in the Darling household for so many generations, one no longer gave a thought to their strangeness. Especially these sisters. Bonkers, the lot.

Lara frowned as she walked Goldie back to the small barn behind Lady Tattenbaum's mansion. Sitting on an old bench at the back of the barn wall was a man who looked rather like her father.

Of course, it could not be but . . . "Father?" she said as she came closer.

He glanced up.

Lara stopped in her tracks. "It *is* you," she said in shock.

He smiled at her as if it should be normal that he was there. "Good morning, dear," he said. And then stared back at the ground.

Lara glanced around. Could she possibly be seeing a ghost? Was she truly out of her mind?

"What are you doing here?" she asked slowly, very afraid that the apparition before her might drift away, or blow up, or talk to her. Any of those things would mean that she really *had* lost her mind.

The man squinted at the ground and did not answer her.

Yes, it was definitely her father. Lara dropped Goldie's reins and sat beside him. "I am sure you were not worried about me. You couldn't possibly be here on a social outing," she suddenly grabbed her father's arm. "Has someone been hurt? Are the girls all right?" She shook him a bit to get him to acknowledge her.

He glanced up and smiled again. "It is good the rain came," he said. "But we do need a patch more, I think."

"Father," Lara said loudly. "Are any of my sisters hurt?"

"Hurt?" he asked. "I don't think so. Reggie looked fine enough when we finally got here, though she has now gone up for a nap."

So, Reggie had turned up as well. "What are you doing here?" Lara asked again, though, of course she knew that she ought to give up and just seek out Reggie.

Still, she did not want to move. She had not heard so many words from her father's mouth in a very long time, and she wished to stay with him. She wanted him to talk to her.

He pulled something from his pocket and,

hunching over his lap, began working on whatever it was. His attention was focused completely on his task. She had seen him in this
position most of her life, she thought.

Lara glanced over his shoulder, expecting to
see steel pipe or perhaps cog wheels. Instead, she
saw that her father had a lap full of daisies, and
he was quite intent on weaving them into a chain.

"Father," she said in surprise. "What are you
doing?" Though that would seem to be obvious, Lara had to imagine a higher purpose in
her father weaving a daisy chain. Her father
did not just weave daisy chains.

Actually, that conclusion was most completely wrong, if her eyes did not deceive her.

"I used to weave chains for your mother's
hair," he said then and glanced at her. "She loved
that I did that. She is the one who told me to use
my hands. She said they were like magic."

Lara held her breath. She had never in her life
heard her father talk about her mother.

"I've made something now that she would be
so proud of. But she's gone."

Lara stared at the chain. She doubted her
mother would have been so enthusiastic about
the bit of frippery. But then she thought again.
On the other hand, perhaps she would have
treasured it forever.

"It's an invention that would finally give her what I wanted to. You know Lord Braithwaite asked for her hand at one time? He is nearly the richest man in England, next to the king, of course."

Lara had heard of the man, of course. But she had never known that her mother could have married him.

"She married me, though. Happiest day of my life. But I wanted to make her happy." Her father quit his braiding and let his hands lie, palms up, on his lap. "She said she was, but I wanted to make her truly happy. I should have believed her, shouldn't I?" He sighed. "I didn't feel like I deserved her. I wanted her to be happy, but I also wanted to prove that I deserved her. Selfish, really.

Lara closed her eyes for a moment. What was going on? she wondered.

"Now I have finally done what I set out to do all those years ago. My hands have made something that will take away all of your mother's drudgery. Give her an inkling of what she would have had with Braithwaite."

Lara swallowed. Her father was speaking of her mother in the present tense. That could not be good.

"Don't worry, dear. I've heard your sisters. They are worried. I know she's gone. I went in the dead of night to sit by her sickbed. Every night I cried as I knelt beside her." He went back to his braiding. "And I know your mother didn't want anything Braithwaite had at all. She just wanted me. It is too bad that we sometimes learn things when it is too late, isn't it?" he asked.

Lara bit at her bottom lip and looked at her father; he was watching her. "Yes," she said softly.

"I'm not too late for you, though," he said.

Lara did not know what to say.

"Anyway," her father returned his attention to his daisy chain. "It will take practice. I am not good at speaking my feelings." He plucked the chain from his lap and placed it on her head. "But you, dear, are not very good at knowing your true feelings, I fear." He smiled at her, stood and walked away.

Chapter 17

*Fear is an interesting emotion, I think. We are
so afraid of it after all, that we sometimes forget
the thing we fear and begin to fear the fear. I say,
jump in full go, it's usually nothing anyway.*
                    The Duchess Diaries, Volume One

Really, Lara should have felt more excited
than she ever had in her life. She was
dressed as a boy, after all, running about London in the dark on a clandestine mission.

She was not excited at all, though. Rather she
was terribly cold. And she just wished that she
could drop out of the race and go home.

The only reason she didn't was because she
wanted Griff to be safe. And she wanted him to
win his fortune. She gripped the contraption
her father had handed over to her that evening.

Her father had explained to her how his invention worked and how he wanted her to put it just behind the back axle of her carriage so that London would be flabbergasted at how well her coach handled. According to her father, they would make a fortune on the sales.

She knew, of course, that one of the coaches in the Great London Race had to have her father's invention in it. But she had decided, as she listened to her father, that it would not be her coach and four.

Both of the coaches they would use in the race were in Lord Rutherford's stables. And as Lara finally turned into the alley behind Lord Rutherford's home, she gave a long sigh.

She dearly wanted to be at home in bed.

The night was dark and clear and crisp. Actually, crisp was putting it mildly. Lara would not have been surprised to see snow fall from the sky, it was so damn cold.

She shivered and stared at the wall behind Lord Rutherford's house. She was pretty sure the man had the tallest wall in all of London. And she was going to have to climb the thing. She glared at it as if, perhaps, her stare would burn a hole through the brick.

But the wall did not crumble.

Lara sighed, settled the cap covering her pinned-up hair so it came farther down her forehead, found a good foothold and started her ascent.

Halfway up, she promised God that she would never do anything unladylike again, if He only let her make it over Lord Rutherford's wall alive. She slipped twice, and each time she heard bits of mortar *plink* their way down and hit the ground.

It was rather a terrifying sound, when one realized that it could be one's bones making that noise. Lara finally levered herself onto the top of the wall. She lay there for a moment, just breathing.

And then she heard a noise.

Lara stayed as still as she could on the top of the wall, listening. Someone was walking down the alleyway she had just left.

Lara closed her eyes like a child. Perhaps if she couldn't see them, they wouldn't see her?

The footfalls came closer, went by and then stopped.

Damn.

And then she heard a clang and a squeak, and realized that it was a gate opening. Lara slowly tilted her head up and blinked in the dark. There was a gate through Lord Rutherford's wall. She had nearly killed herself climbing the damn thing, and there was a gate.

She rolled her eyes, but then remembered that someone was creeping through that gate in the middle of the night. That was just plain scary. She peered over the edge, but couldn't make out much but a shadow, as a person—a rather big person—carefully pulled the gate closed and then tiptoed through what looked to be an herb-and-vegetable garden.

The large figure was most definitely trying to be as quiet as possible. She watched until the shadowy form became completely lost in the darkness. And then she waited for a very long time.

It must have been a servant coming back late, she thought. Yes, of course, that was exactly who it was. She waited another few minutes. Then she swung her legs over the wall and started the perilous climb down.

At least she knew that she could go through the gate on her way home. Lara jumped the last few feet. The ground was hard, probably frozen through it was so cold, and she seemed to bounce and then fall. She landed very hard on her backside.

She made a small sound of pain, reached down and rubbed her bum. It was covered in something wet and mushy.

"Ewww!" she cried, and then bit her tongue.

She put her fingers to her nose and realized that she had crushed a tomato plant.

Lovely.

She wiped her hand on her pantleg and shoved herself up to her feet. *All this for Griff*, she thought petulantly. But then she smiled. Yes, all of this was for Griff. He would win the race easily and get his fortune. He would find his place again in Society.

Her heart felt warm even though she was freezing.

Wiping her hands together to dislodge the remnants of dirt and tomato pulp, Lara picked her way carefully through the garden to the back wall of the stable. She pressed against the bricks as she moved to the corner.

She could see the back of the main house from here, and it was a bit disconcerting. She did not like the idea of being in full view of the house. Lara waited for a minute, said a little prayer, and then scurried around to the front of the stable and through the doors she knew would take her into the room with the coaches.

Fortunately, Lord Rutherford was richer than sin. He had a huge stable with a completely separate area for the horses. If she had tried to sneak into a stable full of horses, they probably would have put up a fuss that would have the groom running out to check on them.

As it was, she was alone in a cavernous room filled with Lord Rutherford's conveyances. Lara tiptoed to the very back, where Griff's coach stood.

It only took her a few minutes to install the small bit of metal on the rear axle, and she was able to do it without even striking a match.

Lara was congratulating herself when she again heard a noise. Her heart thumped, and she dropped the tools she had just used. They clattered against each other as they hit the hay on the floor, and she grimaced.

She waited as quietly as she could. Maybe it was just a rat, or even one of the horses from the next building. Lara's breathing steadied and she carefully gathered her tools.

Thunk, thunk!

Lara stopped. No. That was not a rat. It had sounded very much like boots hitting planked flooring.

Someone was in the room with her.

Lara stifled a scream. As quietly as she could, she crawled across the floor toward the back wall. She would find a window, climb through and run. She was a fast runner. She could make it.

And then suddenly something very large and heavy dropped onto her back and pinned her to the floor. Hard hands grabbed her arms, and a dark voice breathed in her ear. "What are you doing here?"

Lara lay flat against the ground. "Get off!" she cried. "Griff Hallsbury, you get off me!"

He laughed and rolled off of her.

Lara pushed herself up quickly, making sure her tools were nicely tucked in her coat so Griff wouldn't see them. "You scared the life out of me, Griff! How dare you!"

"Well, you can't blame me. I thought you were some bounder stealing away with something that wasn't yours." Griff took a step closer to her, and lowered his voice. "Imagine my surprise when I jumped on you and rose water filled my senses."

"Imagine my surprise when someone twice my weight smashed me flat," Lara grumbled at him, retreating a step.

"What are you doing here, Lara?" Griff asked.

"What are *you* doing here, Griff?" she returned.

Griff closed the gap between them again. She could feel the heat from his body. "I couldn't sleep," he said.

Lara stumbled backward. "Well, I couldn't either."

Griff reached forward and fingered the lapel of Lara's boy's jacket. "Interesting fashion decision," he said, taking a determined step toward her.

Lara scooted backward, her back coming up against a hard surface. Damn. She narrowed her eyes on the large, dark figure hovering over her. She felt like a rabbit, backed into a corner by a wolf.

She didn't like feeling trapped, she decided.

Lara cocked her head to the side and raised a brow at the hungry wolf in front of her. "Grabbed the first thing I could find," she said, and folded her arms across her chest.

They stood staring at each other for a long moment. "Lara," Griff said finally. "Don't race. You will not lose anything if you just do not show up tomorrow. No one knows who you are . . . now."

Lara took a deep breath. Did he care, really, she wondered, about her reputation, or had it all been about the Baron's own ego?

She had fallen in love with a man who cared: a man who did not run from his mistakes. But maybe she was a mistake to him. A mistake he had to fix.

She hated that idea. It hurt down to her toes.

"If you step down," she said quietly. "I will."

It was not fair at all. And she did not mean it, not really. She wanted Griff to race. She wanted him to win. She wanted to give him back what he had lost. And she wanted that because she did love him.

But a small part of her self wanted at least the spoken proof that he felt the same for her. That he would save her again over himself.

Griff drew in a deep breath and blew it out slowly. "I have spoken to Thomas . . . Lord Rutherford," he said. "I know that he threatened my well-being. I know that you tried to get out of the race, and he forced your hand by saying he would hurt me."

"You spoke to Lord Rutherford?"

"Listen," Griff took her hands in his. "Thomas will not hurt me."

Lara bit her lip. "So I can back down now. But you will not."

"Lara," Griff said quickly.

"No," Lara stopped him. "It doesn't matter."

"It does!" Griff's fingers squeezed hers so hard they hurt. "You have made mistakes that have hurt you, but this will ruin you completely. And *then* what will you do?"

"I am not making a mistake. I'm doing something I believe in. And anyway, no one is even going to know that it is me. I promise you. Reggie and I have a plan."

Griff made a sound like a choked laugh. "Now I really am petrified, I think."

"You should be, dearest, I am not to be taken lightly, you know," Lara said with a laugh.

But Griff was not laughing. He just stared at her in the dark. Lara shivered.

He closed the distance between them quickly, his mouth taking hers before she knew what was happening.

Lara started to protest, realized that was the last thing she wished to do, and slipped her arms around Griff's neck so she could better return the kiss.

With a soft moan, Griff pulled her tightly against him. Lara sighed, going up on her tiptoes so that she could feel all of this man against her. She curled her fingers into the hair at his nape and opened her mouth to his taste.

Griff settled one large hand at the back of her head, his other hand resting on her hip. She was not a tiny woman. She was tall and well rounded, but Griff's hand dwarfed her hip, making her feel something that she did not understand at first.

And then she did, suddenly.

She had tried so hard to be ladylike during this season in London. She had sat primly listening to hour-long conversations about weather, sipped tea with her little finger crooked just so, quietly labored over her embroidery. And, always, it seemed distressingly futile.

She did not feel ladylike or feminine.

But now, here, with Griff, Lara felt soft. She felt beautiful and fragile. But at the same time, she knew that her very fragility held a power that was stronger and more complete than being able to outshoot Lord Cartwright. Or win any race, ever.

She slipped her tongue over her lover's teeth and felt the muscles of his neck tremble beneath her fingers.

Oh yes, she was enjoying her femininity immensely.

"Lara," Griff said against her mouth. "I want to show you something."

"Yes?" she asked, nipping at Griff's lower lip. She trailed kisses along his jaw, and trailed her fingers down his neck and to the opening of his shirt.

"I . . ." Griff began again, but then bent and kissed Lara's lips again.

She bit him lightly and began to undo his buttons as she continued to kiss Griff's jaw. And then she tongued her way down his neck.

She opened Griff's shirt and slid her hands inside and around his bare chest.

Griff shuddered and groaned deep in his throat. And then he lifted his hands and cupped Lara's face, bringing her mouth back to his. They kissed deeply.

Lara loved Griff's mouth. He tasted of mint and he smelled of musk, and when she kissed him, it was as if she could inhale his entire being into her soul.

She also loved his hands, so strong and large and capable against her body. They made her feel like a woman.

A woman who was adored.

When life intruded, she was not sure. But when he touched her like this, she felt invincible. She felt loved and cherished and important.

Griff brushed Lara's hat off her head and pulled at the pins that confined her hair. "I want you," he said.

Lara laughed lightly. "I know."

He shoved her jacket off one shoulder, and Lara had a moment of panic at the thought of all of her tools spilling to the ground at their feet. She stepped away quickly and shrugged out of her coat.

She carefully folded it and shoved it away from them. Griff was watching her, and she did not want him to be suspicious about her carefulness with the coat. So she started to undress quickly, but then she slowed.

She pulled off her borrowed shirt and glanced up from under her lashes. Griff had stilled. He was the wolf this time. But Lara was not a rabbit.

She felt like a hunter, perhaps. A hunter that would never kill, but seduce.

Lara undid the buttons of her pants slowly, one at a time as she listened to Griff's breathing quicken. She slipped the trousers down over her hips and then stepped out of them with a flourish.

"You want me," she said. "And you get to have me." With a naughty grin, Lara slid her naked body against Griff's half-clothed one.

His arms went around her, his mouth found hers. But then he let go of her. Still kissing her, Griff relieved himself of his own clothes, and then took her down with him onto the floor.

He was awfully good at this, Lara thought as she realized that he had made sure his clothing stretched out in a way that protected them from lying directly on the hay.

Griff hovered over her, kissing her and touching her. But Lara pushed at him, and he fell back.

"What's wrong?" he asked breathlessly.

Without saying anything, Lara got on top of him, straddling his hips. "Shh," she said.

Griff grinned. "All right," he answered.

His hardness was hot against her as Lara trailed her hands over Griff's chest, ran her fingers along his stomach.

She loved the feel of his skin, soft, but with the steel of his muscles beneath. It was exactly like who Griff Hallsbury was. He was a good man, just like Lady Tattenbaum had said. A man who could touch her softly, yet protect her with strength.

She bit her lip, her heart beating hard in her chest as she realized that she wanted to feel this way about Griff Hallsbury forever. And she wanted him to love her forever.

It made her sad.

Griff was watching her, she knew. But she did not look at him. She bent quickly and kissed his stomach. She trailed her lips up his chest and tongued his neck. And then she was at his mouth again.

They kissed, and Griff curled his fingers around her hips. She moved slightly against him, and he groaned.

Griff guided her up, his manhood sliding wetly against her. She shivered, her skin tingling and her heart beating faster. She felt Griff enter her, slowly filling her, and then she could feel him hard inside of her.

Lara made a soft sound as Griff gripped her hips and slid his tongue along her teeth. She was warm and cold at the same time, and she was excited and thrilled and at peace all at once. She moved then, lifting and lowering slowly.

Her blood warmed and then burned as she moved.

Griff cupped her breasts, his thumbs lightly flicking at her nipples. Lara groaned and moved faster against him, her blood on fire in her veins.

Her woman's place tightened and then convulsed and she spiraled with it as Griff groaned into her mouth and she felt his seed pour into her body.

Lara collapsed on Griff's chest, her lips against his throat. They lay there, breathing heavily, for a long moment.

"You wanted to show me something?" she finally asked. And Griff laughed out loud.

"I don't remember," he said then. "I don't even think I remember my name."

Lara giggled.

Griff rubbed her back, trailing his fingers up and down her spine as they laughed together.

Finally, Lara moved off her lover, turning onto her back beside him and staring at the ceiling.

"I was hoping you had decided to stay on top of me forever," he said.

There was that *forever* word. Lara did not say anything.

Griff propped himself up on his elbow and looked down at her. "I remember," he said then. He pushed himself up and stood beside her. "Come with me," he said, holding out his hand.

She took it, letting Griff help her up. He bent, picked up his oiled coachmen's cloak and wrapped it around her shoulders. And then he guided her over to one of the high windows at the back of Lord Rutherford's stable.

"Look," he said, and pointed.

Lara peered into the darkness beyond the window, wondering what she was supposed to see.

And then suddenly she realized that Griff meant the moon. It was nearly full, round and large and white in the dark sky. It was a clear night and the moon looked very tranquil and peaceful in the blackness.

"I was pacing," Griff said. "My stomach was churning, my mind going over every single bad thing that could possibly happen tomorrow, and I turned and there was the moon shining through my window."

Lara nodded without looking away from the moon.

"It settled me. I don't know why, really. It's just so serene, I guess," Griff said. "Anyway, I wanted to show you."

He was silent for a moment. "I was afraid," he said then. "The last time we were together, I thought that perhaps you were laughing at me. Using me as other women have tried. Excited with what I represent rather than who I am."

Lara shook her head. "No," she said.

Griff put his arm around her shoulders and pulled her tightly against his side. "My heart has always felt restless, Lara. I always felt as if I was not good enough for my father, and I did not want what he wanted. And I went after things that gave me pleasure for a moment, but were fleeting. Even in the last few years with this goal, which is actually noble, I have never felt settled. I have never felt at peace with myself." He stopped.

Lara stared into the night. Peace with herself. That is what she wanted, to do something that would help her make peace with who she was.

Griff cleared his throat, and his arm against her neck trembled as if he were nervous. "When I hold your hand, Lara," he said softly, "I find that peace."

Lara had not moved, but in that moment she became completely still. The world seemed to slow.

"I was angry the last time I was with you. I had decided that I would not speak to you again after we got this damned race behind us. But it struck me just now, that I had to tell you how I felt. I had to tell you that I love you."

Lara swallowed hard, her legs nearly gave out beneath her. But Griff was holding onto her.

"If I had not told you, it would have been because I was afraid you did not feel the same," he said. "I know you don't want to marry me. And I fear you don't feel the same intense feelings I do."

He turned toward her then, and Lara pulled her eyes away from the moon and stared into Griff Hallsbury's piercing blue ones.

"But I cannot live like that. I love you. And I want you to know that I think you are a beautiful person. I love to listen to you, and I love to laugh with you. And I adore you."

Lara blinked.

She loved him, too. She knew that with all of her heart. But if she gave herself completely, what would happen to her? What if it burned out? What if the fire did not stay? What if Griff did not love her like this forever?

The pain would be so much more awful.

And anyway, was it real?

Lara wished suddenly she could just take this moment and live in it forever. She did not want to put it all to the test of real life.

Real life was that Griff had taken her maidenhood. Real life was that Griff felt responsible. Real life was that he would always think of her as a mistake.

Lara bit her lip. And then, instead of telling Griff how she felt, she kissed him.

He folded her into his arms and kissed her back.

There was a world happening around her, full of scary things and difficult things and confusing things, and she did not care in the least. With a long sigh, Lara melted against Griff, put her arms around his neck and let him take her to the beautiful world of soft caresses and scintillating nibbles.

He loved her carefully and thoroughly, and Lara did not remember anything about the confusion of her life until the midnight black beyond the window lightened to a dull gray. And the moon had dropped from the sky.

And then she watched her lover sleep for a few moments, wishing she could just let him stay there next to her forever.

Forever.

And she finally gave in to reality and kissed Griff awake. "We have to go," she said. "'Tis nearly morning."

He blinked at her, one side of his mouth lifting in a lazy smile. She could not help but smile in the face of such beauty. And cry, inside, at the face of the man she would love to wake up with every morning of her life.

But only if he would look at her like this every morning. And even true love could not promise that.

Lara knew then that she could not continue this affair. After the race she would go home with Reggie. Her father seemed to think he could make quite a lot of money with his invention.

Perhaps he would let her travel. She would do something, find that thing that would bring her peace.

And she would always know that she had been loved completely at one time in her life. This love they had right now would live forever, if she stopped it now. Forever in her memory, Griff would love her like this.

Lara stood quickly and started dressing, finding her clothes strewn about the cold stable.

"Lara," Griff said as she determinedly kept her eyes off of him.

"Don't, Griff." She stopped him, her back to him as she buttoned up her boy's jacket and then wound her hair under the hat. "We both know this can't continue."

"I don't know that," Griff said.

She turned. He had found his clothing as well. He stood before her, looking very much as he had the very first time she had seen him. Tall and magnificent. But now she knew that the cocky way he stood—his hip forward, head back as if he could conquer the world with just his smile—hid a man who did not want to make any more mistakes in his life.

But he wasn't afraid, she remembered.

"Griff, the race is going to change your life. And I'm glad," Lara said.

"What if it changes yours?" he asked.

Lara shook her head. "It doesn't matter." She closed her eyes for a moment, and then took a deep breath and looked up into Griff's eyes. "I loved you tonight. It was not the excitement of what you represent. I loved you."

"'Loved'?" he asked.

But Lara couldn't stand it anymore. He had asked her to marry him once. And she knew that she could still change everything right now. She could tell him she wanted to marry him now, and he would do it. His integrity, at the very least, would force his hand in that.

Lara's stomach churned with fear at the thought of marrying someone she adored and loved more than life. He might feel that way toward her now, but what of tomorrow? Or the next day?

What pain would be hers if she ended up alone crying into her pillow like her mother?

Her brain hurt with it all—her heart as well. Amanda had quite a shock coming if she thought that love was so incredibly wonderful. It was an ache, really, like nothing she had ever known.

Griff watched her closely, his summer blue eyes so clear, she felt she might be able to dive into them, like the pond at home. She looked away, finally. And then she ran.

She had always been very fast, and she knew that since she had surprised Griff, she could probably get away from him. She did not want to hurt anymore. And standing there watching him hurt.

She heard him behind her as she shoved through the gate in Lord Rutherford's back wall. She felt him nearly snatch at her sleeve as she rounded the corner of the alley. But once she had gained the street, the rain started.

One huge raindrop smacked her face. Lara ducked her head and kept running as she heard Griff skid behind her, say a really foul word and smack against something hard.

She took a moment to glance behind her and make sure Griff was all right. He was moving, at least. And swearing a blue streak.

With a prayer of thanks, Lara darted down another alley and never looked back again.

The rain poured down in sheets. If he did not know that Lara had her father's invention on her coach, he would force her to quit. But with the added maneuverability the gadget gave her, Griff believed she could do it.

He glanced at her coach. A young boy held the reins as Lara checked each harness one by one. Griff grinned and had to look away, for Lara had outdone herself with her costume. If anyone recognized her, it would be a miracle. She had a mask on, of course, as well as a blonde wig. She wore boots that must be too big and she had padded her bum and her bosom.

He did notice that the eyes of the mask were cut very wide so as to let Lara see well enough to drive, but she had also painted kohl onto the skin around her eyes.

Because of the rain, the crowd was not quite as large as he had expected, but it was still more people than he had ever seen together at once, including most of the young bucks that showed up for the monthly carriage races.

Thomas was scarce, as well as Mrs. Braxton. The last caused him a bit of anxiety. But since he was so nervous already, it hardly signified.

Funny, that. He had raced many times in his life, so many he could not count. And now, here, with a fortune at stake and half of London watching, certainly, he did not feel even the slightest bit of the thrill he usually experienced.

Of course, he knew that he would not win. But mostly, he decided that the reason for this phenomenon was quite simple. It simply did not matter to him. In that moment, only one thing mattered: Lara. He wanted her safe. That was all he could think about.

Well, that was not entirely true, he was also thinking about kissing her again—ravaging her, really—but beyond that, he did not care a whit about anything else.

Griff scanned the crowd again and suddenly did a double take. He blinked. Lady Tattenbaum's high phaeton, which he could place a mile away by its horrendous shade of magenta, sat at the side of the road just behind him. And in the conveyance sat Lady Tattenbaum, wrapped in a concoction of bright pink and . . . Griff closed his eyes, shook his head and then opened them again.

Yes, it was Lara.

He whipped his head around to look again at the coach beside him. Mrs. Hastings was levering herself onto the box seat. He peered at her through the rain. She grinned at him and wiggled the fingers of her right hand in greeting.

It was Lara, he could swear.

He bounced between the two women for a minute. What on earth?

And then he looked closer at the Lara with Lady Tattenbaum. She wore a poke hat that covered all of her hair, but there was a tiny curl that had escaped the brim. Lara's hair would never curl like that.

Even when it was wet, Lara Darling's hair was straight as a stick.

But her sister Reggie: Now, her hair curled. It was about the same color as Lara's, and they were the same height. Reggie, though, was more angular.

Griff squinted at the woman with Lady Tattenbaum. It had to be Reggie. She had padded herself as well, and wore a dress Griff had seen Lara wear. He blew out a puff of air. A fine idea, but really, fraught with pitfalls.

They were sisters, so they resembled each other to a degree, and with the rain hampering the view, one could mistake them easily. Still, the minute anyone actually walked up to one of them and spoke to her, they would know which one was not Lara.

And then, over the cacophony of the crowd, Griff heard the bellow of a deep, masculine voice.

"Lara Darling," it cried.

It was as if the entire city turned toward Lara's sister and Lady Tattenbaum. Griff realized that he was holding his breath. He glanced quickly around for the source of the voice.

"Lara, Darling," the voice said again, and

Griff saw Lara's father elbowing his way through the crowd toward Lady Tattenbaum's phaeton. He would ruin everything when he discovered that the girl he thought was Lara was not Lara at all.

Griff stood. He should not be standing on the box without his full attention focused on his team, but he suddenly knew that something terrible was about to happen. A million thoughts went through his head. And then he slammed back down on the box and decided that he would set his team in motion there and then.

That would bring all attention away from the debacle about to happen.

But, just before he cracked his whip, he heard Lara's father say, "You'll catch your death, girl. I told you to stay home!"

Griff's hands were shaking as he stilled his whip. And then he watched as Lady Tattenbaum cracked her own whip. The pink atrocity of a conveyance turned smartly and whisked away from them down the road.

Brilliant.

Griff grinned, relief flooding him like sweet nectar. He looked over at Lara. She nodded at him and gave him a thumbs-up.

He was definitely going to kiss her later. She

was brilliant. That had been brilliant. The entire world had just seen Lara Darling *and* Mrs. Hastings in the same place, at the same time.

Just then a huge yellow umbrella caught Griff's eye. Beneath it stood none other than Amelia Braxton. Her jaw was somewhere near her feet as her gaze followed Lady Tattenbaum's phaeton.

Try and ruin her now, Griff wanted to yell. He whooped then, loud and clear, suddenly excited for the race to start. It might actually be fun, now. Lara was on her way to gaining her fortune, and Amelia Braxton would be hardpressed to get anyone to believe that Mrs. Hastings was Lara Darling.

He glanced over at Lara, and she grinned back at him.

And then they both looked forward as Thomas stepped before them. A silence descended as Lord Rutherford held aloft a sodden red handkerchief.

And then he dropped it.

Both teams jumped against their traces, and they were off.

It was tricky, to say the least. Lara and Griff ran right beside each other through the narrow streets, turning and then straightening out. They were on a circuitous route that took them along the fringes of London, and then there would be a straightaway to the finish, which had also been the start.

The raindrops smashed against his face like rocks as Griff picked up speed. He was amazed at how well his team was managing the sharper turns.

He had never done so well, actually. His peripheral vision confirmed that Lara was still right beside him. They jockeyed at each turn, but in the straights, they were always about level. She really ought to be way out ahead of him, with the advantage she had, given her father's invention.

There weren't as many people scattered along this part of the route, and all Griff could hear were the horses' shoes hitting the stones, the huff of their breath and the jangling of the traces.

They turned another corner, and Griff saw the finish before them. He glanced over at Lara. How on earth had he kept up with her?

She glanced at him at the same time, and even with the mask, he could tell that she was baffled as well. And suddenly it came to him.

She knew about the invention. She must have put it in his coach, too. Of course, now that he figured it out, he wondered how he could not have known immediately. The tight corners had been much too easy to handle.

He laughed against the pelting rain, even though he really did feel like thrashing Lara Darling. And then kissing her until she begged for mercy.

They both ran for the finish, right beside each other. It would be a tie, obviously. Except that Griff had a plan. He bent to his task then, concentrating on keeping all four horses in line with each other. Each rein had to hit all four mouths at the same time to ensure safety as they came up on the finish line.

It leaped toward them, and just before he crossed, Griff dragged on the reins, slowing his coach so that Lara would rush across before him. He glanced over, but she had disappeared.

He blinked. What?

He looked in front of him, the finish line disappearing under his lead horses, and then he grabbed the edge of his seat and craned around to look behind him.

It was a move he would never have done in a right state of mind. It was absolutely the most dangerous thing he could do in that moment, and, quite frankly, he could have killed himself then and taken a few of the onlookers with him to their eternal reward.

Fortunately that did not happen.

But one could not blame Griff Hallsbury, because when he ratcheted around on the box, he saw exactly what his mind had told him had happened, but his heart had not believed.

Lara sat just behind the finish line, her team at a full stop.

His own team slowed and halted about fifty yards past the finish. The people of London screamed as one, a deafening sound, and converged on his coach.

It came to him slowly, the clarity of what had just happened. As he blinked at the crazy mishmash of faces around him, Griff realized that he had just won a fortune.

Lady Lara had *handed* him a fortune.

Chapter 18

Do not kiss a man during a party. No matter the lengths you go to secret yourself. You will always be found out.

The Duchess Diaries, Volume One

ara's father was waiting for her just where they had planned, dressed in the clothes of a farmer, sitting atop a rickety-looking cart, holding the reins of a sorry-looking mule.

Lara plunged into the back of the cart and threw the tarp over her head. Her father took off without a word.

She had jumped from her perch on the coach and four just as soon as she knew that Griff had truly won, and lost herself quickly in the cheering crowd.

She had a bonnet stuck down the front of her dress: That had gone on, and the mask had been thrown off. And now she breathed deeply as her father drove her off to safety.

She felt giddy and excited, more so than if she had actually won, really. Lara giggled.

"A bit 'o fun for you, dear?" her father said from above her.

Lara pulled the tarp aside so she could see her father's back. He had his head bent against the rain that still slicked the skies above them gray.

"It was, Father," Lara said. It still seemed strange to have a father who actually spoke to her. Her father had mostly just looked right through her.

She watched him nod, but then he went quiet. Lara snuggled into the blankets Reggie had thoughtfully lined the cart with, but she kept the tarp steepled so she could watch her father drive.

He was very good at it, always had been. He loved driving. Lara remembered as a child, making old Tumley teach her the art so that she might get her father's attention.

"Reggie wants me to tell you something," her father said then. The cart hit a rock and thumped over it, hard.

"Ouch," Lara cried.

"Damn roads," her father grumbled.

They rode silently again. Lara waited, figuring that probably her father had forgotten he was speaking to her when they hit the rock.

"I was a horrible father, a worse husband," he said.

"No . . ."

But her father waved a hand in the air and glanced down at her out of the corner of his eye. " 'Course I was."

Lara swallowed hard.

"I wanted to do something to prove myself. Prove that I was worthy of your mother. I was afraid that I wasn't, really." He shook his head.

The raindrops made a sad, lonely plopping sound against the tarp over Lara.

"What a big mistake," her father sighed.

And then he was quiet. She could tell he had gone into the world he lived in when his mind was working furiously, and he was trying to keep up. Lara let the tarp fall closed, shutting out the cold day.

She bounced along in the quiet, thinking about fear and mistakes. A sadness beat in her heart as she thought about her mother. If only her father had just thrown his fears to the wind and lived.

Of course, she knew very well, that was a very scary thing to do.

A part of her wanted to do it, run and find Griff, throw all of her fears behind her like so many petals on the wind.

Another part of her wanted to find a very safe place and stay there forever.

The party at Lady Tattenbaum's was raucous and loud. Mrs. Braxton and her husband had not even come. Too bad for her, actually, because the regent had.

It was one of those amazing moments. The quartet was playing, couples were dancing, older people were drinking, the young bucks were fast becoming inebriated.

And the regent walked in.

A hush had gone over the crowd, and since then, there had not been any more moments of quiet. It was now loud and, really, almost dangerous.

Still, it had been most gratifying to watch the regent go up and talk to Lord Ashton. It seemed his little invention was exciting even royalty.

Lady Tattenbaum came up to Griff as he stood with a glass of water by the fireplace. "Goodness, boy, you are not getting into the mood at all, are you? You won today, don't you remember? How much money did you make, boy? Are you any closer to using my help to re-gain your foothold in Society?" She grinned.

Griff did not want to encourage her. She was already giddy enough. "I will let you know," he told her.

"Good, good," she said, crossing her arms over her considerable midriff and glanced around. She was all in pink tonight. A pink tur-ban, pink feather in the pink turban and pink crystals on the pink feather.

"I love you, Lady Tattenbaum," Griff said softly so that she wouldn't hear him.

"And I heard you, young man." She put her hand on his arm. "Don't be doing anything you'll regret anymore, Griff. It really puts a damper on the party."

He chuckled as she left him. But still, he re-ally could not get into the mood of the party. He had not seen Lara since he had been engulfed by the people at the end of the race.

She had yet to show up at the party. And he needed to see her. But he did not dare climb up to her window during the day, and he did not dare go looking for her now. He did not want to tempt fate. She had gotten away with her cha-rade, Amelia Braxton be damned. But Griff knew that everything could still tumble with one person seeing the wrong thing, or one person saying the wrong thing.

Add to that, he did not know what to do with Lara in the least. He just wanted her to marry him, damn it.

But she was so incredibly stubborn!

And she was so incredibly absent. Where the hell was the woman?

Reggie was there. Lady Tattenbaum had sat her next to the Sinclair sisters, and told them that if she even moved they were to sit on her.

Obviously, though she would not admit it to anyone, the last few months with Lara had given Lady Tattenbaum enough worry to last a lifetime. And, as she'd already promised to sponsor each of the sisters, she was clearly just beginning to realize what was in store for her. The very thought made Griff shudder.

Lara times six? Holy hell.

And Lord Ashton was there, of course. But he had taken himself off to the library after a while to tinker with some nuts and bolts that looked nothing like the gadget that still needed a name. He was probably starting on another twenty-year quest to invent something.

Lord Rutherford was absent as well.

Griff stared down at the gleaming Hessians

on his feet. Thomas had left without saying good-bye. Griff had not even seen the man after the race.

But Sterling had found Griff. The small, dark butler brought memories flooding back to him. Sterling had been Thomas's trusted servant for years. He had been with Rutherford's father, after all.

Sterling had delivered a large box and a bank draft, explaining that Lord Rutherford had already left. He was traveling to China, of all places.

The bank draft, of course, was enough for Griff to buy back his father's unentailed estate. The very place where Griff had grown up. He grinned, just thinking about it.

The box had contained a pair of brand-new boots.

They felt damn good.

Griff searched the room again. He wanted to show Lara his boots. He wanted to tell her all about Thomas. He wanted to try one more time at a proposal. And, he thought as he sipped his water, if she did not accept his suit, he just might have to enlist her sisters to help break down the stubborn chit's defenses.

Griff rubbed a suddenly damp palm against

the bottom of his waistcoat. He did have one fear that niggled, though. What if she really had just wanted a roll with the coachman?

No, she had put her father's invention in his coach. Lara had risked her name because she thought Thomas was going to hurt Griff if she did not race. She had given him her body.

Griff tapped his brand-new Hessian boots in agitation.

Where was Lara?

And then he saw her. She drifted down the stairs, slender hand trailing along the banister, pale pink dress like a cloud around her beautiful, curved body.

Griff suddenly felt like he was thirteen again, about to make an attempt at a first kiss.

He remembered how she had looked, sitting on the box of his coach in Lower Tunsburrow, her eyes lit from the inside and her smile bigger than the entire country.

And now, here she was, that same woman, and that same smile.

Surely, every male from ten to ninety would clamber over each other to get to her. She was radiant.

Griff swiped his palm across his chest. Maybe he should leave. Maybe it would be more gentlemanly of him to back out of the room and leave Lara to find someone who could give her the status she deserved.

He had money now, at least. But he still had an uphill climb before him in terms of regaining his footing in Society. That climb seemed more like an idyllic country stroll, though, when he imagined Lara beside him during the whole of it.

Griff plunked down his glass on the mantel beside him. Damn being gentlemanly. He wasn't half what she deserved, but he loved her more than any man ever could.

And he rather thought that was exactly what she needed.

With the stairs as his goal, Griff wound his way through the bodies that were making Lady Tattenbaum's rather small ballroom smell a bit like Lower Tunsburrow's public room on a hot day.

The dancers that clogged the middle of the room were not helping, either.

He was stopped a dozen times. Mostly by men, young men. And they each had an urgent question.

"Do you whip the horses at the crest of a hill?" asked young Roddy. "If they went faster right then, wouldn't you have slack on the traces?"

Griff smiled and spoke to Roddy, though for the life of him, he wanted to thump the boy on the head. Slack on the traces on the way *up* a hill? What balderdash.

But he very nicely told the boy that he was completely wrong, and then explained exactly how to get a coach and four up and then down a small hill without incident.

By the time Griff had made it to the door of the ballroom, it had been a good half hour. He stopped and took a deep breath of the air in the hall.

Lara, of course, was gone.

Damn.

"You have new boots," Lara said from behind him.

Griff turned on his shiny new heel. "You noticed," he said.

She smiled. "If nothing else, this sojourn in Town has given me a new appreciation for footwear and the enjoyment of acquiring it."

"That is all you have acquired?" he asked, lifting his eyebrows and giving her one of his famously wicked grins.

"Among other things." She stepped closer to him. And then stepped closer still.

Every single nerve ending in his body went on high alert. Lara in the vicinity: breathe in lovely scent, remember feel of soft bosom, bring lower extremity to upright position.

He was definitely thirteen again. Except that he was not. And he was with the woman who would give him children.

"You tried to let me win," she whispered.

Griff bent his head so that his mouth was at a level with Lara's ear. It was a lovely ear. "But you are too good. I can't even lose to you when I wish."

She giggled and then moved her head slightly so that she whispered into his ear, "You put my father's invention in my coach."

Griff shivered at the feel of her breath against his skin, and then lowered his mouth to her ear again. "You put your father's invention in *my* coach." And then he licked the lobe of Lara's delicate ear.

She grabbed his hand. A reflex, obviously. A very, very nice reflex. "Why did you race if you were going to let me win?" She kissed the skin just behind his ear.

Griff felt his knees turn a bit wobbly. "You, my dear, had a private conversation in a public place. Amelia Braxton found out who Mrs. Hastings was. Long story short, if I did not drive, she was going to reveal your secret."

Lara stood very still for a long moment. And

then she tilted her head up and put her mouth against his ear. "I don't mind a long story," she took his lobe between her teeth. "Not when we get to talk to each other like this."

He just could not do it anymore. Grabbing Lara's hand, Griff glanced up and down the hall and then went into the first door he found. It turned out to be a closet.

A large closet, but a closet just the same.

And it was dark.

He took her in his arms immediately. And, even though he could not see her face so that he could gauge her reactions, he said, "I know you just want to be my mistress so that I will never grow bored of you, but I absolutely refuse to accept that, Lara. Marry me."

She didn't answer him right away, and suddenly he felt as if his heart had turned to stone and dropped like a rock to his stomach. She was going to make this difficult.

"You love me," she said.

He wasn't sure whether that was a question or a statement.

He answered her anyway, "Yes," he said. "More than anyone will ever love you, Lara."

"But love does not ensure that we shall always take care of each other."

He held her tighter. "If you ever think I am

not taking care of you, tell me. I will listen. I will always listen to you."

"I always thought that I would be something and do something, other than simply be a wife," she said then.

Griff held his breath.

"But today I realized that the something I want to be is Lady Trenton. And the something I want to do is build our life together. I love you, Griff Hallsbury."

Griff smiled. Ah yes, Lady Lara had handed him a fortune this day. He found her mouth then, kissing her as he held her tightly to him.

And then someone knocked at the door of their closet.

"Don't you dare make love to her in my broom closet, Griff Hallsbury," Lady Tattenbaum barked through the closed door.

Lara buried her head against Griff's chest, her shoulders shaking in mirth.

"Can we announce the engagement, Lara?" Reggie asked then. "Father is dying to do it."

"Have you said yes yet?" Lord Ashton bellowed. "We need to get this over with. I need to get home. Can't leave four girls to themselves for too long, they'll burn the house down."

"Oh dear," Lara whispered.

"Shall we get this over with, then?" Griff asked.

He felt Lara reach up and brush at her hair. "Yes," she said then. "The quicker we get it over with, the quicker we can find a closet more out of the main thoroughfare."

Griff decided he loved Lara even more. "Good thinking."

And together they opened the door to their new life.

Epilogue

One year later

The Darling sisters and Old Tumley, the groom, stood at the side of a long, winding road just outside of Lord and Lady Trenton's Lincolnshire estate.

They were waiting.

Emma held little Thomas Hallsbury, who was just a month old.

"Here they come," Reggie announced.

"Finally, I swear I am getting a red nose, and that will absolutely never do. Lady Tattenbaum has promised that she will introduce me in court when I am seventeen, which is in only two years. I cannot burn my nose ever again," Amanda told them all.

"I don't understand how you can be related to me," Emma said as she bounced the baby. One had to bounce when holding little Thomas. He cried, a lot. Griff said it was because he was to have Lara's personality.

"Who is in the lead?" Rachel asked.

"Lara is. She always is," Lissie said.

Old Tumley grunted.

Reggie squinted into the sun, and then grinned. "'Tis Lara, but Griff is close behind her."

The coaches came up fast, the dust flying behind them, and passed the girls in a rush.

"So," Amanda asked, "Who won? Because I really could not tell."

"It was Lara, by Amanda's red nose," Reggie yelled, after the couple had brought their respective coaches to a halt. "Lara, you are the best driver in Christendom!"

"I completely resent the red-nose thing, Reggie." Amanda pouted.

Lara grinned as she jumped from her seat and gave her lead horse a pat. "I am, aren't I?" she said softly to her horse. "I always knew that I would be something."

Griff sauntered over to her. "Yes, darling, you are something, all right."

Lara cocked her head and narrowed her gaze on her husband. "Are you teasing me by any chance, Grifford?"

"Me? Never." He laughed. "Re-match, one month's time. One of these days, I'm going to win."

Lara smiled sweetly. "Well, you can certainly keep trying, darling." She held her hand out, palm up. "You owe me a pound."

Griff nodded. "Put it on my bill. Perhaps you wouldn't mind consoling me, though? My ego is trampled, my pride dust . . ."

Lara rolled her eyes, put her arms around her husband and kissed him full on the mouth.

Her sisters tittered.

"I will never tire of that, I promise you," he said against her mouth. "All right then," Griff yelled out when his wife backed away and winked. "Everyone in. We're off for some shopping to commemorate yet another win by my most charming and beautiful wife. And, yes, Lissie you can sit up front with me." He grinned at the youngest Darling sister.

Lara watched as Old Tumley took the coach seat she had just vacated, and the rest of her family tumbled into Griff's coach. Everything was so incredibly wonderful that it scared her sometimes.

But instead of letting that fear curb her life, she let it fill her life with joy. She jumped in, full go.

Anyway, look at what had happened to her. She had left for her first season scared that she would marry some horrible man who would make her be ladylike always, and never allow her to do anything more exciting than arrange menus for dinner parties.

Instead she had learned to love to be ladylike when it suited her. And she had married a man who let her drive and shoot . . . and win whenever she wanted.

Start the New Year with these thrilling new romances
coming in January from Avon Books

MARRIED TO THE VISCOUNT by Sabrina Jeffries
An Avon Romantic Treasure

Abigail Mercer had married Viscount Ravenswood by proxy, but when she arrives on his doorstep, the dashing rogue denies their union! Now, rather than risk a scandal, the Viscount has proposed a marriage in name only, but Abigail has other plans.

DO NOT DISTURB by Christie Ridgway
An Avon Contemporary Romance

Investigative reporter Angel Buchanan has just uncovered a whopper: her deadbeat dad is actually a man famous for his family values. But legendary lawyer C.J. Jones is determined to keep Angel quiet . . . and he'll gladly woo her into submission.

NO ORDINARY GROOM by Gayle Callen
An Avon Romance

Jane Whittington wants excitement and adventure, not marriage to a fop! But William Chadwick is more than he seems. And if excitement is what Jane seeks, then he'll give her what she desires . . . one kiss at a time.

SEEN BY MOONLIGHT by Kathleen Eschenburg
An Avon Romance

Annabelle Hallston will do anything to keep her younger brother safe—which is the only reason she agreed to marry Royce Kincaid. The notorious black sheep of an aristocratic family, Royce does not believe in love . . . until Anabelle unlocks his true passion and frees his wounded soul.

Avon Romances—
the best in exceptional authors
and unforgettable novels!

Avon Romantic Treasures

*Unforgettable, enthralling love stories,
sparkling with passion and adventure
from Romance's bestselling authors*